D0295875

BUCHAN. J

The Best Short Stories
of
JOHN BUCHAN

Edited by David Daniell

LONDON
MICHAEL JOSEPH

To
Alice, John and William,
and in memory of Alastair,
with love.

First published in this edition in Great Britain by
Michael Joseph Limited
44 Bedford Square, London WC1
May 1980
Second impression October 1980

Copyright in the stories of John Buchan,
Lord Tweedsmuir of Elsfield
© Introduction and selection by David Daniell, 1980

ISBN 0 7181 1906 1

Phototypeset in V.I.P. Garamond by
Western Printing Services Ltd, Bristol
Printed and bound by
Billing and Sons Ltd, Guildford and Worcester

Contents

While acknowledging with gratitude the permission of Lord Tweedsmuir to reprint these stories, I take the opportunity to thank the members of John Buchan's family for their most generous interest, help and encouragement: this book is warmly dedicated to them.

Introduction

John Buchan wrote over a hundred books, and very many of them are still read, with delight, by a countless host of people across the world. He was a biographer of distinction: his lives of Scott and Montrose remain standard works. He wrote lucid history, notably of the First World War, which he regarded with horror but explained with insight even while it was being fought, often writing from the Front. He was a fine editor, effectively of the *Spectator* for a spell, for which journal alone he wrote nearly a thousand articles, as well as so far uncounted regular columns for the daily, weekly and monthly press on both sides of the Atlantic. He was a pleasing poet, and a great contributor to considered collections of discussion and commentary. He was by formal training a classicist, principally at home in pastoral Greece and Augustan Rome. He wrote a technical book about the law relating to the taxation of foreign income.

In his official life he was, after Oxford, one of Lord Milner's Young Men in South Africa at the end of the Boer War, and then barrister, publisher, wartime Director of Information, a director of Reuters, MP for the Scottish Universities, and Governor-General of Canada as Lord Tweedsmuir. He was a profoundly happy family man with a great wealth of friendships, a fine fisherman, a clever climber and a prodigious walker. He was a man much loved and much admired. Several generations of young people owe to his friendship and interest the confidence to begin their own special endeavours. He died in Canada in February 1940 at the age of sixty-four, and he is still much missed.

And of course he wrote fiction: nearly thirty novels and seven collections of short stories. Some of the novels, like *Witch Wood*, set in seventeenth-century Scotland, or *Salute to Adventures*, in eighteenth-century Virginia, or *The Blanket of the Dark*, in Tudor England, continue to surprise the unwary modern reader who does not quite expect such clarity, atmosphere, character-isation and grasp of large affairs. Other novels, such as those in which the lawyer Sir Edward Leithen plays a major part, like *John Macnab*, *The Dancing Floor* or *Sick Heart River*, treat, with unusual organisation, far profounder matters than their ease of reading might suggest. Buchan is most widely known, of course, for the adventure stories containing the South African ex-mining engineer Richard Hannay. The first, *The Thirty-Nine Steps*, his twenty-seventh book, written at great speed while he was confined to bed in the second year of the War, has become a record-breaking best-seller, and is his single best-known book. This has been not altogether to his advantage, as early in the book a terrified young American spy makes to the South African engineer Hannay an anti-semitic remark which has, absurdly, been taken to represent the considered judgements of the author. Buchan has not been helped here either by the three curious films of the book, little recognisable as having any connection.

Some of Buchan's most enjoyable writing is in his short stories, and he found good form astonishingly early, when he was not yet twenty, and an undergraduate at Brasenose College, Oxford. He had won scholarships there from the University of Glasgow, where he had been an outstanding pupil of the star young professor Gilbert Murray, appointed to the Chair when he was only twenty-three.

The Greek and Latin texts and philosophy that were Buchan's prime occupation influenced his writing all his life. He wrote, at his best, with Attic lucidity and a Roman strength. But from his first year at Brasenose College he also supported himself as a publisher's reader, and through many of the manuscripts that the enterprising London publisher John Lane sent him he was kept in touch with modern developments in fiction: he recommended for publication, for example, the first novel by Arnold Bennett, *The Man from the North*. Like many others at the time, he was happy to confess himself captive to the skills of R. L. Stevenson, an admirable master. The young John Buchan spent much of his early life in the Lowland Scottish countryside – his mother's family were Upper Tweeddale sheep-farmers – and he very early showed R. L. Stevenson's knack of catching pace, landscape, atmosphere and tension and making the writing 'feel' on all the senses: indeed, there are those who would say that at his best he betters Stevenson, and he certainly brought more to conclusion. On his own account, he loved the English tradition of prose writing, especially in seventeenth-century men like Sir Thomas Browne and Bunyan, or the eighteenth-century Burke. He wrote about these with love and understanding but, more importantly, they are often present as effects below the surface of his own prose. Very little that he wrote does not hold such hidden power in its rhythms and words, and this makes him a unique writer of adventure-stories. There are passages at high points of even the more brittle Hannay novels where seventeenth-century felicities are at work. It is noticeable that at the major climax of *Mr Standfast* Buchan echoes, and indeed uses, some of Bunyan's most admired sentences in a First World War context, and far from producing mawkishness can make a serious effect.

Though short tales are as old as mankind, there is a sense in which the short story had only just appeared in Britain when Buchan began to write. Those characteristics of the form that we now recognise were developed in America, in Russia and in France in the middle of the nineteenth century. American writers, finding themselves swamped by all the longer European fiction which was pirated and printed there, were quick to nurture a native talent for the short story. Edgar Allan Poe first practised, and first analysed, the technique of that 'certain unique or single *effect'*, the search for a single impression of mood, or emotion, or situation, which became the dominant force in short-story writing. The inner tensions in the psychology of the super-Romantic Gothic tale (as in Mary Shelley's *Frankenstein*) could be made to marry with the perpetual inner soundings of Puritan narrative, and the resulting 'impressionism' developed some force in America. The great Russian novelists too were bold explorers of the shorter form: H. E. Bates has quoted Gorky on the modern European short story, saying that 'We all spring from Gogol's *Overcoat'*. In France, Maupassant sharpened the ironies. In Britain, there was detectable a concern that though the mid-century had been copious with novelists and poets, England had produced in fiction neither the experiments nor the theories to match what was seen to be happening elsewhere, especially in France. Then, in the last decades of Victoria's reign, the continental and American impulse reached Britain with a rush. Stevenson, Kipling, Conrad and — to some extent — James (two Scots, a Pole and an American) created the English short story. In the earliest years of that new tradition, Buchan began to write, using the new techniques, but at the same time creating something with an altogether simpler appearance.

In his short stories Buchan's interest, from the very first, is in the small moment at the point of balance of very large events. He understands that the small frame allows for fineness of perspective, so that the matter at issue can be viewed obliquely. This in turn gives him the chance to use different effects of off-centre narration. The tale may be told by someone quite out of sympathy with the matter implicit in the story. The narrator may be a reticent countryman whose stolid and understated heroism, for example, colours the reader's view of the shifting rhetoric of distant Westminster, as in 'The Herd of Standlan'. In this story the politician spends most of the tale in the Tweeddale river-pool, not merely deprived of speech but quite unconscious. His life is saved – just – and he lives to become a leading Tory, causing, it is hinted, national disaster. Here, by devices of perspective and narrative, oppositions of human judgement and decision are held in a tiny delicate balance. Moreover, the Herd's vivid imaginative experiences make a quite different scale, producing another kind of vertical dimension. The young aristocrat, elevated both socially and politically, lacks all imagination. The Herd, at the foot of both scales, is in touch with great forces, which may or may not be partly supernatural, but are certainly recognisably human. There are other forces, too, most pleasingly balanced, in this and in the other tales. The more the reader digs, the more gold is found, which is the sign of a certain artistry.

Buchan's first collection, *Grey Weather* (1899) contains thirteen short tales, all set in or near Tweeddale, and a poem, *The Ballad of Grey Weather*. The subtitle of the book is *Moorland Tales of My Own People*. His next collection, and his thirteenth book, was *The Watcher by the Threshold* (1902), containing six long stories, all on the characteristic theme of 'a line, a thread, a sheet of glass' between modern civilisation and the primitive. *The Moon Endureth* (1912), the most mixed bag, contains eight new stories, two older ones from *Grey Weather*, and nine poems interspersed between the tales in the manner of Kipling. *The Path of the King* (1921) is a book of fourteen historical short stories, linked by a cunning thread, and *The Runagates Club* (1928) contains twelve stories in a dining-club frame. Two other volumes, the children's books *Sir Walter Raleigh* (1911) and *The Long Traverse* (1941) are also made up of loosely-connected separate tales. In all the collections there are seventy-two stories.

I found the selection of twelve for this volume particularly hard to make. I began with some imperatives. There must, I felt, be a *locus amoenus* story, about a special, powerful place. There must be a 'flight North' story. So much of Buchan appeared in *Blackwood's*, with major contributions to forty-six issues and eight books published by that firm, that I should have to take one from there. Readers might reasonably expect a Hannay story. I very much wanted to include a classical story like 'The Lemnian', and a historical romance with a 'faerie' heroine. Above all, Buchan would not be seen to be Buchan without Scottish, moorland, adventures.

I ran into difficulties straight away. There were too many good stories. Sorrowfully I had to turn favourites away. One imperative, however, I allowed to have full force. I have thought for years that some of Buchan's earliest stories from *Grey Weather* ought to be available again, and I wanted half the collection, at least, to be from that volume. And so it has turned out. Six of the stories here have not been in print for eighty years. The others I chose as being typical of Buchan in six different ways. But I chose them all for the pleasure they continued to give me, and I wanted to share that pleasure.

David Daniell
University College, London

The Company of the Marjolaine

This story was written in 1908, when John Buchan was thirty-three. He was living in Hyde Park Square, at the beginning of his deeply happy marriage to the former Susan Grosvenor. He already had seventeen books to his name, and nearly a hundred and fifty shorter pieces, as well as a vast amount of distinguished journalism. He had diminished his practice as a barrister specialising in tax affairs to join Nelson's, the publishers, as chief literary adviser. The story first appeared simultaneously in February 1909 in Blackwood's *and* The Atlantic Monthly, *and the following month in the Boston, Massachusetts journal,* The Living Age, *before becoming the opening story in the volume* The Moon Endureth *in April 1912.*

It is a story which, while fully in the tradition of Romance, learned from Stevenson, also locates itself beautifully in a time and a place in reality. An acute sense of landscape and atmosphere — always a Buchan gift — is linked to a gradual focusing on to one significant moment in history. Buchan is able to look not only historically backward but also far forward from the final clarifying second — 'I do not think [it] longer.' His narrator, an alert, relaxed, late-eighteenth-century Whig gentleman, is broad enough in his sympathies to compass many kinds of judgement.

The Company of the Marjolaine

Qu'est-c' qui passe ici si tard,
Compagnons de la Marjolaine?

CHANSONS DE FRANCE*

[This extract from the unpublished papers of the Manorwater family has seemed to the Editor worth printing for its historical interest. The famous Lady Molly Carteron became Countess of Manorwater by her second marriage. She was a wit and a friend of wits, and her nephew, the Honourable Charles Hervey-Townshend (afterwards our Ambassador at The Hague), addressed to her a series of amusing letters while making, after the fashion of his contemporaries, the Grand Tour of Europe. Three letters, written at various places in the Eastern Alps and dispatched from Venice, contain the following short narrative.* (JB)]

I

. . . I came down from the mountains and into the pleasing valley of the Adige in as pelting a heat as ever mortal suffered under. The way underfoot was parched and white; I had newly come out of a wilderness of white limestone crags, and a sun of Italy blazed blindingly in an azure Italian sky. You are to suppose, my dear aunt, that I had had enough and something more of my craze for foot-marching. A fortnight ago I had gone to Belluno in a post-chaise, dismissed my fellow to carry my baggage by way of Verona, and with no more than a valise on my back plunged into the fastnesses of those mountains. I had a fancy to see the little sculptured hills which made backgrounds for Gianbellin, and there were rumours of great mountains built wholly of marble which shone like the battlements of the

* An asterisk denotes an entry in the notes on p. 221.

Celestial City. So at any rate reported young Mr Wyndham, who had travelled with me from Milan to Venice. I lay the first night at Piave, where Titian had the fortune to be born, and the landlord at the inn displayed a set of villainous daubs which he swore were the early works of that master. Thence up a toilsome valley I journeyed to the Ampezzan country, where indeed I saw my white mountains, but, alas! no longer Celestial. For it rained like Westmoreland for five endless days, while I kicked my heels in an inn and turned a canto of Ariosto into halting English couplets. By and by it cleared, and I headed westward towards Bozen, among the tangle of wild rocks where the Dwarf King had once his rose garden. The first night I had no inn, but slept in the vile cabin of a forester, who spoke a tongue half Latin, half Dutch, which I could not master. The next day was a blaze of heat, the mountain paths lay thick with dust, and I had no wine from sunrise to sunset. Can you wonder that, when the following noon I saw Santa Chiara sleeping in its green circlet of meadows, my thought was only of a deep draught and a cool chamber? I protest that I am a great lover of natural beauty, of rock and cascade, and all the properties of the poet; but the enthusiasm of M. Rousseau himself would sink from the stars to earth if he had marched since breakfast in a cloud of dust with a throat like the nether millstone.

Yet I had not entered the place before Romance revived. The little town — a mere wayside halting-place on the great mountain road to the North — had the air of mystery which foretells adventure. Why is it that a dwelling or a countenance catches the fancy with the promise of some strange destiny? I have houses in my mind which I know will some day and somehow be intertwined oddly with my life; and I have faces in memory of which I know nothing save that I shall undoubtedly cast eyes again upon them. My first glimpses of Santa Chiara gave me this earnest of romance. It was walled and fortified, the streets were narrow pits of shade, old tenements with bent fronts swayed to meet each other. Melons lay drying on flat roofs, and yet now and then would come a high-pitched northern gable. Latin and Teuton met and mingled in the place, and, as Mr Gibbon has taught us, the offspring of this admixture is something fantastic and unpredictable. I forgot my grievous thirst and my tired feet in admiration and a certain vague expectation of wonders. Here, ran my thought, it is fated, maybe, that Romance and I shall at last compass a meeting. Perchance some princess is in need of my arm, or some affair of high policy is afoot in this jumble of old masonry. You will laugh at my folly, but I had an excuse for it. A fortnight in strange mountains disposes a man to look for something at his next encounter with his kind, and the sight of Santa Chiara would have fired the imagination of a judge in Chancery.

I strode happily into the courtyard of the Tre Croci, and presently had my expectation confirmed. For I found my fellow, Gianbattista — a faithful rogue I got in Rome on a Cardinal's recommendation — hot in dispute with a lady's maid. The woman was old, harsh-featured — no Italian clearly, though she spoke fluently in the tongue. She rated my man like a pickpocket, and the dispute was over a room.

'The signor will bear me out,' said Gianbattista. 'Was not I sent to Verona with his baggage, and thence to this place of ill manners? Was I not bidden engage for him a suite of apartments? Did I not duly choose these fronting on the gallery, and dispose therein the signor's baggage? And lo! an hour ago I found it all turned into the yard and this woman installed in its place. It is monstrous, unbearable! Is this an inn for travellers, or haply the private mansion of these Magnificences?'

'My servant speaks truly,' I said, firmly yet with courtesy, having had no mind to spoil adventure by urging rights. 'He had orders to take these rooms for me, and I know not what higher power can countermand me.'

The woman had been staring at me scornfully, for no doubt in my dusty habit I was a figure of small count; but at the sound of my voice she started, and cried out, 'You are English, signor?'

I bowed an admission.

'Then my mistress shall speak with you,' she said, and dived into the inn like an elderly rabbit.

Gianbattista was for sending for the landlord and making a riot in that hostelry; but I stayed him, and bidding him fetch me a flask of white wine, three lemons, and a glass of *eau de vie*, I sat down peaceably at one of the little tables in the courtyard and prepared for the quenching of my thirst. Presently, as I sat drinking that excellent compound which was my own invention, my shoulder was touched, and I turned to find the maid and her mistress. Alas for my hopes of a glorious being, young and lissom and bright with the warm riches of the south! I saw a short, stout little lady, well on the wrong side of thirty. She had plump red cheeks, and fair hair dressed indifferently in the Roman fashion. Two candid blue eyes redeemed her plainness, and a certain grave and gentle dignity. She was notably a gentlewoman, so I got up, doffed my hat, and awaited her commands.

She spoke in Italian. 'Your pardon, signor, but I fear my good Cristine has done you unwittingly a wrong.'

Cristine snorted at this premature plea of guilty, while I hastened to assure the fair apologist that any rooms I might have taken were freely at her service.

I spoke unconsciously in English, and she replied in a halting parody of that tongue. 'I understand him,' she said, 'but I do not speak him happily. I will discourse, if the signor pleases, in our first speech.'

She and her father, it appeared, had come over the Brenner, and arrived that morning at the Tre Croci, where they purposed to lie for some days. He was an old man, very feeble, and much depending upon her constant care. Wherefore it was necessary that the rooms of all the party should adjoin, and there was no suite of the size in the inn save that which I had taken. Would I therefore consent to forgo my right, and place her under an eternal debt?

I agreed most readily, being at all times careless where I sleep, so the bed be clean, or where I eat, so the meal be good. I bade my servant see the landlord and have my belongings carried to other rooms. Madame thanked me sweetly, and would have gone, when a thought detained her.

'It is but courteous,' she said, 'that you should know the names of those whom you have befriended. My father is called the Count d'Albani, and I am his only daughter. We travel to Florence, where we have a villa in the environs.'

'My name,' said I, 'is Hervey-Townshend, an Englishman travelling abroad for his entertainment.'

'Hervey?' she repeated. 'Are you one of the family of Miladi Hervey?'

'My worthy aunt,' I replied, with a tender recollection of that preposterous woman.

Madame turned to Cristine, and spoke rapidly in a whisper.

'My father, sir,' she said, addressing me, 'is an old frail man, little used to the company of strangers; but in former days he has had kindness from members of your house, and it would be a satisfaction to him, I think, to have the privilege of your acquaintance.'

She spoke with the air of a vizier who promises a traveller a sight of the Grand Turk. I murmured my gratitude, and hastened after Gianbattista. In an hour I had bathed, rid myself of my beard, and arrayed myself in decent clothing. Then I strolled out to inspect the little city, admired an altar-piece, chaffered with a Jew for a cameo, purchased some small necessaries, and returned early in the afternoon with a noble appetite for dinner.

The Tre Croci had been in happier days a bishop's lodging, and possessed a dining-hall ceiled with black oak and adorned with frescoes. It was used as a general *salle à manger* for all dwellers in the inn, and there accordingly I sat down to my long-deferred meal. At first there were no other diners, and I had two maids, as well as Gianbattista, to attend on my wants.

Presently Madame d'Albani entered, escorted by Cristine and
by a tall gaunt serving-man, who seemed no part of the hostelry.
The landlord followed, bowing civilly, and the two women
seated themselves at the little table at the farther end. 'Il Signor
Conte dines in his room,' said Madame to the host, who
withdrew to see to that gentleman's needs.

I found my eyes straying often to the little party in the cool
twilight of that refectory. The man-servant was so old and
battered, and yet of such a dignity, that he lent a touch of
intrigue to the thing. He stood stiffly behind Madame's chair,
handing dishes with an air of silent reverence — the lackey of a
great noble, if ever I had seen the type. Madame never glanced
towards me, but conversed sparingly with Cristine, while she
pecked delicately at her food. Her name ran in my head with a
tantalising flavour of the familiar. Albani! D'Albani! It was a
name not uncommon in the Roman States, but I had never
heard it linked to a noble family. And yet I had — somehow,
somewhere; and in the vain effort at recollection I had almost
forgotten my hunger. There was nothing bourgeois in the little
lady. The austere servants, the high manner of condescension,
spake of a stock used to deference, though, maybe, pitifully
decayed in its fortunes. There was a mystery in these quiet folk
which tickled my curiosity. Romance after all was not destined
to fail me at Santa Chiara.

My doings of the afternoon were of interest to myself alone.
Suffice it to say that when I returned at nightfall I found
Gianbattista the trustee of a letter. It was from Madame,
written in a fine thin hand on a delicate paper, and it invited me
to wait upon the signor, her father, that evening at eight
o'clock. What caught my eye was a coronet stamped in a corner.
A coronet, I say, but in truth it was a crown, the same as
surmounts the Arms Royal of England on the signboard of a
Court tradesman. I marvelled at the ways of foreign heraldry.
Either this family of d'Albani had higher pretensions than I had
given it credit for, or it employed an unlearned and imaginative

stationer. I scribbled a line of acceptance and went to dress.

The hour of eight found me knocking at the Count's door. The grim serving-man admitted me to the pleasant chamber which should have been mine own. A dozen wax candles burned in sconces, and on the table, among fruits and the remains of supper, stood a handsome candelabra of silver. A small fire of logs had been lit on the hearth, and before it in an armchair sat a strange figure of a man. He seemed not so much old as aged. I should have put him at sixty, but the marks he bore were clearly less those of Time than of Life. There sprawled before me the relics of noble looks. The fleshy nose, the pendulous cheek, the drooping mouth, had once been cast in the lines of manly beauty. Heavy eyebrows above and heavy bags beneath spoiled the effect of a choleric blue eye, which age had not dimmed. The man was gross and yet haggard; it was not the padding of good living which clothed his bones, but a heaviness as of some dropsical malady. I could picture him in health a gaunt loose-limbed being, high-featured and swift and eager. He was dressed wholly in black velvet, with fresh ruffles and wrist-bands, and he wore heeled shoes with antique silver buckles. It was a figure of an older age which rose slowly to greet me, in one hand a snuff-box and a purple handkerchief, and in the other a book with finger marking place. He made me a great bow as Madame uttered my name, and held out a hand with a kindly smile.

'Mr Hervey-Townshend,' he said, 'we will speak English, if you please. I am fain to hear it again, for 'tis a tongue I love. I make you welcome, sir, for your own sake and for the sake of your kin. How is her honourable ladyship, your aunt? A week ago she sent me a letter.'

I answered that she did famously, and wondered what cause of correspondence my worthy aunt could have with wandering nobles of Italy.

He motioned me to a chair between Madame and himself, while a servant set a candle on a shelf behind him. Then he proceeded to catechise me in excellent English, with now and then a phrase of French, as to the doings in my own land. Admirably informed this Italian gentleman proved himself. I defy you to find in Almack's more intelligent gossip. He inquired as to the chances of my Lord North and the mind of my Lord Rockingham. He had my Lord Shelburne's foibles at his fingers' ends. The habits of the Prince, the aims of their ladyships of Dorset and Buckingham, the extravagance of this noble Duke and that right honourable gentleman were not hid from him. I answered discreetly yet frankly, for there was no illbreeding in his curiosity. Rather it seemed like the inquiries of some fine lady, now buried deep in the country, as to the doings of a forsaken Mayfair. There was humour in it and something of pathos.

'My aunt must be a voluminous correspondent, sir,' I said.

He laughed. 'I have many friends in England who write to me, but I have seen none of them for long, and I doubt I may never see them again. Also in my youth I have been in England.' And he sighed as at a sorrowful recollection.

Then he showed the book in his hand. 'See,' he said, 'here is one of your English writings, the greatest book I have ever happened on.' It was a volume of Mr Fielding.

For a little he talked of books and poets. He admired Mr Fielding profoundly, Dr Smollett somewhat less, Mr Richardson not at all. But he was clear that England had a monopoly of good writers, saving only my friend M. Rousseau, whom he valued, yet with reservations. Of the Italians he had no opinion. I instanced against him the plays of Signor Alfieri. He groaned, shook his head, and grew moody.

'Know you Scotland?' he asked suddenly.

I replied that I had visited Scotch cousins, but had no great estimation for the country. 'It is too poor and jagged,' I said, 'for the taste of one who loves colour and sunshine and suave outlines.'

He sighed. 'It is indeed a bleak land, but a kindly. When the

sun shines at all he shines on the truest hearts in the world. I love
its bleakness too. There is a spirit in the misty hills, and the
harsh sea-wind which inspires men to great deeds. Poverty and
courage go often together, and my Scots, if they are poor, are as
untamable as their mountains.'

'You know the land, sir?' I asked.

'I have seen it, and I have known many Scots. You will find
them in Paris and Avignon and Rome, with never a plack in
their pockets. I have a feeling for exiles, sir, and I have pitied
these poor people. They gave their all for the cause they followed.'

Clearly the Count shared my aunt's views of history – those
views which have made such sport for us often at Carteron.
Stalwart Whig as I am, there was something in the tone of the
old gentleman which made me feel a certain majesty in the lost
cause.

'I am a Whig in blood and Whig in principle,' I said, 'but I
have never denied that those Scots who followed the Chevalier
were too good to waste on so trumpery a leader.'

I had no sooner spoken the words than I felt that somehow I
had been guilty of a *bêtise*.

'It may be so,' said the Count. 'I did not bid you here, sir, to
argue on politics, on which I am assured we should differ. But I
will ask you one question. The King of England is a stout
upholder of the right of kings. How does he face the defection of
his American possessions?'

'The nation takes it well enough, and as for His Majesty's
feelings, there is small inclination to inquire into them. I
conceive of the whole war as a blunder out of which we have
come as we deserved. The day is gone by for the assertion of
monarchic rights against the will of a people.'

'May be. But take note that the King of England is suffering
today as – how do you call him? – the Chevalier suffered forty
years ago. "The wheel has come full circle", as your Shakespeare
says. Time has wrought his revenge.'

He was staring into a fire, which burned small and smokily.

'You think the days for kings is ended. I read it differently. The world will ever have need of kings. If a nation cast out one it will have to find another. And mark you, those later kings, created by the people, will bear a harsher hand than the old race who ruled as of right. Some day the world will regret having destroyed the kindly and legitimate line of monarchs and put in their place tyrants who govern by the sword or by flattering an idle mob.'

This belated dogma would at other times have set me laughing, but the strange figure before me gave no impulse to merriment. I glanced at Madame, and saw her face grave and perplexed, and I thought I read a warning gleam in her eye. There was a mystery about the party which irritated me, but good breeding forbade me to seek a clue.

'You will permit me to retire, sir,' I said. 'I have but this morning come down from a long march among the mountains east of this valley. Sleeping in wayside huts and tramping those sultry paths make a man think pleasantly of bed.'

The Count seemed to brighten at my words. 'You are a marcher, sir, and love the mountains? Once I would gladly have joined you, for in my youth I was a great walker in hilly places. Tell me, now, how many miles will you cover in a day?'

I told him thirty at a stretch.

'Ah,' he said, 'I have done fifty, without food, over the roughest and mossiest mountains. I lived on what I shot, and for drink I had spring water. Nay, I am forgetting. There was another beverage, which I wager you have never tasted. Heard you ever, sir, of that *eau de vie* which the Scots call *usquebagh*? It will comfort a traveller as no thin Italian wine will comfort him. By my soul, you shall taste it. Charlotte, my dear, bid Oliphant fetch glasses and hot water and lemons. I will give Mr Hervey-Townshend a sample of the brew. You English are all *têtes-de-fer*, sir, and are worthy of it.'

The old man's face had lighted up, and for the moment his air

had the jollity of youth. I would have accepted the entertainment had I not again caught Madame's eye. It said, unmistak-
ably and with serious pleading, 'Decline.' I therefore made my
excuses, urged fatigue, drowsiness, and a delicate stomach,
bade my host goodnight, and in deep mystification left the
room.

Enlightenment came upon me as the door closed. There on
the threshold stood the man-servant whom they called
Oliphant, erect as a sentry on guard. The sight reminded me of
what I had once seen at Basle when by chance a Rhenish Grand
Duke had shared the inn with me. Of a sudden a dozen clues
linked together – the crowned notepaper, Scotland, my aunt
Hervey's politics, the tale of old wanderings.

'Tell me,' I said in a whisper. 'Who is the Count d'Albani,
your master?' and I whistled softly a bar of *Charlie is my darling*.

'Ay,' said the man, without relaxing a muscle of his grim
face. 'It is the King of England – my king and yours.'

II

In the small hours of the next morning I was awoke by a most
unearthly sound. It was as if all the cats on all the roofs of Santa
Chiara were sharpening their claws and wailing their battle-
cries. Presently out of the noise came a kind of music – very
slow, solemn, and melancholy. The notes ran up in great flights
of ecstasy, and sunk anon to the tragic deeps. In spite of my
sleepiness I was held spellbound, and the musician had concluded with certain barbaric grunts before I had the curiosity to
rise. It came from somewhere in the gallery of the inn, and as I
stuck my head out of my door I had a glimpse of Oliphant,
nightcap on head and a great bagpipe below his arm, stalking
down the corridor.

The incident, for all the gravity of the music, seemed to give
a touch of farce to my interview of the past evening. I had gone

to bed with my mind full of sad stories of the deaths of kings.
Magnificence in tatters has always affected my pity more deeply
than tatters with no such antecedent, and a monarch out at
elbows stood for me as the last irony of our mortal life. Here was
a king whose misfortunes could find no parallel. He had been in
his youth the hero of a high adventure, and his middle age had
been spent in fleeting among the courts of Europe, and waiting
as pensioner on the whims of his foolish but regnant brethren. I
had heard tales of a growing sottishness, a decline in spirit, a
squalid taste in pleasures. Small blame, I had always thought,
to so ill-fated a princeling. And now I had chanced upon the
gentleman in his dotage, travelling with a barren effort at
mystery, attended by a sad-faced daughter and two ancient
domestics. It was a lesson in the vanity of human wishes which
the shallowest moralist would have noted. Nay, I felt more than
the moral. Something human and kindly in the old fellow had
caught my fancy. The decadence was too tragic to prose about,
the decadent too human to moralise on. I had left the chamber of
the − shall I say *de jure* King of England? − a sentimental
adherent of the cause. But this business of the bagpipes touched
the comic. To harry an old valet out of bed and set him droning
on pipes in the small hours smacked of a theatrical taste, or at
least of an undignified fancy. Kings in exile, if they wish to keep
the tragic air, should not indulge in such fantastic serenades.

My mind changed again when after breakfast I fell in with
Madame on the stair. She drew aside to let me pass, and then
made as if she would speak to me. I gave her good-morning,
and, my mind being full of her story, addressed her as 'Excel-
lency'.

'I see, sir,' she said, 'that you know the truth. I have to ask
your forbearance for the concealment I practised yesterday. It
was a poor requital for your generosity, but it is one of the shifts
of our sad fortune. An uncrowned king must go in disguise or
risk the laughter of every stable-boy. Besides, we are too poor to
travel in state, even if we desired it.'

Honestly, I knew not what to say. I was not asked to sympathise, having already revealed my politics, and yet the case cried out for sympathy. You remember, my dear aunt, the good Lady Culham, who was our Dorsetshire neighbour, and tried hard to mend my ways at Carteron? This poor Duchess — for so she called herself — was just such another. A woman made for comfort, housewifery, and motherhood, and by no means of racing about Europe in charge of a disreputable parent. I could picture her settled equably on a garden seat with a lapdog and needlework, blinking happily over green lawns and mildly rating an errant gardener. I could fancy her sitting in a summer parlour, very orderly and dainty, writing lengthy epistles to a tribe of nieces. I could see her marshalling a household in the family pew, or riding serenely in the family coach behind fat bay horses. But here, on an inn staircase, with a false name and a sad air of mystery, she was woefully out of place. I noted little wrinkles forming in the corners of her eyes, and the ravages of care beginning in the plump rosiness of her face. Be sure there was nothing appealing in her mien. She spoke with the air of a great lady, to whom the world is matter only for an after-thought. It was the facts that appealed and grew poignant from her courage.

'There is another claim upon your good nature,' she said. 'Doubtless you were awoke last night by Oliphant's playing upon the pipes. I rebuked the landlord for his insolence in protesting, but to you, a gentleman and a friend, an explanation is due. My father sleeps ill, and your conversation seems to have cast him into a train of sad memories. It has been his habit on such occasions to have the pipes played to him, since they remind him of friends and happier days. It is a small privilege for an old man, and he does not claim it often.'

I declared that the music had only pleased, and that I would welcome its repetition. Whereupon she left me with a little bow and an invitation to join them that day at dinner, while I departed into the town on my own errands. I returned before midday, and was seated at an arbour in the garden, busy with letters, when there hove in sight the gaunt figure of Oliphant. He hovered around me, if such a figure can be said to hover, with the obvious intention of addressing me. The fellow had caught my fancy, and I was willing to see more of him. His face might have been hacked out of grey granite, his clothes hung loosely on his spare bones, and his stockinged shanks would have done no discredit to Don Quixote. There was no dignity in his air, only a steady and enduring sadness. Here, thought I, is the one of the establishment who most commonly meets the shock of the world's buffets. I called him by name and asked him his desires.

It appeared that he took me for a Jacobite, for he began a rigmorale about loyalty and hard fortune. I hastened to correct him, and he took the correction with the same patient despair with which he took all things. 'Twas but another of the blows of Fate.

'At any rate,' he said in a broad Scotch accent, 'ye come of kin that has helpit my maister afore this. I've many times heard tell o' Herveys and Townshends in England, and a' folk said they were on the richt side. Ye're maybe no a freend, but ye're a freend's freend, or I wadna be speirin' at ye.'

I was amused at the prologue, and waited on the tale. It soon came. Oliphant, it appeared, was the purse-bearer of the household, and woeful straits that poor purse-bearer must have been often put to. I questioned him as to his master's revenues, but could get no clear answer. There were payments due next month in Florence which would solve the difficulties for the winter, but in the meantime expenditure had beaten income. Travelling had cost much, and the Count must have his small comforts. The result, in plain words, was that Oliphant had not the wherewithal to frank the company to Florence; indeed, I doubted if he could have paid the reckoning in Santa Chiara. A loan was therefore sought from a friend's friend, meaning myself.

I was very really embarrassed. Not that I would not have given willingly, for I had ample resources at the moment and was mightily concerned about the sad household. But I knew that the little Duchess would take Oliphant's ears from his head if she guessed that he had dared to borrow from me, and that, if I lent, her back would for ever be turned against me. And yet, what would follow on my refusal? In a day or two there would be a pitiful scene with mine host, and as like as not some of their baggage detained as security for payment. I did not love the task of conspiring behind the lady's back, but if it could be contrived 'twas indubitably the kindest course. I glared sternly at Oliphant, who met me with his pathetic, dog-like eyes.

'You know that your mistress would never consent to the request you have made of me?'

'I ken,' he said humbly. 'But payin' is *my* job, and I simply havena the siller. It's no' the first time it has happened, and it's a sair trial for them both to be flung out o' doors by a foreign hostler because they canna meet his charges. But, sir, if ye can lend to me, ye may be certain that her leddyship will never hear a word o't. Puir thing, she takes nae thocht o' where the siller comes frae, ony mair than the lilies o' the field.'

I became a conspirator. 'You swear, Oliphant, by all you hold sacred, to breathe nothing of this to your mistress, and if she should suspect, to lie like a Privy Councillor?'

A flicker of a smile crossed his face. 'I'll lee like a Scots packman, and the Father o' lees could do nae mair. You need have no fear for your siller, sir. I've aye repaid when I borrowed, though you may have to wait a bittock.' And the strange fellow strolled off.

At dinner no Duchess appeared till long after the appointed hour, nor was there any sign of Oliphant. When she came at last with Cristine, her eyes looked as if she had been crying, and she greeted me with remote courtesy. My first thought was that Oliphant had revealed the matter of the loan, but presently I found that the lady's trouble was far different. Her father, it seemed, was ill again with his old complaint. What that was I did not ask, nor did the Duchess reveal it.

We spoke in French, for I had discovered that this was her favourite speech. There was no Oliphant to wait on us, and the inn servants were always about, so it was well to have a tongue they did not comprehend. The lady was distracted and sad. When I inquired feelingly as to the general condition of her father's health she parried the question, and when I offered my services she disregarded my words. It was in truth a doleful meal, while the faded Cristine sat like a sphinx staring into vacancy. I spoke of England and of her friends, of Paris and Versailles, of Avignon where she had spent some years, and of the amenities of Florence, which she considered her home. But it was like talking to a nunnery door. I got nothing but 'It is indeed true, sir,' or 'Do you say so, sir?' till my energy began to sink. Madame perceived my discomfort, and, as she rose, murmured an apology. 'Pray forgive my distraction, but I am poor company when my father is ill. I have a foolish mind, easily frightened. Nay, nay!' she went on when I again offered help, 'the illness is trifling. It will pass off by tomorrow, or at the latest the next day. Only I had looked forward to some ease at Santa Chiara, and the promise is belied.'

As it chanced that evening, returning to the inn, I passed by the north side where the windows of the Count's room looked over a little flower garden abutting on the courtyard. The dusk was falling, and a lamp had been lit which gave a glimpse into the interior. The sick man was standing by the window, his figure flung into relief by the lamplight. If he was sick, his sickness was of a curious type. His face was ruddy, his eye wild, and, his wig being off, his scanty hair stood up oddly round his head. He seemed to be singing, but I could not catch the sound through the shut casement. Another figure in the room, probably Oliphant, laid a hand on the Count's shoulder, drew him from the window, and closed the shutter.

It needed only the recollection of stories which were the

property of all Europe to reach a conclusion on the gentleman's illness. The legitimate King of England was very drunk.

As I went to my room that night I passed the Count's door. There stood Oliphant as sentry, more grim and haggard than ever, and I thought that his eye met mine with a certain intelligence. From inside the room came a great racket. There was the sound of glasses falling, then a string of oaths, English, French, and for all I knew, Irish, rapped out in a loud drunken voice. A pause, and then came the sound of maudlin singing. It pursued me along the gallery, an old childish song, delivered as if 'twere a pot-house catch —

> *Qu'est-c' qui passe ici si tard,*
> *Compagnons de la Marjolaine* —

One of the late-going company of the Marjolaine hastened to bed. This king in exile, with his melancholy daughter, was becoming too much for him.

III

It was just before noon next day that the travellers arrived. I was sitting in the shady loggia of the inn, reading a volume of De Thou*, when there drove up to the door two coaches. Out of the first descended very slowly and stiffly four gentlemen; out of the second four servants and a quantity of baggage. As it chanced there was no one about, the courtyard slept its sunny noontide sleep, and the only movement was a lizard on the wall and a buzz of flies by the fountain. Seeing no sign of the landlord, one of the travellers approached me with a grave inclination.

'This is the inn called the Tre Croci, sir?' he asked.

I said it was, and shouted on my own account for the host. Presently that personage arrived with a red face and a short wind, having ascended rapidly from his own cellar. He was awed by the dignity of the travellers, and made none of his usual protests of incapacity. The servants filed off solemnly with the baggage, and the four gentlemen set themselves down beside me in the loggia and ordered each a modest flask of wine.

At first I took them for our countrymen, but as I watched them the conviction vanished. All four were tall and lean beyond the average of mankind. They wore suits of black, with antique starched frills to their shirts; their hair was their own and unpowdered. Massive buckles of an ancient pattern adorned their square-toed shoes, and the canes they carried were like the yards of a small vessel. They were four merchants, I had guessed, of Scotland, maybe, or of Newcastle, but their voices were not Scotch, and their air had no touch of commerce. Take the heavy-browed preoccupation of a Secretary of State, add the dignity of a bishop, the sunburn of a fox-hunter, and something of the disciplined erectness of a soldier, and you may perceive the manner of these four gentlemen. By the side of them my assurance vanished. Compared with their Olympian serenity my person seemed fussy and servile. Even so, I mused, must Mr Franklin have looked when baited in Parliament by the Tory pack. The reflection gave me the cue. Presently I caught from their conversation the word 'Washington', and the truth flashed upon me. I was in the presence of four of Mr Franklin's countrymen. Having never seen an American in the flesh, I rejoiced at the chance of enlarging my acquaintance.

They brought me into the circle by a polite question as to the length of road to Verona. Soon introductions followed. My name intrigued them, and they were eager to learn of my kinship to Uncle Charles. The eldest of the four, it appeared, was Mr Galloway* out of Maryland. Then came two brothers, Sylvester by name, of Pennsylvania, and last Mr Fish, a lawyer of New York. All four had campaigned in the late war, and all four were members of the Convention, or whatever they call their rough-and-ready Parliament. They were modest in their behaviour, much disinclined to speak of their past, as great men might be whose reputation was world-wide. Somehow the names stuck in my memory. I was certain that I had heard them linked with some stalwart fight or some moving civil deed or some defiant manifesto. The making of history was in their steadfast eye and the grave lines of the mouth. Our friendship flourished mightily in a brief hour, and brought me the invitation, willingly accepted, to sit with them at dinner.

There was no sign of the Duchess or Cristine or Oliphant. Whatever had happened, that household today required all hands on deck, and I was left alone with the Americans. In my day I have supped with the Macaronies, I have held up my head at the Cocoa Tree, I have avoided the floor at hunt dinners, I have drunk glass to glass with Tom Carteron. But never before have I seen such noble consumers of good liquor as those four gentlemen from beyond the Atlantic. They drank the strong red Cyprus as if it had been spring water. 'The dust of your Italian roads takes some cleansing, Mr Townshend,' was their only excuse, but in truth none was needed. The wine seemed only to thaw their iron decorum. Without any surcease of dignity they grew communicative, and passed from lands to peoples and from peoples to constitutions. Before we knew it we were embarked upon high politics.

Naturally we did not differ on the war. Like me, they held it to have been a grievous necessity. They had no bitterness against England, only regret for her blunders. Of His Majesty they spoke with respect, of His Majesty's advisers with dignified condemnation. They thought highly of our troops in America; less highly of our generals.

'Look you, sir,' said Mr Galloway, 'in a war such as we have witnessed the Almighty is the only strategist. You fight against the forces of Nature, and a newcomer little knows that the success or failure of every operation he can conceive depends not upon generalship, but upon the conformation of a vast country. Our generals, with this in mind and with fewer men, could make all your schemes miscarry. Had the English soldiery not been of such stubborn stuff, we should have been victors from the first. Our leader was not General Washington, but General America, and his brigadiers were forests, swamps, lakes, rivers, and high mountains.'

'And now,' I said, 'having won, you have the greatest of human experiments before you. Your business is to show that the Saxon stock is adaptable to a republic.'

It seemed to me that they exchanged glances.

'We are not pedants,' said Mr Fish, 'and have no desire to dispute about the form of a constitution. A people may be as free under a king as under a senate. Liberty is not the lackey of any type of government.'

These were strange words from a member of a race whom I had thought wedded to the republicanism of Helvidius Priscus.

'As a loyal subject of a monarchy,' I said, 'I must agree with you. But your hands are tied, for I cannot picture the establishment of a House of Washington, and – if not, where are you to turn for your sovereign?'

Again a smile seemed to pass among the four.

'We are experimenters, as you say, sir, and must go slowly. In the meantime, we have an authority which keeps peace and property safe. We are at leisure to cast our eyes round and meditate on the future.'

'Then, gentleman,' said I, 'you take an excellent way of meditation in visiting this museum of old sovereignties. Here you have the relics of any government you please – a dozen republics, tyrannies, theocracies, merchant confederations, kingdoms, and more than one empire. You have your choice. I am tolerably familiar with the land, and if I can assist you I am at your service.'

They thanked me gravely. 'We have letters,' said Mr Galloway; 'one in especial is to a gentleman whom we hope to meet in this place. Have you heard in your travels of the Count of Albany?'

'He has arrived,' said I, 'two days ago. Even now he is in the chamber above us at dinner.'

The news interested them hugely.

'You have seen him?' they cried. 'What is he like?'

'An elderly gentleman in poor health, a man who has travelled much, and, I judge, has suffered something from fortune. He has a fondness for the English, so you will be welcome, sirs; but he was indisposed yesterday, and may still be unable to receive you. His daughter travels with him and tends his old age.'

'And you – you have spoken with him?'

'The night before last I was in his company. We talked of many things, including the late war. He is somewhat of your opinion on matters of government.'

The four looked at each other, and then Mr Galloway rose.

'I ask your permission, Mr Townshend, to consult for a moment with my friends. The matter is of some importance, and I would beg you to await us.' So saying, he led the others out of doors, and I heard them withdraw to a corner of the loggia. Now, thought I, there is something afoot, and my long-sought romance approaches fruition. The company of the Marjolaine, whom the Count had sung of, have arrived at last.

Presently they returned and seated themselves at the table.

'You can be of great assistance to us, Mr Townshend, and we would fain take you into our confidence. Are you aware who is this Count of Albany?'

I nodded. 'It is a thin disguise to one familiar with history.'

'Have you reached any estimate of his character or capabilities? You speak to friends, and, let me tell you, it is a matter which deeply concerns the Count's interests.'

'I think him a kindly and pathetic old gentleman. He naturally bears the mark of forty years' sojourn in the wilderness.'

Mr Galloway took snuff.

'We have business with him, but it is business which stands in need of an agent. There is no one in the Count's suite with whom we could discuss affairs?'

'There is his daughter.'

'Ah, but she would scarcely suit the case. Is there no man – a friend, and yet not a member of the family, who can treat with us?'

I replied that I thought that I was the only being in Santa Chiara who answered the description.

'If you will accept the task, Mr Townshend, you are amply qualified. We will be frank with you and reveal our business. We are on no less an errand than to offer the Count of Albany a crown.'

I suppose I must have had some suspicion of their purpose, and yet the revelation of it fell on me like a thunderclap. I could only stare owlishly at my four grave gentlemen.

Mr Galloway went on unperturbed. 'I have told you that in America we are not yet republicans. There are those among us who favour a republic, but they are by no means a majority. We have got rid of a king who misgoverned us, but we have no wish to get rid of kingship. We want a king of our own choosing, and we would get with him all the ancient sanctions of monarchy. The Count of Albany is of the most illustrious stock in Europe – he is, if legitimacy goes for anything, the rightful King of Britain. Now, if the republican party among us is to be worsted, we must come before the nation with a powerful candidate for its favour. You perceive my drift? What more potent appeal to American pride than to say: "We have got rid of King George; we choose of our own free will the older line and King Charles"?'

I said foolishly that I thought monarchy had had its day, and that 'twas idle to revive it.

'That is a sentiment well enough under a monarchical government; but we, with a clean page to write upon, do not share it. You know your ancient historians. Has not the repository of the chief power always been the rock on which republicanism has shipwrecked? If that power is given to the chief citizen, the way is prepared for the tyrant. If it abides peacefully in a royal house, it abides with cyphers who dignify, without obstructing, a popular constitution. Do not mistake me, Mr Townshend. This is no whim of a sentimental girl, but the reasoned conclusion of the men who achieved our liberty. There is every reason to believe that General Washington shares our views, and Mr Hamilton, whose name you may know, is the inspirer of our mission.'

'But the Count is an old man,' I urged; for I knew not where to begin in my exposition of the hopelessness of their errand.

'By so much the better. We do not wish a young king who may be fractious. An old man tempered by misfortune is what our purpose demands.'

'He has also his failings. A man cannot lead his life for forty years and retain all the virtues.'

At that one of the Sylvesters spoke sharply. 'I have heard such gossip, but I do not credit it. I have not forgotten Preston and Derby.'

I made my last objection. 'He has no posterity — legitimate posterity — to carry on his line.'

The four gentlemen smiled. 'That happens to be his chiefest recommendation,' said Mr Galloway. 'It enables us to take the House of Stuart on trial. We need a breathing-space and leisure to look around; but unless we establish the principle of monarchy at once the republicans will forestall us. Let us get our king at all costs, and during the remaining years of his life we shall have time to settle the succession problem. We have no wish to saddle ourselves for good with a race who might prove burdensome. If King Charles fails he has no son, and we can look elsewhere for a better monarch. You perceive the reason of my view?'

I did, and I also perceived the colossal absurdity of the whole business. But I could not convince them of it, for they met my objections with excellent arguments. Nothing save a sight of the Count would, I feared, disillusion them.

'You wish me to make this proposal on your behalf?' I asked.

'We shall make the proposal ourselves, but we desire you to prepare the way for us. He is an elderly man, and should first be informed of our purpose.'

'There is one person whom I beg leave to consult — the Duchess, his daughter. It may be that the present is an ill moment for approaching the Count, and the affair requires her sanction.'

They agreed, and with a very perplexed mind I went forth to seek the lady. The irony of the thing was too cruel, and my heart ached for her. In the gallery I found Oliphant packing some very shabby trunks, and when I questioned him he told me that the family were to leave Santa Chiara on the morrow. Perchance the Duchess had awakened to the true state of their exchequer, or perchance she thought it well to get her father on the road again as a cure for his ailment.

I discovered Cristine, and begged for an interview with her mistress on an urgent matter. She led me to the Duchess's room, and there the evidence of poverty greeted me openly. All the little luxuries of the menage had gone to the Count. The poor lady's room was no better than a servant's garret, and the lady herself sat stitching a rent in a travelling cloak. She rose to greet me with alarm in her eyes.

As briefly as I could I set out the facts of my amazing mission. At first she seemed scarcely to hear me. 'What do they want with him?' she asked. 'He can give them nothing. He is no friend to the Americans or to any people who have deposed their sovereign.' Then, as she grasped my meaning, her face flushed.

'It is a heartless trick, Mr Townshend. I would fain think you no party to it.'

'Believe me, dear madame, it is no trick. The men below are in sober earnest. You have but to see their faces to know that theirs is no wild adventure. I believe sincerely that they have the power to implement their promise.'

'But it is madness. He is old and worn and sick. His day is long past for winning a crown.'

'All this I have said, but it does not move them.' And I told her rapidly Mr Galloway's argument.

She fell into a muse. 'At the eleventh hour! Nay, too late, too

late. Had he been twenty years younger, what a stroke of
fortune! Fate bears too hard on us, too hard!'

Then she turned to me fiercely. 'You have no doubt heard,
sir, the gossip about my father, which is on the lips of every fool
in Europe. Let us have done with this pitiful make-believe. My
father is a sot. Nay, I do not blame him. I blame his enemies and
his miserable destiny. But there is the fact. Were he not old, he
would still be unfit to grasp a crown and rule over a turbulent
people. He flees from one city to another, but he cannot flee
from himself. That is his illness on which you condoled with me
yesterday.'

The lady's control was at breaking-point. Another moment
and I expected a torrent of tears. But they did not come. With a
great effort she regained her composure.

'Well, the gentlemen must have an answer. You will tell
them that the Count, my father – nay, give him his true title if
you care – is vastly obliged to them for the honour they have
done him, but would decline on account of his age and infir-
mities. You know how to phrase a decent refusal.'

'Pardon me,' said I, 'but I might give them that answer till
doomsday and never content them. They have not travelled
many thousand miles to be put off by hearsay evidence. Nothing
will satisfy them but an interview with your father himself.'

'It is impossible,' she said sharply.

'Then we must expect the renewed attentions of our American friends. They will wait till they see him.'

She rose and paced the room.

'They must go,' she repeated many times. 'If they see him
sober he will accept with joy, and we shall be the laughing-stock
of the world. I tell you it cannot be. I alone know how immense
is the impossibility. He cannot afford to lose the last rags of his
dignity, the last dregs of his ease. They must not see him. I will
speak with them myself.'

'They will be honoured, madame, but I do not think they
will be convinced. They are what we call in my land "men of

business". They will not be content till they get the Count's reply from his own lips.'

A new Duchess seemed to have arisen, a woman of quick action and sharp words.

'So be it. They shall see him. Oh, I am sick to death of fine sentiments and high loyalty and all the vapouring stuff I have lived among for years. All I ask for myself and my father is a little peace, and, by Heaven! I shall secure it. If nothing will kill your gentlemen's folly but truth, why, truth they shall have. They shall see my father, and this very minute. Bring them up, Mr Townshend, and usher them into the presence of the rightful King of England. You will find him alone.' She stopped her walk and looked out of the window.

I went back in a hurry to the Americans. 'I am bidden to bring you to the Count's chamber. He is alone and will see you. These are the commands of madame his daughter.'

'Good!' said Mr Galloway, and all four, grave gentlemen as they were, seemed to brace themselves to a special dignity as befitted ambassadors to a king. I led them upstairs, tapped at the Count's door, and, getting no answer, opened it and admitted them.

And this was what we saw. The furniture was in disorder, and on a couch lay an old man sleeping a heavy drunken sleep. His mouth was open and his breath came stertorously. The face was purple, and large purple veins stood out on the mottled forehead. His scanty white hair was draggled over his cheek. On the floor was a broken glass, wet stains still lay on the boards, and the place reeked of spirits.

The four looked for a second – I do not think longer – at him whom they would have made their king. They did not look at each other. With one accord they moved out, and Mr Fish, who was last, closed the door very gently behind him.

In the hall below Mr Galloway turned to me. 'Our mission is ended, Mr Townshend. I have to thank you for your courtesy.' Then to the others, 'If we order the coaches now, we may get well on the way to Verona ere sundown.'

An hour later two coaches rolled out of the courtyard of the Tre Croci. As they passed, a window was half-opened on the upper floor, and a head looked out. A line of a song came down, a song sung in a strange quavering voice. It was the catch I had heard the night before:

> *Qu'est-c' qui passe ici si tard,*
> *Compagnons de la Marjolaine—e?*

It was true. The company came late indeed – too late by forty years. . . .

The Herd of Standlan

This early story, written when Buchan was an Oxford undergraduate in the 1890s, illustrates something that he never lost, a deep love for the places and people of the valleys of the Upper Tweed in southern Scotland, where much of his childhood and youth was spent. Some forty years later he took his title as First Baron from the upland village of Tweedsmuir.

The story uses the idea of a moment in history to very different effect. British national events are seen here very obliquely indeed, and put in a context both cosmic and comic. Buchan, though a serious theologian, could always sit lightly to aspects of his Calvinist inheritance. Yet the ironies of individual, local pain, as well as cosmic horrors, linked with distant Tory policies, do not in fact quite register on the conventional, vacuous narrator — a device Buchan uses, even so early, with great confidence.

The Herd of Standlan *first appeared in 1899 in the collection of stories and poems Buchan called* Grey Weather: Moorland Tales of My Own People. *It has not been reprinted until now.*

The Herd of Standlan

When the wind is nigh and the moon is high
   And the mist on the riverside,
Let such as fare have a very good care
   Of the Folk who come to ride.
For they may meet with the riders fleet
   Who fare from the place of dread;
And hard it is for a mortal man
   To sort at ease with the Dead.

THE BALLAD OF GREY WEATHER

When Standlan Burn leaves the mosses and hags which gave it birth, it tumbles over a succession of falls into a deep, precipitous glen, whence in time it issues into a land of level green meadows, and finally finds its rest in the Gled. Just at the opening of the ravine there is a pool shut in by high, dark cliffs, and black even on the most sunshiny day. The rocks are never dry but always black with damp and shadow. There is scarce any vegetation save stunted birks, juniper bushes, and draggled fern; and the hoot of owls and the croak of hooded crows is seldom absent from the spot. It is the famous Black Linn where in winter sheep stray and are never more heard of, and where more than once an unwary shepherd has gone to his account. It is an Inferno on the brink of a Paradise, for not a stone's throw off is the green, lawn-like turf, the hazel thicket, and the broad, clear pools, by the edge of which on that July day the Herd of Standlan and I sat drowsily smoking and talking of fishing and the hills. There he told me this story, which I here set down as I remember it, and as it bears repetition.

'D'ye mind Airthur Morrant?' said the shepherd, suddenly.

I did remember Arthur Mordaunt. Ten years past he and I had been inseparables, despite some half-dozen summers differ-

ence in age. We had fished and shot together, and together we
had tramped every hill within thirty miles. He had come up
from the South to try sheep-farming, and as he came of a great
family and had no need to earn his bread, he found the profession pleasing. Then irresistible fate had swept me southward to
college, and when after two years I came back to the place, his
father was dead and he had come into his own. The next I heard
of him was that in politics he was regarded as the most promis-
ing of the younger men, one of the staunchest and ablest upstays
of the Constitution. His name was rapidly rising into promi-
nence, for he seemed to exhibit that rare phenomenon of a man
of birth and culture in direct sympathy with the wants of the
people.

'You mean Lord Brodakers?' said I.

'Dinna call him by that name,' said the shepherd, darkly. 'I
hae nae thocht o' him now. He's a disgrace to his country,
servin' the Deil wi' baith hands. But nine year syne he was a bit
innocent callant wi' nae Tory deevilry in his heid. Well, as I was
sayin', Airthur Morrant has cause to mind that place till his
dying day;' and he pointed his finger to the Black Linn.

I looked up the chasm. The treacherous water, so bright and
joyful at our feet, was like ink in the great gorge. The swish and
plunge of the cataract came like the regular beating of a clock,
and though the weather was dry, streams of moisture seamed
the perpendicular walls. It was a place eerie even on that bright
summer's day.

'I don't think I ever heard the story,' I said casually.

'Maybe no,' said the shepherd. 'It's no yin I like to tell;' and
he puffed sternly at his pipe, while I awaited the continuation.

'Ye see it was like this,' he said, after a while. 'It was just the
beginning o' the back-end, and that year we had an awfu' spate
o' rain. For near a week it poured hale water, and a' doon by
Drumeller and the Mossfennan haughs was yae muckle loch.
Then it stopped, and an awfu' heat came on. It dried the grund
in nae time, but it hardly touched the burns; and it was rale

queer to be pourin' wi' sweat and the grund aneath ye as dry as a
potato-sack, and a' the time the water neither to haud nor bind.
A' the waterside fields were clean stripped o' stooks, and a guid
wheen hay-ricks gaed doon tae Berwick, no to speak o' sheep
and nowt beast. But that's anither thing.

'Weel, ye'll mind that Airthur was terrible keen on fishing.
He wad gang oot in a' weather, and he wasna feared for only
mortal or naitural thing. Dod, I've seen him in Gled wi' the
water rinnin' ower his shouthers yae cauld March day playin' a
saumon. He kenned weel aboot the fishing, for he had traivelled
in Norroway and siccan outlandish places, where there's a heap
o' big fish. So that day — and it was a Setterday tae and far ower
near the Sabbath — he maun gang awa' up Standlan Burn wi' his
rod and creel to try his luck.

'I was bidin' at that time, as ye mind, in the wee cot-house at
the back o' the faulds. I was alane, for it was three year afore I
mairried Jess, and I wasna begun yet to the coortin'. I had been
at Gledsmuir that day for some o' the new stuff for killing
sheep-mawks, and I wasna very fresh on my legs when I gaed oot
after my tea that night to hae a look at the hill-sheep. I had had a
bad year on the hill. First the lambin'-time was snaw, snaw ilka
day, and I lost mair than I wad like to tell. Syne the grass a'
summer was so short wi' the drought that the puir beasts could
scarcely get a bite and were as thin as pipe-stapples. And then,
to crown a', auld Will Broun, the man that helpit me, turned ill
wi' his back, and had to bide at hame. So I had twae man's work
on yae man's shouthers, and was nane so weel pleased.

'As I was saying, I gaed oot that nicht, and after lookin' a' the
Dun Rig and the Yellow Mire and the back o' Cramalt Craig, I
cam down the burn by the road frae the auld faulds. It was geyan
dark, being about seven o'clock o' a September nicht, and I
keepit weel back frae that wanchancy hole o' a burn. Weel, I was
comin' kind o' quick, thinkin' o' supper and a story-book that I
was readin' at the time, when just abune that place there, at the
foot o' the Linn, I saw a man fishing. I wondered what ony body

in his senses could be daein' at that time o' nicht in sic a dangerous place, so I gave him a roar and bade him come back. He turned his face round and I saw in a jiffey that it was Mr Airthur.

'"O, sir," I cried, "What for are ye fishing there? The water's awfu' dangerous, and the rocks are far ower slid."

'"Never mind, Scott," he roars back cheery-like. "I'll take care o' mysel'."

'I lookit at him for twa-three meenutes, and then I saw by his rod he had yin on, and a big yin tae. He ran it up and doon the pool, and he had uncommon wark wi' 't, for it was strong and there was little licht. But bye and bye he got it almost tae his feet, and was just about to lift it oout when a maist awfu' thing happened. The tackets o' his boots maun hae slithered on the stane, for the next thing I saw was Mr Airthur in the muckle hungry water.

'I dinna exactly ken what happened after that, till I found myself on the very stone he had slipped off. I maun hae come doon the face o' the rocks, a thing I can scarcely believe when I look at them, and a thing no man ever did afore. At ony rate I ken I fell the last fifteen feet or sae, and lichted on my left airm, for I felt it crack like a rotten branch, and an awfu' sairness ran up it.

'Now, the pool is a whirlpool as ye ken, and if anything fa's in, the water first smashes it against the muckle rock at the foot, then it brings it round below the fall again, and syne at the second time it carries it doon the burn. Weel, that was what happened to Mr Airthur. I heard his heid gang dunt on the stane wi' a sound that made me sick. This must hae dung him clean senseless, and indeed it was a wonder it didna knock his brains oot. At ony rate there was nae mair word o' swimming, and he was swirled round below the fa' just like a corp.

'I kenned fine that nae time was to be lost, for if he once gaed doon the burn he wad be in Gled or ever I could say a word, and nae wad ever see him mair in life. So doon I got on my hunkers on the stane, and waited for the turnin'. Round he came, whirling in the foam, wi' a lang line o' blood across his brow where the stane had cut him. It was a terrible meenute. My heart fair stood still. I put out my airm, and as he passed I grippit him and wi' an awfu' pu' got him out o' the current into the side.

'But now I found that a waur thing still was on me. My left airm was broken, and my richt sae numbed and weak wi' my fall that, try as I micht, I couldna raise him ony further. I thocht I wad burst a blood-vessel i' my face and my muscles fair cracked wi' the strain, but I would make nothing o' 't. There he stuck wi' his heid and shouthers abune the water, pu'd close until the edge of a rock.

'What was I to dae? If I once let him slip he wad be into the stream and lost forever. But I couldna hang on here a' nicht, and as far as I could see there wad be naebody near till the mornin', when Ebie Blackstock passed frae the Head o' the Hope. I roared wi' a' my power; but I got nai answer, naething but the rummle o' the water and the whistling o' some whaups on the hill.

'Then I turned very sick wi' terror and pain and weakness and I kenna what. My broken airm seemed a great lump o' burnin' coal. I maun hae given it some extra wrench when I hauled him out, for it was sae sair now that I thocht I could scarcely thole it. Forbye, pain and a', I could hae gone off to sleep wi' fair weariness. I had heard tell o' men sleepin' on their feet, but I never felt it till then. Man, if I hadna warstled wi' mysel, I wad hae dropped off as deid's a peery.

'Then there was the awfu' strain o' keepin' Mr Airthur up. He was a great big man, twelve stone I'll warrant, and weighing a terrible lot mair wi' his fishing togs and things. If I had had the use o' my ither airm I micht hae taen off his jacket and creel and lichtened the burden, but I could do naething. I scarcely like to tell ye how I was tempted in that hour. Again and again I says to mysel, "Gidden Scott," say I, "what do ye care for this man?

He's no a drap's bluid to you, and forbye ye'll never be able to
save him. Ye micht as weel let him gang. Ye've dune a' ye
could. Ye're a brave man, Gidden Scott, and ye've nae cause to
be ashamed o' givin' up the fecht." But I says to mysel again:
"Gidden Scott, ye're a coward. Wad ye let a man die, when
there's a breath in your body? Think shame o' yoursel, man." So
I aye kept haudin' on, although I was very near bye wi' 't.
Whenever I lookit at Mr Airthur's face, as white's death and a'
blood, and his een sae stelled-like, I got a kind o' groo and felt
awfu' pitiful for the bit laddie. Then I thocht on his faither, the
auld Lord, wha was sae built up in him, and I couldna bear to
think o' his son droonin' in that awfu' hole. So I set mysel to the
wark o' keepin' him up a' nicht, though I had nae hope in the
matter. It wasna what ye ca' bravery that made me dae't, for I
had nae ither choice. It was just a kind o' dourness that runs in
my folk, and a kind o' vexedness for sae young a callant in sic an
ill place.

'The nicht was hot and there was scarcely a sound o' wind. I
felt the sweat standin' on my face like frost on tatties, and abune
me the sky was a' misty and nae mune visible. I thocht very
likely that it micht come a thunder-shower and I kind o' lookit
forrit tae 't. For I was aye feared at lichtning, and if it came that
nicht I was bound to get clean dazed and likely tummle in. I was
a lonely man wi' nae kin to speak o', so it wouldna maitter
muckle.

'But now I come to tell ye about the queer side o' that nicht's
wark, whilk I never telled to nane but yoursel, though a' the
folk about here ken the rest. I maun hae been geyan weak, for I
got into a kind o' doze, no sleepin', ye understand, but awfu'
like it. And then a' sort o' daft things began to dance afore my
een. Witches and bogles and brownies and things oot o' the
Bible, and leviathans and brazen bulls – a' cam fleerin' and
flauntin' on the tap o' the water straucht afore me. I didna pay
muckle heed to them, for I half kenned it was a' nonsense, and
syne they gaed awa'. Then an auld wife wi' a mutch and a hale

procession o' auld wives passed, and just about the last I saw yin I thocht I kenned.

'"Is that you, grannie?" says I.

'"Ay, it's me, Gidden,' says she; and as shüre as I'm a leevin' man, it was my auld grannie, whae had been deid thae sax year. She had on the same mutch as she aye wore, and the same auld black stickie in her hand, and, Dod, she had the same snuff-box I made for her out o' a sheep's horn when I first took to the herdin'. I thocht she was lookin' rale weel.

'"Losh, Grannie," says I, "Where in the warld hae ye come frae? It's no canny to see ye danderin' about there."

'"Ye've been badly brocht up," she says, "and ye ken nocht about it. Is't no a decent and comely thing that I should get a breath o' air yince in the while?"

'"Deed," said I, "I had forgotten. Ye were sae like yoursel I never had a mind ye were deid. And how d' ye like the Guid Place?"

'"Wheesht, Gidden," says she, very solemn-like, "I'm no there."

'Now at this I was fair flabbergasted. Grannie had aye been a guid contentit auld wumman, and to think that they hadna let her intil Heeven made me think ill o' my ain chances.

'"Help us, ye dinna mean to tell me ye're in Hell?" I cries.

'"No exactly," says she, "But I'll trouble ye, Gidden, to speak mair respectful about holy things. That's a name ye uttered the noo whilk we dinna daur to mention."

'"I'm sorry, Grannie," says I, "but ye maun allow it's an astonishin' thing for me to hear. We aye counted ye shüre, and ye died wi' the Buik in your hands."

'"Weel," she says, "it was like this. When I gaed up till the gate o' Heeven a man wi' a lang white robe comes and says, 'Wha may ye be?' Says I, 'I'm Elspeth Scott.' He gangs awa' and consults a wee and then he says, 'I think, Elspeth my wumman, ye'll hae to gang doon the brae a bit. Ye're no quite guid eneuch for this place, but ye'll get a very comfortable doonsittin' whaur

' to a place whaur the air was like
at the Lodge. They took me in
le comfortable. Ye see they keep
the reg'lar bad folk, but they've a
re the likes o' me stop."
ny hae ye?"
"There's maist o' the ministers o'
irmers, tho' the maist o' them are
n Jock, your ain faither, Gidden,
lage, and oh, I'm nane sae bad."
e wad like then, Grannie?"
e each yae thing which we canna
e hae. Mine's butter. I canna get
ye see it winna keep, it just melts.
:e, whilk is rale sair on the teeth.

ng but some tobaccy. D' ye want

Na, na, says she. I get plenty o' tobaccy doon bye. The
pipe's never out o' the folks' mouth there. But I'm no speakin'
about yoursel, Gidden. Ye're in a geyan ticht place."

'"I'm a' that," I said. "Can ye no help me?"

'"I micht try." And she raxes out her hand to grip mine. I put
out mine to tak it, never thinkin' that that wasna the richt side,
and that if Grannie grippit it she wad pu' the broken airm and
haul me into the water. Something touched my fingers like a
hot poker; I gave a great yell; and ere ever I kenned I was awake,
a' but off the rock, wi' my left airm aching like hell-fire. Mr
Airthur I had let slunge ower the heid and my ain legs were in
the water.

'I gae an awfu' whammle and edged my way back though it
was near bye my strength. And now anither thing happened.
For the cauld water roused Mr Airthur frae his dwam. His een
opened and he gave a wild look around him. "Where am I?" he
cries, "Oh God!" and he gaed off intil anither faint.

'I can tell ye, sir, I never felt anything in this warld and I hope never to feel anything in anither sae bad as the next meenutes on that rock. I was fair sick wi' pain and weariness and a kind o' fever. The lip-lap o' the water, curling round Mr Airthur, and the great *crush* o' the Black Linn itsel dang me fair silly. Then there was my airm, which was bad eneuch, and abune a' I was gotten into sic a state that I was fleyed at ilka shadow just like a bairn. I felt fine I was gaun daft, and if the thing had lasted anither score o' meenutes I wad be in a madhouse this day. But soon I felt the sleepiness comin' back, and I was off again dozin' and dreamin'.

'This time it was nae auld wumman but a muckle black-avised man that was standin' in the water glowrin' at me. I kenned him fine by the bandy-legs o' him and the broken nose (whilk I did mysel), for Dan Kyle the poacher deid thae twae year. He was a man, as I remembered him weel, wi' a great black beard and een that were stuck sae far in his heid that they looked like twae wull-cats keekin' oot o' a hole. He stands and just stares at me, and never speaks a word.

'"What d'ye want?" I yells, for by this time I had lost a' grip o' mysel. "Speak, man, and dinna stand there like a dummy."

'"I want naething," he says in a mournfu' sing-song voice; "I'm just thinkin'."

'"Whaur d' ye come frae?" I asked, "and are ye keepin' weel?"

'"Weel," he says bitterly. "In this warld I was ill to my wife, and twa-three times I near killed a man, and I stole like a pyet, and I was never sober. How d' ye think I should be weel in the next?"

'I was sorry for the man. "D' ye ken I'm vexed for ye, Dan," says I; "I never likit ye when ye were here, but I'm wae to think ye're sae ill off yonder."

'"I'm no alane," he says. "There's Mistress Courhope o' the Big House, she's waur. Ye mind she was awfu' fond o' gum-flowers. Weel, she canna keep them Yonder, for they a' melt wi' the heat. She's in an ill way about it, puir body." Then he broke off. "Whae's that ye've got there? Is't Airthur Morrant?"

'"Ay, it's Airthur Morrant," I said.

'"His family's weel kent doon bye," says he. "We've maist o' his forbears, and we're expectin' the auld Lord every day. May be we'll sune get the lad himsel."

'"That's a damned lee," says I, for I was angry at the man's presumption.

'Dan lookit at me sorrowfu'-like. "We'll be gettin' you tae, if ye swear that gate," says he, "and then ye'll ken what it's like."

'Of a sudden I fell into a great fear. "Dinna say that, Dan," I cried; "I'm better than ye think. I'm a deacon, and 'll maybe sune be an elder, and I never swear except at my dowg."

'"Tak care, Gidden," said the face afore me. "Where I am, a' things are taken into account."

'"Then they'll hae a gey big account for you," says I. "What-like do they treat you, may be?"

'The man groaned.

'"I'll tell ye what they dae to ye doon there," he said. "They put ye intil a place a' paved wi' stanes and wi' four square walls around. And there's naething in 't, nae grass, nae shadow. And abune you there's a sky like brass. And sune ye get terrible hot and thirsty, and your tongue sticks to your mouth, and your eyes get blind wi' lookin' on the white stane. Then ye gang clean fey, and dad your heid on the ground and the walls to try and kill yoursel. But though ye dae 't till a' eternity ye couldna feel pain. A' that ye feel is just the awfu' devourin' thirst, and the heat and the weariness. And if ye lie doon the ground burns ye and ye're fain to get up. And ye canna lean on the walls for the heat, and bye and bye when ye're fair perished wi' the thing, they tak ye out to try some ither ploy."

'"Nai mair," I cried, "nae mair, Dan!"

'But he went on malicious-like, —

'"Na, na, Gidden, I'm no dune yet. Syne they tak you to a fine room but awfu' warm. And there's a big fire in the grate and thick woollen rugs on the floor. And in the corner there's a braw feather bed. And they lay ye down on 't, and then they pile on the tap o' ye mattresses and blankets and sacks and great rolls o' woollen stuff miles wide. And then ye see what they're after, tryin' to suffocate ye as they dae to folk that a mad dowg has bitten. And ye try to kick them off, but they're ower heavy, and ye canna move your feet nor your airms nor gee your heid. Then ye gang clean gyte and skirl to yoursel, but your voice is choked and naebody is near. And the warst o' 't is that ye canna die and get it ower. It's like death a hundred times and yet ye're aye leevin'. Bye and bye when they think ye've got eneuch they tak you out and put ye somewhere else."

'"Oh," I cries, "stop, man, or you'll ding me silly."

'But he says never a word, just glowrin' at me.

'"Aye, Gidden, and waur than that. For they put ye in a great loch wi' big waves just like the sea at the Pier o' Leith. And there's nae chance o' soomin', for as sune as ye put out your airms a billow gulfs ye down. Then ye swallow water and your heid dozes round and ye're chokin'. But ye canna die, ye must just thole. And down ye gang, down, down, in the cruel deep, till your heid's like to burst and your een are fu' o' bluid. And there's a' kind o' fearfu' monsters about, muckle slimy things wi' blind een and white scales, that claw at ye wi' claws just like the paws o' a drooned dog. And ye canna get away though ye fecht and fleech, and bye and bye ye're fair mad wi' horror and choking and the feel o' thae awfu' things. Then – "

'But now I think something snapped in my heid, and I went daft in doonricht earnest. The man before me danced about like a lantern's shine on a windy nicht and then disappeared. And I woke yelling like a pig at a killing, fair wud wi' terror, and my skellochs made the rocks ring. I found mysel in the pool a' but yae airm – the broken yin – which had hankit in a crack o' rock. Nae wonder I had been dreaming o' deep waters among the torments o' the Ill Place, when I was in them mysel. The pain in my airm was sae fearsome and my heid was gaun round sae wi' horror that I just skirled on and on, shrieking and groaning wi'oot a thocht what I was daein'. I was as near death as ever I will be, and as for Mr Airthur he was on the very nick o' 't, for by this time he was a' in the water, though I still kept a grip o' him.

'When I think ower it often I wonder how it was possible that I could be here the day. But the Lord's very gracious, and he works in a queer way. For it so happened that Ebie Blackstock, whae had left Gledsmuir an hour afore me and whom I thocht by this time to be snorin' in his bed at the Head o' the Hope, had gone intil the herd's house at the Waterfit, and had got sae muckle drink there that he was sweered to start for hame till aboot half-past twal i' the night. Weel, he was comin' up the burnside, gae happy and contentit, for he had nae wife at hame to speir about his ongaeings, when, as he's telled me himsel, he heard sic an uproar doon by the Black Linn that made him turn pale and think that the Deil, whom he had long served, had gotten him at last. But he was a brave man, was Ebie, and he thinks to himsel that some fellow-creature micht be perishin'. So he gangs forrit wi' a' his pith, trying to think on the Lord's Prayer and last Sabbath's sermon. And, lookin' ower the edge, he saw naething for a while, naething but the black water wi' the awfu' yells coming out o' 't. Then he made out something like a heid near the side. So he rins doon by the road, no ower the rocks as I had come, but round by the burnside road, and soon he gets to the pool, where the crying was getting aye fainter and fainter. And then he saw me. And he grips me by the collar, for he was a sensible man, was Ebie, and hauls me oot. If he hadna been geyan strong he couldna hae dune it, for I was a deid wecht, forbye having a heavy man hanging on to me. When he got me up, what was his astonishment to find anither man at the end o' my airm, a man like a corp a' bloody about the heid. So he got us baith out, and we wae baith senseless; and he laid us in a safe bit back frae the water, and syne gaed off for help. So bye and bye we were baith got home, me to my house and Mr Airthur up to the Lodge.'

'And was that the end of it?' I asked.

'Na,' said the shepherd. 'I lay for twae month there raving wi' brain fever, and when I cam to my senses I was as weak as a bairn. It was many months ere I was mysel again, and my left airm to this day is stiff and no muckle to lippen to. But Mr Airthur was far waur, for the dad he had gotten on the rock was thocht to have broken his skull, and he lay long atween life and death. And the warst thing was that his faither was sae vexed about him that he never got ower the shock, but dee'd afore Airthur was out o' bed. And so when he cam out again he was My Lord, and a monstrously rich man.'

The shepherd puffed meditatively at his pipe for a few minutes.

'But that's no a' yet. For Mr Airthur wad tak nae refusal but that I maun gang awa' doon wi' him to his braw house in England and be a land o' factor or steward or something like that. And I had a rale fine cottage a' to mysel, wi' a very bonny gairden and guid wages, so I stayed there maybe sax month and then I gaed up till him. "I canna bide nae longer," says I. "I canna stand this place. It's far ower laigh, and I'm fair sick to get hills to rest my een on. I'm awfu' gratefu' to ye for your kindness, but I maun gie up my job." He was very sorry to lose me, and was for giein' me a present o' money or stockin' a fairm for me, because he said that it was to me he owed his life. But I wad hae nane o' his gifts. "It wad be a terrible thing," I says, "to tak siller for daein' what ony body wad hae dune out o' pity." So I cam awa' back to Standlan, and I maun say I'm rale contentit here. Mr Airthur used whiles to write to me and ca' in and see me when he cam North for the shooting; but since he's gane sae far wrang wi' the Tories, I've had naething mair to dae wi' him.'

I made no answer, being busy pondering in my mind on the depth of the shepherd's political principles, before which the ties of friendship were as nothing.

'Ay,' said he, standing up, 'I did what I thocht my duty at the time and I was rale glad I saved the callant's life. But now, when

I think on a' the ill he's daein' to the country and the Guid Cause, I whiles think I wad hae been daein' better if I had just drappit him in.

'But whae kens? It's a queer warld.' And the shepherd knocked the ashes out of his pipe.

The Last Crusade

In the mid-1920s, Buchan, rooted and settled with his young family at Elsfield Manor, on a Cotswold upland four miles from Oxford, was giving half of every weekday to his publishing work with Nelson's in London and Edinburgh, and half to Reuters, of which he was Deputy Chairman, having been a very hard-working Director since 1919. He also had a massive programme of writing: not only revision of his own million-and-a-half words for a new edition of Nelson's History of the War, but much history, biography and full-length fiction as well.   .

He works again in this story at his interest in the 'ifs' of history — a prime subject for a romancer. He liked to quote Burke's remark, 'A common soldier, a child, a girl at the door of an inn, have changed the face of fortune, and almost of Nature.' His narrator in this story, Francis Martendale (his only appearance in Buchan) shares with the author a South African period, war service in France, publishing, Agency work and an interest in philosophy. Otherwise he is, of course, in his dining-club setting, a fictional character. The point has to be laboured because some modern casuistry, understandably dismayed by Martendale's off-hand use of the word 'nigger', instantly damns the whole of Buchan and sweeps him from the shelves. More sophisticated readers may relish the use of the specifics of international affairs, of literature, history and religion, the easy handling of detailed knowledge of the world's press, and the curious topicality of some of the names and situations.

By the time the story appeared in print, in July 1928, Buchan had begun his Parliamentary career as Member for the Scottish universities.

The Last Crusade

It is often impossible, in these political inquiries, to find any
proportion between the apparent force of any moral causes we
may assign, and their known operation. We are therefore
obliged to deliver up that operation to mere chance; or, more
piously (perhaps more rationally), to the occasional interposi-
tion and the irresistible hand of the Great Disposer.

BURKE*

One evening the talk at dinner turned on the Press. Lamancha
was of opinion that the performances of certain popular newspapers in recent years had killed the old power of the anonymous
printed word. 'They bluffed too high,' he said, 'and they had
their bluff called. All the delphic oracle business has gone from
them. You haven't today what you used to have — papers from
which the ordinary man docilely imbibes all his views. There
may be one or two still, but not more.'

Sandy Arbuthnot, who disliked journalism as much as he
liked journalists, agreed, but there was a good deal of difference
of opinion among the others. Pallister-Yeates thought that the
Press had more influence than ever, though it might not be
much liked; a man, he said, no longer felt the kind of loyalty
towards his newspaper that he felt towards his club and his
special brand of cigar, but he was mightily influenced by it all
the same. He might read it only for its news, but in the selection
of news a paper could wield an uncanny power.

Francis Martendale was the only journalist among us, and he
listened with half-closed sleepy eyes. He had been a war correspondent as far back as the days of the South African War, and
since then had seen every serious row on the face of the globe. In

France he had risen to command a territorial battalion, and that seemed to have satisfied his military interest, for since 1919 he had turned his mind to business. He was part-owner of several provincial papers, and was connected in some way with the great Ladas news agency. He had several characters which he kept rigidly separate. One was a philosopher, for he had translated Henri Poincaré, and published an acute little study of Bergson; another was a yachtsman, and he used to race regularly in the twelve-metre class at Cowes. But these were his relaxations, and five days in the week he spent in an office in the Fleet Street neighbourhood. He was an enthusiast about his hobbies and a cynic about his profession, a not uncommon mixture; so we were surprised when he differed from Lamancha and Sandy and agreed with Palliser-Yeates.

'No doubt the power of the leader-writer has waned,' he said. 'A paper cannot set a Cabinet trembling because it doesn't like its policy. But it can colour the public mind most damnably by a steady drip of tendencious news.'

'Lies?' Sandy asked.

'Not lies — truths judiciously selected — half-truths with no context. Facts — facts all the time. In these days the Press is obliged to stick to facts. But it can make facts into *news*, which is a very different class of goods. And it can interpret facts — don't forget that. It can report that Burminster fell asleep at a public dinner — which he did — in such a way as to make everybody think that he was drunk — which he wasn't.'

'Rather a dirty game?' someone put in.

'Sometimes — often perhaps. But now and then it works out on the side of the angels. Do any of you know Roper Willinck?'

There was a general confession of ignorance.

'Pity. He would scarcely fit in here, but he is rather a great man and superbly good company. There was a little thing that Willinck once did — or rather helped to do, with about a million other people who hadn't a notion what was happening. That's the fun of journalism. You light a match and fling it away, and the fire goes smouldering round the globe, and ten thousand miles off burns down a city. I'll tell you about it if you like, for it rather proves my point.'

It all began – said Martendale – with an old Wesleyan parson of the name of Tubb, who lived at a place called Rhenosterspruit on the east side of the Karroo. He had been a missionary, but the place had grown from a small native reserve to an ordinary up-country dorp; the natives were all Christians now, and he had a congregation of store-keepers, and one or two English farmers, and the landlady of the hotel, and the workmen from an adjacent irrigation dam. Mr Tubb was a man of over seventy, a devoted pastor with a gift of revivalist eloquence, but not generally considered very strong in the head. He was also a bachelor. He had caught a chill and had been a week in bed, but he rose on the Sunday morning to conduct service as usual.

Now about that time the Russian Government had been rather distinguishing themselves. They had had a great function at Easter, run by what they called the Living Church, which had taken the shape of a blasphemous parody of the Christian rites and a procession of howling dervishes who proclaimed that God was dead and Heaven and Hell wound up. Also they had got hold of a Patriarch, a most respected Patriarch, put him on trial for high treason, and condemned him to death. They had postponed the execution, partly by way of a refinement of cruelty, and partly, I suppose, to see just how the world would react; but there seemed not the slightest reason to doubt that they meant to have the old man's blood. There was a great outcry, and the Archbishop of Canterbury and the Pope had something to say, and various Governments made official representations, but the Bolshies didn't give a hoot. They felt that they needed to indulge in some little bit of extra blackguardism just to show what stout fellows they were.

Well, all this was in the cables from Riga and Warsaw and Helsingfors, and it got into the weekly edition of the *Cape*

Times. There Mr Tubb read it, as he lay sick in bed, and, having nothing else to worry about, it fretted him terribly. He could not bear to think of those obscene orgies in Moscow, and the story of the Patriarch made him frantic. This, it seemed to him, was a worse persecution than Nero's or Diocletian's, and the Patriarch was a nobler figure than any martyr of the Roman amphitheatre; and all the while the Christian peoples of the world were doing nothing. So Mr Tubb got out of bed on that Sunday morning, and, having had no time to prepare a sermon, delivered his soul from the pulpit about the Bolshies and their doings. He said that what was needed was a new crusade, and he called on every Christian man and woman to devote their prayers, their money, and, if necessary, their blood to this supreme cause. Old as he was, he said, he would gladly set off for Moscow that instant and die beside the Patriarch, and count his life well lost in such a testimony of his faith.

I am sure that Mr Tubb meant every word he said, but he had an unsympathetic audience, who were not interested in Patriarchs; and the hotel-lady slumbered, and the store-keepers fidgeted and the girls giggled and whispered just as usual. There the matter would have dropped, had not a young journalist from Cape Town been spending his holidays at Rhenosterspruit and out of some caprice been present at the service. He was an ambitious lad, and next morning despatched to his paper a brightly written account of Mr Tubb's challenge. He wrote it with his tongue in his cheek, and headed it, 'Peter the Hermit at Rhenosterspruit' with, as a sub-title, 'The Last Crusade'. His editor cut it savagely, and left out all his satirical touches, so that it read rather bald and crude. Still it got about a quarter of a column.

That week the Ladas representative at Cape Town was rather short of material, and just to fill up his budget of outgoing news put in a short message about Rhenosterspruit. It ran: 'On Sunday Tubb Wesleyan Minister Rhenosterspruit summoned congregation in name Christianity release Patriarch and announced intention personally lead crusade Moscow.' That was the result of the cutting of the bright young correspondent's article. What he had meant as fantasy and farce was so summarised as to appear naked facts. Ladas in London were none too well pleased with the message. They did not issue it to the British Press, and they cabled to the Cape Town people that, while they welcomed 'human interest' stories, they drew the line at that sort of thing. What could it matter to the world what a Wesleyan parson in the Karroo thought about Zinovieff? They wanted news, not nonsense.

Now behold the mysterious workings of the Comic Spirit. Ladas, besides their general service to the Canadian Press, made special services to several Canadian papers. One of these was called, shall we say? the *Toronto Watchman*. The member of the Ladas staff who had the compiling of the *Watchman* budget was often hard-pressed, for he had to send news which was not included in the general service. That week he was peculiarly up against it, so he went through the files of the messages that had come in lately and had not already been transmitted to Canada, and in the Cape Town section he found the Rhenosterspruit yarn. He seized on it joyfully, for he did not know of the disfavour with which his chief had regarded it, and he dressed it up nicely for Toronto. The *Watchman* he knew was a family paper, with a strong religious connection, and this would be meat and drink to it. So he made the story still more matter-of-fact. Mr Tubb had sounded a call to the Christian Church, and was himself on the eve of setting out against Trotsky like David against Goliath. He left the captions to the Toronto sub-editors, but of his own initiative he mentioned John Knox. That, he reflected comfortably, as he closed up and went off to play golf, would fetch the Presbyterian-minded *Watchman*.

It did. The Editor of the *Watchman*, who was an elder of the Kirk and Liberal Member of Parliament, had been getting very anxious about the ongoings in Russia. He was not very clear what a Patriarch was, but he remembered that various Anglican ecclesiastics had wanted to affiliate the English and Greek Churches, so he concluded that he was some kind of Protestant. He had, like most people, an intense dislike of Moscow and its ways, and he had been deeply shocked by the Easter sacrilege. So he went large on the Ladas message. It was displayed on his chief page, side by side with all the news he could collect about the Patriarch, and he had no less than two leaders on the subject. The first, which he wrote himself, was headed 'The Weak Things of the World and the Strong'. He said that Mr Tubb's clarion-call, 'the voice of a simple man of God echoing from the lonely veld', might yet prove a turning-point in history, and he quoted Burke about a child and a girl at an inn changing the fate of nations. It might – it should – arouse the conscience of the Christian world, and inaugurate a new crusade, which would lift mankind out of the rut of materialism and open its eyes to the eternal verities. Christianity had been challenged by the miscreants in Russia, and the challenge must be met. I don't think he had any very clear idea what he meant, for he was strongly opposed to anything that suggested war, but it was a fine chance for 'uplift' writing. The second leader was called 'The Deeper Obligations of Empire', and, with a side glance at Mr Tubb, declared that unless the British Empire was a spiritual and moral unity it was not worth talking about.

The rest of the Canadian Press did not touch the subject. They had not had the Rhenosterspruit message, and were not going to lift it. But the *Watchman* had a big circulation, and Mr Tubb began to have a high, if strictly local, repute. Several prominent clergymen preached sermons on him, and a weekly paper printed a poem in which he was compared to St Theresa and Joan of Arc.

The thing would have been forgotten in a fortnight, if McGurks had not chosen to take a hand. McGurks, as you probably know, is the biggest newspaper property in the world directed by a single hand. It owns outright well over a hundred papers, and has a controlling interest in perhaps a thousand. Its tone is strictly national, not to say chauvinistic; its young men in Europe at that time were all hundred-per-cent Americans, and returned to the States a hundred and twenty per cent, to allow for the difference in the exchange. McGurks does not love England, for it began with strong Irish connections, and it has done good work in pointing out to its immense public the predatory character of British Imperialism and the atrocities that fill the shining hours in India and Egypt. As a matter of fact, however, its politics are not very serious. What it likes is a story that can be told in thick black headlines, so that the stupidest of its free-born readers, glancing in his shirt-sleeves at the first page of his Sunday paper, can extract nourishment. Murders, rapes, fires and drownings are its daily bread, and it fairly revels in details — measurements and plans, names and addresses of witnesses, and appalling half-tone blocks. Most unfairly it is called sensational, for the stuff is as dull as a directory.

With regard to Russia, McGurks had steered a wavy course. It had begun in 1917 by flaunting the banner of freedom, for it disliked monarchies on principle. In 1919 it wanted America to recognise the Russian Government, and take hold of Russian trade. But a series of rebuffs to its special correspondents changed its view, and by 1922 it had made a speciality of Bolshevik horrors. The year 1923 saw it again on the fence, from which in six months it had tumbled off in a state of anti-Bolshevik hysteria. It was out now to save God's country from foreign microbes, and it ran a good special line of experts who proved that what America needed was a *cordon sanitaire* to protect her purity from a diseased world. At the time of which I speak it had worked itself up into a fine religious enthusiasm, and had pretty well captured the 'hick' public. McGurks was first and foremost a business proposition, and it had decided that crime and piety were the horses to back. I should add that, besides its papers, it ran a news agency, the P.U., which stood for Press Union, but which was commonly and affectionately known as Punk.

McGurks seized upon the story in the *Toronto Watchman* as a gift from the gods, and its headlines were a joy for ever. All over the States men read 'Aged Saint Defies Demoniacs – Says That In God's Name He Will Move Mountains' – 'Vengeance From The Veld' – 'The First Trumpet Blast' – 'Who Is On The Lord's Side – WHO?' I daresay that in the East and beyond the Rockies people were only mildly interested, but in the Middle West and in the South the thing caught like measles. McGurks did not leave its stunts to perish of inanition. As soon as it saw that the public was intrigued it started out to organise that interest. It circularised every parson over big areas, it arranged meetings of protest and sympathy, it opened subscription lists, and, though it refrained from suggesting Government action, it made it clear that it wanted to create such a popular feeling that the Government would be bound to bestir itself. The home towns caught fire, the Bible Belt was moved to its foundations, every Methodist minister rallied to his co-religionist of Rhenoster-spruit, the Sunday Schools uplifted their voice, and even the red-blooded he-men of the Rotary Clubs got going. The Holiness Tabernacle of Sarcophagus, Neb., produced twenty volunteers who were ready to join Mr Tubb in Moscow, and the women started knitting socks for them, just as they did in the War. The First Consecration Church of Jumpersville, Tenn., followed suit, and McGurks made the most of the doings of every chapel in every one-horse township. Punk, too, was busy, and cabled wonderful stories of the new crusade up and down the earth. Old-established papers did not as a rule take the Punk service, so only a part of it was printed, but it all helped to create an atmosphere.

Presently Concord had to take notice. This, as you know, is the foremost American press agency – we call it the C.C. – and it had no more dealings with Punk than the Jews with the Samaritans. It was in close alliance with Ladas, so it cabled testily wanting to know why it had not received the Rhenosterspruit message. Ladas replied that they had considered the story too absurd to waste tolls on, but, since the C.C. was now carrying a lot of stuff about the new crusade, they felt obliged to cable to Cape Town to clear things up. Punk had already got on to that job, and was asking its correspondents for pictures of Rhenosterspruit, interviews with the Reverend Tubb, details about what he wore and ate and drank, news of his mother and his childhood, and his premonitions of future greatness. Half a dozen anxious journalists converged upon Rhenosterspruit.

But they were too late. For Mr Tubb was dead -- choked on a chicken-bone at his last Sunday dinner. They were only in time to attend the funeral in the little, dusty, sun-baked cemetery. Very little was to be had from his congregation, which, as I have said, had been mostly asleep during the famous sermon; but a store-keeper remembered that the minister had not been quite like himself on that occasion and that he had judged from his eyes that he had still a bad cold. McGurks made a great fuss with this scrap of news. The death of Mr Tubb was featured like the demise of a President or a film star, and there was a moving picture of the old man, conscious that he was near his end (the chicken-bone was never mentioned), summoning his failing strength to one supreme appeal – 'his eyes,' said McGurks, 'now wet with tears for the world's sins, now shining with the reflected radiance of the Better Country'.

I fancy that the thing would have suddenly died away, for there was a big prize-fight coming on, and there seemed to be a risk of the acquittal of a nigger who had knifed a bootlegger in Chicago, and an Anti-Kink Queen was on the point of engaging herself to a Dentifrice King, and similar stirring public events were in the offing. But the death of Mr Tubb kept up the excitement, for it brought in the big guns of the Fundamentalists. It seemed to them that the old man had not died but had been miraculously translated, just like Elijah or William Jennings Bryan after the Dayton trial. It was a Sign, and they were bound to consider what it signified.

This was much heavier metal than the faithful of Sarcophagus

and Jumpersville. The agitation was now of national importance; it had attained 'normalcy', as you might say, the 'normalcy' of the periodic American movement. Conventions were
summoned and addressed by divines whose names were known
even in New York. Senators and congressmen took a hand, and
J. Constantine Buttrick, the silver trumpet of Wisconsin, gave
tongue, and was heard by several million wireless outfits.
Articles even appeared about it in the intellectual weeklies.
Congress wasn't in session, which was fortunate, but Washington began to be uneasy, for volunteers for the crusade were
enrolling fast. The C.C. was compelled to carry long
despatches, and Ladas had to issue them to the English Press,
which usually printed them in obscure corners with the names
misspelt. England is always apathetic about American news,
and, besides, she had a big strike on her hands at the time.
Those of us who get American press-clippings realised that
quite a drive was starting to do something to make Moscow
respectful to religion, but we believed that it would be dropped
before any serious action could be taken. Meanwhile Zinovieff
and Trotsky carried on as usual, and we expected any day to hear
that the Patriarch had been shot and buried in the prison yard.

Suddenly Fate sent Roper Willinck mooning round to my
office. I suppose Willinck is the least known of our great men,
for you fellows have never even heard his name. But he *is* a great
man in his queer way, and I believe his voice carries farther than
any living journalist's, though most people do not know who is
speaking. He doesn't write much in the Press here, only now
and then a paper in the heavy monthlies, but he is the prince of
special correspondents, and his 'London Letters' in every known
tongue are printed from Auckland to Seattle. He seems to have
found the common denominator of style which is calculated to
interest the whole human family. On the Continent he is the
only English journalist whose name is known to the ordinary
reader — rather like Maximilian Harden before the War. In
America they reckon him a sort of Pope, and his stuff is

syndicated in all the country papers. His enthusiasms make a funny hotch-potch — the League of Nations and the British Empire, racial purism and a sentimental socialism; but he is a devout Catholic, and Russia had become altogether too much for him. That was why I thought he would be interested in McGurks' stunt, of which he had scarcely heard; so he sat down in an armchair and, during the consumption of five caporal cigarettes, studied my clippings.

I have never seen a man so roused. 'I see light,' he cried, pushing his double glasses up on his forehead. 'Martendale, this is a revelation. Out of the mouths of babes and sucklings . . . Master Ridley, Master Ridley, we shall this day kindle a fire which will never be extinguished . . .'

'Nonsense,' I said. 'The thing will fizzle out in a solemn protest from Washington to Moscow with which old Trotsky will light his pipe. It has got into the hands of highbrows, and in a week will be clothed in the jargon of the State Department, and the home towns will wonder what has been biting them.'

'We must retrieve it,' he said softly. 'Get it back to the village green and the prayer-meeting. It was the prayer-meeting, remember, which brought America into the War.'

'But how? McGurks has worked that beat to death.'

'McGurks!' he cried contemptuously. 'The time is past for slobber, my son. What they want is the prophetic, the apocalyptic, and by the bones of Habbakuk they shall have it. I am going to solemnise the remotest parts of the great Republic, and then,' he smiled serenely, 'I shall interpret that solemnity to the world. First the fact and then the moral — that's the lay-out.'

He stuffed my clippings into his pocket and took himself off, and there was that in his eye which foreboded trouble. Someone was going to have to sit up when Willinck looked like that. My hope was that it would be Moscow, but the time was getting terribly short. Any day might bring the news that the Patriarch had gone to his reward.

I heard nothing for several weeks, and then Punk suddenly

became active, and carried some extraordinary stuff. It was
mostly extracts from respectable papers in the Middle West and
the South, reports of meetings which seemed to have worked
themselves into hysteria, and rumours of secret gatherings of
young men which suggested the Ku-Klux-Klan. Moscow had a
Press agency of its own in London, and it began to worry Ladas
for more American news. Ladas in turn worried the C.C., but
the C.C. was reticent. There was a Movement, we were told,
but the Government had it well in hand, and we might dis-
regard the scare-stuff Punk was sending; everything that was
important and reliable would be in its own service. I thought I
detected Willinck somewhere behind the scenes, and tried to
get hold of him, but learned that he was out of town.

One afternoon, however, he dropped in, and I noticed that
his high-boned face was leaner than ever, but that his cavernous
eyes were happy. '"The good work goes cannily on",' he said –
he was always quoting – and he flung at me a bundle of green
clippings.

They were articles of his own in the American Press, chiefly
the Sunday editions, and I noticed that he had selected the really
influential country papers – one in Tennessee, one in Kentucky,
and a batch from the Corn States.

I was staggered by the power of his stuff – Willinck had never
to my knowledge written like this before. He didn't rave about
Bolshevik crimes – people were sick of that – and he didn't bang
the religious drum or thump the harmonium. McGurks had
already done that to satiety. He quietly took it for granted that
the crusade had begun, and that plain men all over the earth,
who weren't looking for trouble, felt obliged to start out and
abolish an infamy or never sleep peacefully in their beds again.
He assumed that presently from all corners of the Christian
world there would be an invading army moving towards Moscow, a thing that Governments could not check, a people's
rising as irresistible as the change of the seasons. Assuming this,
he told them just exactly what they would see.

I can't do justice to Willinck by merely describing these articles; I ought to have them here to read to you. Noble English they were, and as simple as the Psalms . . . He pictured the constitution of the army, every kind of tongue and dialect and class, with the same kind of discipline as Cromwell's New Model — Ironsides every one of them, rational, moderate-minded fanatics, the most dangerous kind. It was like *Paradise Lost* — Michael going out against Belial . . . And then the description of Russia — a wide grey world, all pale colours and watery lights, broken villages, tattered little towns ruled by a few miscreants with rifles, railway tracks red with rust, ruinous great palaces plastered over with obscene posters, starving hopeless people, children with old vicious faces . . . God knows where he got the stuff from — mainly his *macabre* imagination, but I daresay there was a lot of truth in the details, for he had his own ways of acquiring knowledge.

But the end was the masterpiece. He said that the true rulers were not those whose names appeared in the papers, but one or two secret madmen who sat behind the screen and spun their bloody webs. He described the crusaders breaking through shell after shell, like one of those Chinese boxes which you open only to find another inside till you end with a thing like a pea. There were layers of Jew officials and Lett mercenaries and camouflaging journalists, and always as you went deeper the thing became more inhuman and the air more fetid. At the end you had the demented Mongol — that was a good touch for the Middle West — the incarnation of the back-world of the Orient. Willinck only hinted at this ultimate camarilla, but his hints were gruesome. To one of them he gave the name of Uriel — a kind of worm-eaten archangel of the Pit, but the worst he called Glubet. He must have got the word out of a passage in Catullus which is not read in schools, and he made a shuddering thing of it — the rancid toad-man, living among the half-lights and blood, adroit and sleepless as sin, but cracking now and then into idiot laughter.

You may imagine how this took hold of the Bible Belt. I never made out what exactly happened, but I have no doubt that there were the rudiments of one of those mass movements, before which Governments and newspapers, combines and Press agencies, Wall Street and Lombard Street and common prudence are helpless. You could see it in the messages C.C. sent and its agitated service cables to its people. The Moscow Agency sat on our doorstep and bleated for more news, and all the while Punk was ladling out fire-water to every paper that would take it.

'So much for the facts,' Willinck said calmly. 'Now I proceed to point the moral in the proper quarters!'

If he was good at kindling a fire he was better at explaining just how hot it was and how fast it would spread. I have told you that he was about the only English journalist with a Continental reputation. Well, he proceeded to exploit that reputation in selected papers which he knew would cross the Russian frontier. He was busy in the Finnish and Latvian and Lithuanian Press, he appeared in the chief Polish daily, and in Germany his stuff was printed in one big Berlin paper and – curiously enough – in the whole financial chain. Willinck knew just how and where to strike. The line he took was very simple. He quietly explained what was happening in America and the British Dominions – that the outraged conscience of Christiandom had awakened among simple folk, and that nothing on earth could hold it. It was a Puritan crusade, the most deadly kind. From every corner of the globe believers were about to assemble, ready to sacrifice themselves to root out an infamy. This was none of your Denikins and Koltchaks and Czarist *emigré* affairs; it was the world's Christian democracy, and a business democracy. No flag-waving or shouting, just a cold steady determination to get the job done, with ample money and men and an utter carelessness of what they spent on both. Cautious Governments might try to obstruct, but the people would compel them to toe the line. It was a militant League of Nations, with the Bible in one hand and the latest brand of munition in the other.

We had a feverish time at Ladas in those days. The British Press was too much occupied with the strike to pay full attention, but the Press of every other country was on its hind legs. Presently things began to happen. The extracts from *Pravda* and *Izvestia*, which we got from Riga and Warsaw, became every day more like the howling of epileptic wolves. Then came the news that Moscow had ordered a very substantial addition to the Red Army. I telephoned this item to Willinck, and he came round to see me.

'The wind is rising,' he said. 'The fear of the Lord is descending on the tribes, and that we know is the beginning of wisdom.'

I observed that Moscow had certainly got the wind up, but that I didn't see why. 'You don't mean to say that you have got them to believe in your precious crusade.'

He nodded cheerfully. 'Why not? My dear Martendale, you haven't studied the mentality of these gentry as I have. Do you realise that the favourite reading of the Russian peasant used to be Milton? Before the War you could buy a translation of *Paradise Lost* at every book kiosk in every country fair. These rootless intellectuals have cast off all they could, but at the back of their heads the peasant superstition remains. They are afraid in their bones of a spirit that they think is in Puritanism. That's why this American business worries them so. They think they are a match for Rome, and they wouldn't have minded if the racket had been started by the Knights of Columbus or that kind of show. But they think it comes from the meeting-house, and that scares them cold.'

'Hang it all,' I said, 'they must know the soft thing modern Puritanism is — all slushy hymns and inspirational advertising.'

'Happily they don't. And I'm not sure that their ignorance is not wiser than your knowledge, my emancipated friend. I'm inclined to think that something may yet come out of the Bible Christian that will surprise the world . . . But not this time. I fancy the trick has been done. You might let me know as soon as you hear anything.' And he moved off, whistling contentedly through his teeth.

He was right. Three days later we got the news from Warsaw, and the Moscow Agency confirmed it. The Patriarch had been released and sent across the frontier, and was now being coddled and fêted in Poland. I rang up Willinck, and listened to his modest *Nunc dimittis* over the telephone.

He said he was going to take a holiday and go into the country to sleep. He pointed out for my edification that the weak things of the world — meaning himself — could still confound the strong, and he advised me to reconsider the foundations of my creed in the light of this surprising miracle.

Well, that is my story. We heard no more of the crusade in America, except that the Fundamentalists seemed to have got a second wind from it and started a large-scale heresy hunt. Several English bishops said that the release of the Patriarch was an answer to prayer; our Press pointed out how civilisation, if it spoke with one voice, would be listened to even in Russia; and Labour papers took occasion to enlarge on the fundamental reasonableness and urbanity of the Moscow Government.

Personally I think that Willinck drew the right moral. But the main credit really belonged to something a great deal weaker than he — the aged Tubb, now sleeping under a painted cast-iron gravestone among the dust-devils and meerkats of Rhenosterspruit.

The Black Fishers

Another tale from the 1890s, lovingly located in Upper Tweed. It has an uneven narrative style and is in places over-written: too many Latinisms in the first paragraph betray Oxford and Greats; but a certain archness elsewhere belongs to fashion as well as youth. Buchan grew out of such mannerisms. What we must never do, as he himself never did, is underestimate the powers of his lowland characters. The Procurator-fiscal, we notice, is reading Maupassant and knows Ibsen. Buchan did not by any means receive all his education from Glasgow and Oxford. In Peebles, on the Tweed, to look no further than his uncle's house, he found during vacation visits not only an excellent and up-to-date library, but comment also on the developments of modern European fiction.

I include this story because, though it has some faults, it is sharp in the Maupassant manner, and has something else: even the over-decoration cannot hide the Buchan sense of place. As so often, writer, characters and reader are made to walk this country, and feel it under the feet, and on all the senses, and receive it in the mind of which the contents are in some cases inappropriately fished for: just as the Procurator-fiscal poaches Maupassant, the minister misappropriates a Bible text (Job 1, 21), and the central characters filch sympathy.

The Black Fishers, too, was printed in Grey Weather (1899) and has not been reprinted until now.

The Black Fishers

Once upon a time, as the story goes, there lived a man in Gledsmuir, called Simon Hay, who had born to him two sons. They were all very proper men, tall, black-avised, formed after the right model of stalwart folk, and by the account of the place in fear of neither God nor devil. He himself had tried many trades before he found the one which suited his talent; but in the various professions of herd, gamekeeper, drover, butcher, and carrier he had not met with the success he deserved. Some makeshift for a conscience is demanded sooner or later in all, and this Simon could not supply. So he flitted from one to the other with decent haste, till his sons came to manhood and settled the matter for themselves. Henceforth all three lived by their wits in defiance of the law, snaring game, poaching salmon, and working evil over the green earth. Hard drinkers and quick fighters, all men knew them and loved them not. But with it all they kept up a tincture of reputability, foreseeing their best interest. Ostensibly their trade was the modest one of the small crofter, and their occasional attendance at the kirk kept within bounds the verdict of an uncensorious parish.

It chanced that in spring, when the streams come down steely-blue and lipping over their brims, there came the most halcyon weather that ever man heard of. The air was mild as June, the nights soft and clear, and winter fled hot-foot in dismay. Then these three girded themselves and went to the salmon-poaching in the long shining pools of the Callowa in the haughlands below the Dun Craigs. The place was far enough and yet not too far from the town, so that an active walker could go there, have four hours' fishing, and return, all well within the confines of the dark.

On this night their sport was good, and soon the sacks were

filled with glittering backs. Then, being drowsy from many nights out o' bed, they bethought them of returning. It would be well to get some hours of sleep before the morning, for they must be up betimes to dispose of their fish. The hardship of such pursuits lies not in the toil but the fate which hardens expediency into necessity.

At the strath which leads from the Callowa vale to Gled they halted. By crossing the ridge of hill they would save three good miles and find a less frequented path. The argument was irresistible; without delay they left the highway and struck over the bent and heather. The road was rough, but they were near its end, and a serene glow of conscious labour began to steal over their minds.

Near the summit is a drystone dyke which girdles the breast of the hill. It was a hard task to cross with a great load of fish even for the young men. The father, a man of corpulent humours and maturing years, was nigh choked with his burden. He mounted slowly and painfully on the loose stones, and prepared to jump. But his foothold was insecure, and a stone slipped from its place. Then something terrible followed. The sack swung round from his neck, and brought him headlong to the ground. When the sons ran forward he was dead as a herring, with a broken neck.

The two men stood staring at one another in hopeless bewilderment. Here was something new in their experience, a disturbing element in their plans. They had just the atom of affection for the fellow-worker to make them feel the practical loss acutely. If they went for help to the nearest town, time would be lost and the salmon wasted; and indeed, it was not unlikely that some grave suspicion would attach to their honourable selves.

They held a hurried debate. At first they took refuge in mutual recriminations and well-worn regrets. They felt that some such sentiments were due to the modicum of respectability in their reputations. But their minds were too practical to linger long in such barren ground. It was demanded by common feeling of decency that they should have their father's body taken home. But were there any grounds for such feeling? None. It could not matter much to their father, who was the only one really concerned, whether he was removed early or late. On the other hand, they had trysted to meet a man seven miles down the water at five in the morning. Should he be disappointed? Money was money; it was a hard world, where one had to work for beer and skittles; death was a misfortune, but not exactly a deterrent. So picking up the old man's sack, they set out on their errand.

It chanced that the shepherd of the Lowe Moss returned late that night from a neighbour's house, and in crossing the march dyke came on the body. He was much shocked, for he recognised it well as the mortal remains of one who had once been a friend. The shepherd was a dull man and had been drinking; so as the subject was beyond his special domain he dismissed its consideration till some more convenient season. He did not trouble to inquire into causes — there were better heads than his for the work — but set out with all speed for the town.

The Procurator-fiscal had been sitting up late reading in the works of M. de Maupassant, when he was aroused by a constable, who told him that a shepherd had come from the Callowa with news that a man lay dead at the back of a dyke. The Procurator-fiscal rose with much grumbling, and wrapped himself up for the night errand. Really, he reflected with Hedda Gabler, people should not do these things nowadays. But, once without, his feelings changed. The clear high space of the sky and the whistling airs of night were strange and beautiful to a town-bred man. The round hills and grey whispering river touched his poetic soul. He began to feel some pride in his vocation.

When he came to the spot he was just in the mood for high sentiment. The sight gave him a shudder. The full-blown face ashen with the grip of death jarred on his finer sensibilities. He remembered to have read of just such a thing in the works of M. Guy. He felt a spice of anger at fate and her cruel ways.

'How sad!' he said; 'this old man, still hale and fit to enjoy life, goes out into the hills to visit a friend. On returning he falls in with those accursed dykes of yours; there is a slip in the darkness, a cry, and then – he can taste of life no more. Ah, Fate, to men how bitter a taskmistress,' he quoted with a far-off classical reminiscence.

The constable said nothing. He knew Simon Hay well, and guessed shrewdly how he had come by his death, but he kept his own counsel. He did not like to disturb fine sentiment, being a philosopher in a small way.

The two fishers met their man and did their business all in the most pleasant fashion. On their way they had discussed their father's demise. It would interfere little with their profits, for of late he had grown less strong and more exacting. Also, since death must come to all, it was better that it should have taken their father unawares. Otherwise he might have seen fit to make trouble about the cottage which was his, and which he had talked of leaving elsewhere. On the whole, the night's events were good; it only remained to account for them.

It was with some considerable trepidation that they returned to the town in the soft spring dawning. As they entered, one or two people looked out and pointed to them, and nodded significantly to one another. The two men grew hotly uncomfortable. Could it be possible? No. All must have happened as they expected. Even now they would be bringing their father home. His finding would prove the manner of his death. Their only task was to give some reason for its possibility.

At the bridge-end a man came out and stood before them.

'Stop,' he cried. 'Tam and Andra Hay, prepare to hear bad news. Your auld faither was fund this morning on the back o'

Callowa hill wi' a broken neck. It's a sair affliction. Try and thole it like men.'

The two grew pale and faltering. 'My auld faither,' said the chorus. 'Oh ye dinna mean it. Say it's no true. I canna believe it, and him aye sae guid to us. What'll we dae wi'oot him?'

'Bear up, my poor fellows,' and the minister laid a hand on the shoulder of one. 'The Lord gave and the Lord has taken away.' He had a talent for inappropriate quotation.

But for the two there was no comfort. With dazed eyes and drawn faces, they asked every detail, fervently, feverishly. Then with faltering voices they told of how their father had gone the night before to the Harehope shepherd's, who was his cousin, and proposed returning in the morn. They bemoaned their remissness, they bewailed his kindness; and then, attended by condoling friends, these stricken men went down the street, accepting sympathy in every public.

At the Rising of the Waters

Buchan, much under the influence of Stevenson in his undergraduate writing, was also a classicist who had studied under the young Gilbert Murray for three years at Glasgow, and then gone to Brasenose to be with Walter Pater.

Some fashionable fellow-classicists of the time were writing of an imaginary rural Arcadia, loosely assembled round the anarchic figure of Pan. Buchan's Arcady was altogether less amateurish. Though his love for the Border country chimed with, as he wrote, 'pastoral . . . the shepherds of Theocritus and Virgil . . . the lyrists of the Greek Anthology, and . . . Horace's Sabine farm', he knew that the reality of life in the open around Tweedsmuir was often harsh. He admired the amused and understated daily courage of the shepherds and drovers with whom he had spent so much of his youth. He knew that the weather could be suddenly treacherous and threaten the whole livelihood, and indeed the life, of even the most experienced Tweeddale farmer. Death from exposure was not sought out, in Buchan's close and formative experience, as a self-conscious, attitudinising fad, as some recent careless commentators on 'the Buchan hero' have supposed.

This story is also from Grey Weather.

At the Rising of the Waters

In mid-September the moors are changing from red to a dusky brown, as the fire of the heather wanes, and the long grass yellows with advancing autumn. Then, too, the rain falls heavily on the hills, and vexes the shallow upland streams, till every glen is ribbed with its churning torrent. This for the uplands; but below, at the rim of the plains, where the glens expand to vales, and trim fields edge the wastes, there is wreck and lamentation. The cabined waters lip over cornland and meadow, and bear destruction to crop and cattle.

This is the tale of Robert Linklater, farmer in Clachlands, and the events which befell him on the night of September 20th, in the year of grace 1880. I am aware that there are characters in the countryside which stand higher in repute than his, for imagination and love of point and completeness in a story are qualities which little commend themselves to the prosaic. I have heard him called 'Leein' Rob', and answer to the same with cheerfulness; but he was wont in private to brag of minutest truthfulness, and attribute his ill name to the universal dullness of man.

On this evening he came home, by his own account, from market about the hour of six. He had had a week of festivity. On the Monday he had gone to a distant cattle-show, and on Tuesday to a marriage. On the Wednesday he had attended upon a cousin's funeral, and, being flown with whisky, brought everlasting disgrace upon himself by rising to propose the health of the bride and bridegroom. On Thursday he had been at the market of Gledsmuir, and, getting two shillings more for his ewes than he had reckoned, returned in a fine fervour of spirit and ripe hilarity.

The weather had been shower and blast for days. The grey

skies dissolved in dreary rain, and on that very morn there had come a downpour so fierce that the highways ran like a hillside torrent. Now, as he sat at supper and looked down at the green vale and red waters leaping by bank and brae, a sudden fear came to his heart. Hitherto he had had no concern — for was not his harvest safely inned? But now he minds of the laigh parks and the nowt beasts there, which he had bought the week before at the sale of Inverforth. They were Kyloe and Galloway mixed, and on them, when fattened through winter and spring, lay great hopes of profit. He gulped his meal down hurriedly, and went forthwith to the garden-foot. There he saw something that did not allay his fears. Gled had split itself in two, at the place where Clachlands water came to swell its flow, and a long, gleaming line of black current stole round by the side of the laigh meadow, where stood the huddled cattle. Let but the waters rise a little, and the valley would be one uniform, turgid sea.

This was pleasing news for an honest man after a hard day's work, and the farmer went grumbling back. He took a mighty plaid and flung it over his shoulders, chose the largest and toughest of his many sticks, and set off to see wherein he could better the peril.

Now, some hundreds of yards above the laigh meadow, a crazy wooden bridge spanned the stream. By this way he might bring his beasts to safety, for no nowt could hope to swim the red flood. So he plashed through the dripping stubble to the river's brink, where, with tawny swirl, it licked the edge of banks which in summer weather stood high and flower-decked. Ruefully he reflected that many good palings would by this time be whirling to a distant sea.

When he came to the wooden bridge he set his teeth manfully and crossed. It creaked and swayed with his weight, and dipped till it all but touched the flow. It could not stand even as the water was, for already its mid prop had lurched forward, like a drunken man, and was groaning at each wave. But if a rise came, it would be torn from its foundations like a reed, and then heigh-ho! for cattle and man.

With painful haste he laboured through the shallows which rimmed the haughlands, and came to the snake-like current which had even now spread itself beyond the laigh meadow. He measured its depth with his eye and ventured. It did not reach beyond his middle, but its force gave him much ado to keep his feet. At length it was passed, and he stood triumphant on the spongy land, where the cattle huddled in mute discomfort and terror.

Darkness was falling, and he could scarcely see the homestead on the affronting hillside. So with all speed he set about collecting the shivering beasts, and forcing them through the ring of water to the bridge. Up to their flanks they went, and then stood lowing helplessly. He saw that something was wrong, and made to ford the current himself. But now it was beyond him. He looked down at the yellow water running round his middle, and saw that it had risen, and was rising inch by inch with every minute. Then he glanced to where aforetime stood the crazy planking of the bridge. Suddenly hope and complacency fled, and the gravest fear settled in his heart; for he saw no bridge, only a ragged, saw-like end of timber where once he had crossed.

Here was a plight for a solitary man to be in at nightfall. There would be no wooden bridge on all the water, and the nearest one of stone was at distant Gledsmuir, over some score of miles of weary moorland. It was clear that his cattle must bide on this farther bank, and he himself, when once he had seen them in safety, would set off for the nearest farm and pass the night. It seemed the craziest of matters, that he should be thus in peril and discomfort, with the lights of his house blinking not a quarter mile away.

Once more he tried to break the water-ring and once more he failed. The flood was still rising, and the space of green which showed grey and black beneath a fitful moon was quickly lessening. Before, irritation had been his upper feeling, now terror succeeded. He could not swim a stroke, and if the field were covered he would drown like a cat in a bag. He lifted up his voice and roared with all the strength of his mighty lungs, 'Sammle', 'Andra', 'Jock', 'come and help 's', till the place rang with echoes. Meantime, with strained eyes he watched the rise of the cruel water, which crept, black and pitiless, over the shadowy grey.

He drove the beasts to a little knoll, which stood somewhat above the meadow, and there they stood, cattle and man, in the fellowship of misfortune. They had been as wild as peat-reek, and had suffered none to approach them, but now with some instinct of peril they stood quietly by his side, turning great billowy foreheads to the surging waste. Upward and nearer came the current, rising with steady gurgling which told of great storms in his hills and roaring torrents in every gorge. Now the sound grew louder and seemed almost at his feet, now it ceased and nought was heard save the dull hum of the main stream pouring its choking floods to the sea. Suddenly his eyes wandered to the lights of his house and the wide slope beyond, and for a second he mused on some alien trifle. Then he was brought to himself with a pull as he looked and saw a line of black water not three feet from the farthest beast. His heart stood still, and with awe he reflected that in half-an-hour by this rate of rising he would be with his Maker.

For five minutes he waited, scarce daring to look around him, but dreading each instant to feel a cold wave lick his boot. Then he glanced timorously, and to his joy it was scarce an inch higher. It was stopping, and he might yet be safe. With renewed energy he cried out for aid, till the very cattle started at the sound and moved uneasily among themselves.

In a little there came an answering voice across the dark, 'Whae's in the laigh meedy?' and it was the voice of the herd of Clachlands, sounding hoarse through the driving of the stream.

'It's me,' went back the mournful response.

'And whae are *ye?*' came the sepulchral voice.

'Your ain maister, William Smail, forewandered among water and nowt beast.'

For some time there was no reply, since the shepherd was engaged in a severe mental struggle; with the readiness of his class he went straight to the heart of the peril, and mentally reviewed the ways and waters of the land. Then he calmly accepted the hopelessness of it all, and cried loudly through the void, —

'There's nae way for't but juist to bide where ye are. The water's stoppit, and gin mornin' we'll get ye aff. I'll send a laddie down to the Dow Pule to bring up a boat in a cairt. But that's a lang gait, and it'll be a sair job gettin' it up, and I misdoot it'll be daylicht or he comes. But haud up hour hert, and we'll get ye oot. Are the beasts a' richt?'

'A' richt, William; but, 'od man! their maister is cauld. Could ye no fling something ower?'

'No, when there's twae hunner yairds o' deep water atween.'

'Then, William, ye maun licht a fire, a great muckle roarin' fire, juist fornenst me. It'll cheer me to see the licht o' 't.'

The shepherd did as he was bid, and for many minutes the farmer could hear the noise of men heaping wood, in the pauses of wind and through the thicker murmur of the water. Then a glare shot up, and revealed the dusky forms of the four serving-men straining their eyes across the channel. The gleam lit up a yard of water by the other bank, but all mid-way was inky shadow. It was about eight o'clock, and the moon was just arisen. The air had coldened and a light chill wind rose from the river.

The farmer of Clachlands, standing among shivering and dripping oxen, himself wet to the skin and cold as a stone, with no wrapping save his plaid, and no outlook save a black moving water and a gleam of fire — in such a position, the farmer of Clachlands collected his thoughts and mustered his resolution. His first consideration was the safety of his stock. The effort gave him comfort. His crops were in, and he could lose nothing there; his sheep were far removed from scaith, and his cattle would survive the night with ease, if the water kept its level. With some satisfaction he reflected that the only care he need have in the matter was for his own bodily comfort in an autumn night. This was serious, yet not deadly, for the farmer was a man of many toils and cared little for the rigours of weather. But he would gladly have given the price of a beast for a bottle of whisky to comfort himself in this emergency.

He stood on a knuckle of green land some twenty feet long, with a crowd of cattle pressing around him and a little forest of horns showing faintly. There was warmth in these great shaggy hides if they had not been drenched and icy from long standing. His fingers were soon as numb as his feet, and it was in vain that he stamped on the plashy grass or wrapped his hands in a fold of plaid. There was no doubt in the matter. He was keenly uncomfortable, and the growing chill of night would not mend his condition.

Some ray of comfort was to be got from the sight of the crackling fire. There at least was homely warmth, and light, and ease. With gusto he conjured up all the delights of the past week, the roaring evenings in market ale-house, and the fragrance of good drink and piping food. Necessity sharpened his fancy, and he could almost feel the flavour of tobacco. A sudden hope took him. He clapped hand to pocket and pulled forth pipe and shag. Curse it! He had left his match-box on the chimney-top in his kitchen, and there was an end to his only chance of comfort.

So in all cold and damp he set himself to pass the night in the midst of that ceaseless swirl of black moss water. Even as he looked at the dancing glimmer of fire, the moon broke forth silent and full, and lit the vale with misty glamour. The great hills, whence came the Gled, shone blue and high with fleecy trails of vapour drifting athwart them. He saw clearly the walls of his dwelling, the light shining from the window, the struggling fire on the bank, and the dark forms of men. Its transient flashes on the waves were scarce seen in the broad belt of moonshine which girdled the valley. And around him, before and behind, rolled the unending desert waters with that heavy, resolute flow, which one who knows the floods fears a thousand-fold more than the boisterous stir of a torrent.

And so he stood till maybe one o'clock of the morning, cold to the bone, and awed by the eternal silence, which choked him, despite the myriad noises of the night. For there are few things more awful than the calm of nature in her madness – the stillness which follows a snow-slip or the monotony of a great flood. By this hour he was falling from his first high confidence. His knees stooped under him, and he was fain to lean upon the beasts at his side. His shoulders ached with the wet, and his eyes grew sore with the sight of yellow glare and remote distance.

From this point I shall tell his tale in his own words, as he has told it me, but stripped of its garnishing and detail. For it were vain to translate Lallan into orthodox speech, when the very salt of the night air clings to the Scots as it did to that queer tale.

'The mune had been lang out,' he said, 'and I had grown weary o' her blinkin'. I was as cauld as death, and as wat as the sea, no to speak o' haein' the rheumatics in my back. The nowt were glowrin' and glunchin', rubbin' heid to heid, and whiles stampin' on my taes wi' their cloven hooves. But I was mortal glad o' the beasts' company, for I think I wad hae gane daft mysel in that muckle dowie water. Whiles I thocht it was risin', and then my hert stood still; an' whiles fa'in', and then it loupit wi' joy. But it keepit geyan near the bit, and aye as I heard it lip-lappin' I prayed the Lord to keep it whaur it was.

'About half-past yin in the mornin', as I saw by my watch, I got sleepy, and but for the nowt steerin', I micht hae drappit aff. Syne I begood to watch the water, and it was rale interestin', for a' sort o' queer things were comin' doun. I could see bits o' brigs and palin's wi'oot end dippin' in the tide, and whiles swirlin' in sae near that I could hae grippit them. Then beasts began to come by, whiles upside doun, whiles soomin' brawly, sheep and stirks frae the farms up the water. I got graund amusement for a wee while watchin' them, and notin' the marks on their necks.

'"That's Clachlands Mains," says I, "and that's Nether Fallo, and the Back o' the Muneraw. Gudesake, sic a spate it maun hae been up the muirs to work siccan a destruction!" I keepit coont o' the stock, and feegured to mysel what the farmer-bodies wad lose. The thocht that I wad keep a' my ain was some kind o' comfort.

'But about the hour o' twae the mune cloudit ower, and I saw nae mair than twenty feet afore me. I got awesome cauld, and a sort o' stound o' fricht took me, as I lookit into that black, unholy water. The nowt shivered sair and drappit their heids, and the fire on the ither side seemed to gang out a' of a sudden, and leave the hale glen thick wi' nicht. I shivered mysel wi' something mair than the snell air, and there and then I wad hae gien the price o' fower stirks for my ain bed at hame.

'It was as quiet as a kirkyaird, for suddenly the roar o' the water stoppit, and the stream lay still as a loch. Then I heard a queer lappin' as o' something floatin' doun, and it sounded miles aff in that dreidfu' silence. I listened wi' een stertin', and aye it cam' nearer and nearer, wi' a sound like a dowg soomin' a burn. It was sae black, I could see nocht, but somewhere frae the edge o' a cloud, a thin ray o' licht drappit on the water, and there, soomin' doun by me, I saw something that lookit like a man.

'My hert was burstin' wi' terror, but, thinks I, here's a droonin' body, and I maun try and save it. So I waded in as far as I daured, though my feet were sae cauld that they bowed aneath me.

'Ahint me I heard a splashin' and fechtin', and then I saw the nowt, fair wild wi' fricht, standin' in the water on the ither side o' the green bit, and lookin' wi' muckle feared een at something in the water afore me.

'Doun the thing came, and aye I got caulder as I looked. Then

it was by my side, and I claught at it and pu'd it after me on to
the land.

'I heard anither splash. The nowt gaed farther into the water,
and stood shakin' like young birks in a storm.

'I got the thing upon the green bank and turned it ower. It
was a drooned man wi' his hair hingin' back on his broo, and his
mouth wide open. But first I saw his een, which glowered like
scrapit lead out o' his clay-cauld face, and had in them a' the fear
o' death and hell which follows after.

'The next moment I was up to my waist among the nowt,
fechtin' in the water aside them, and snowkin' into their wet
backs to hide mysel like a feared bairn.

'Maybe half an 'oor I stood, and then my mind returned to
me. I misca'ed mysel for a fule and a coward. And my legs were
sae numb, and my strength sae far gane, that I kenned fine that
I couldna lang thole to stand this way like a heron in the water.

'I lookit round, and then turned again wi' a stert, for there
were thae leaden een o' that awfu' deid thing staring at me still.

'For anither quarter-hour I stood and shivered, and then my
guid sense returned, and I tried again. I walkit backward, never
lookin' round, through the water to the shore, whaur I thocht
the corp was lyin'. And a' the time I could hear by hert chokin'
in my breist.

'My God, I fell ower it, and for one moment lay aside it, wi'
my heid touchin' its deathly skin. Then wi' a skelloch like a daft
man, I took the thing in my airms and flung it wi' a' my
strength into the water. The swirl took it, and it dipped and
swam like a fish till it gaed out o' sicht.

'I sat doun on the grass and grat like a bairn wi' fair horror and
weakness. Yin by yin the nowt came back, and shouthered
anither around me, and the puir beasts brocht me yince mair to
mysel. But I keepit my een on the grund, and thocht o' hame
and a' thing decent and kindly, for I daurna for my life look out
to the black water in dreid o' what it micht bring.

'At the first licht, the herd and twae ither men cam' ower in a boat to tak me aff and bring fodder for the beasts. They fand me still sitting wi' my heid atween my knees, and my face like a peeled wand. They lifted me intil the boat and rowed me ower, driftin' far down wi' the angry current. At the ither side the shepherd says to me in an awed voice, —

'"There's a fearfu' thing happened. The young laird o' Manorwater's drooned in the spate. He was ridin' back late and tried the ford o' the Cauldshaw foot. Ye ken his wild cantrips, but there's an end o' them noo. The horse cam' hame in the nicht wi' an empty saiddle, and the Gled Water rinnin' frae him in streams. The corp'll be far on to the sea by this time, and they'll never see 't mair.'

'"I ken," I cried wi' a dry throat, "I ken; I saw him floatin' by." And then I broke yince mair into a silly greetin', while the men watched me as if they thocht I was out o' my mind.'

So much the farmer of Clachlands told me, but to the countryside he repeated merely the bare facts of weariness and discomfort. I have heard that he was accosted a week later by the minister of the place, a well-intentioned, phrasing man, who had strayed from his native city with its familiar air of tea and temperance to those stony uplands.

'And what thoughts had you, Mr Linklater, in that awful position? Had you no serious reflection upon your life?'

'Me,' said the farmer; 'no me. I juist was thinkin' that it was dooms cauld, and that I wad hae gien a guid deal for a pipe o' tobaccy.' This in the racy, careless tone of one to whom such incidents were the merest child's play.

The Grove of Ashtaroth*

Buchan was one of Lord Milner's Young Men in South Africa, from 1901 to 1903, winning praise from the London Times for his work in helping to resettle the land after the Boer War. Africa bit deep. He travelled thousands of miles, on horseback and on foot, often alone, and experienced a continued love-affair with the African landscape and a strong interest in its people. Two especial Buchan fascinations were further heightened there: the challenge of the frontiers of religious belief, and that curious magic which can be felt suddenly in certain special places, the unwittingly-discovered sacred τέμενος* in Cicero's locus amoenus*. His Scottish Calvinism, mixed with Oxford Platonism, both then having been developed into something of his own, allowed him to explore mysteries with which he always felt himself surrounded. Most landscapes, across the globe, could speak to Buchan of the possibility of hidden, greatly significant, powers – even Oxfordshire in May allowed 'The Gap in the Curtain'. In Africa, he felt, the frontier of civilisation was even less permanently held.

In this story, he sharpens the conflict by using a narrator who is many things that Buchan is not – dull, insensitive, superficial in religion ('a half-believer in casual faiths'), miserable in Africa ('I wasn't feeling very well and did not care for the country') and patronising towards the main character's Jewishness, referring to the 'grandfather who sold antiques in a back street at Brighton'. One of the points of this powerful story is the vulnerability of some of those with Eastern blood to tremendous mysteries, those atavistic responses themselves, in all their ambivalence, being the ground of the deepest envy on the part of those incapable of them.

The story first appeared in Blackwood's in June 1910, and was reprinted in The Moon Endureth in April 1912.

The Grove of Ashtaroth

C'est enfin que dans leurs prunelles
Rit et pleure — fastidieux —
L'amour des choses éternelles,
Des vieux morts et des anciens dieux!

PAUL VERLAINE*

I

We were sitting around the camp fire, some thirty miles north of a place called Taqui, when Lawson announced his intention of finding a home. He had spoken little the last day or two, and I guessed that he had struck a vein of private reflection. I thought it might be a new mine or irrigation scheme, and I was surprised to find that it was a country-house.

'I don't think I shall go back to England,' he said, kicking a sputtering log into place. 'I don't see why I should. For business purposes I am far more useful to the firm in South Africa than in Throgmorton Street. I have no relations left except a third cousin, and I have never cared a rush for living in town. That beastly house of mine in Hill Street will fetch what I gave for it — Isaacson cabled about it the other day, offering for furniture and all. I don't want to go into Parliament, and I hate shooting little birds and tame deer. I am one of those fellows who are born colonial at heart, and I don't see why I shouldn't arrange my life as I please. Besides, for ten years I have been falling in love with this country, and now I am up to the neck.'

He flung himself back in the camp-chair till the canvas creaked, and looked at me below his eyelids. I remember glancing at the lines of him, and thinking what a fine make of a man he was. In his untanned field-boots, breeches, and grey shirt he looked the born wilderness-hunter, though less than two months before he had been driving down to the City every morning in the sombre regimentals of his class. Being a fair man, he was gloriously tanned, and there was a clear line at his shirt-collar to mark the limits of his sunburn. I had first known him years ago, when he was a broker's clerk working on half-commission. Then he had gone to South Africa, and soon I heard he was a partner in a mining house which was doing wonders with some gold areas in the North. The next step was his return to London as the new millionaire – young, good-looking, wholesome in mind and body, and much sought after by the mothers of marriageable girls. We played polo together, and hunted a little in the season, but there were signs that he did not propose to become a conventional English gentleman. He refused to buy a place in the country, though half the Homes of England were at his disposal. He was a very busy man, he declared, and had not time to be a squire. Besides, every few months he used to rush out to South Africa. I saw that he was restless, for he was always badgering me to go big game hunting with him in some remote part of the earth. There was that in his eyes, too, which marked him out from the ordinary blond type of our countrymen. They were large and brown and mysterious, and the light of another race was in their odd depths.

To hint such a thing would have meant a breach of his friendship, for Lawson was very proud of his birth. When he first made his fortune he had gone to the Heralds to discover his family, and these obliging gentlemen had provided a pedigree. It appeared that he was a scion of the house of Lowson or Lowieson, an ancient and rather disreputable clan on the Scottish side of the Border. He took a shooting in Teviotdale on the strength of it, and used to commit lengthy Border ballads to memory. But I had known his father, a financial journalist who never quite succeeded, and I had heard of a grandfather who sold antiques in a back street in Brighton. The latter, I think, had not changed his name, and still frequented the synagogue. The father was a progressive Christian, and the mother had been a blond Saxon from the Midlands. In my mind there was no doubt, as I caught Lawson's heavy-lidded eyes fixed on me. My friend was of a more ancient race than the Lowsons of the Border.

'Where are you thinking of looking for your house?' I asked. 'In Natal or in the Cape Peninsula? You might get the Fishers' place if you paid a price.'

'The Fishers' place be hanged!' he said crossly. 'I don't want any stuccoed, overgrown Dutch farm. I might as well be at Roehampton as in the Cape.'

He got up and walked to the far side of the fire, where a lane ran down through thorn-scrub to a gully of the hills. The moon was silvering the bush of the plains, forty miles off and three thousand feet below us.

'I am going to live somewhere hereabouts,' he answered at last.

I whistled. 'Then you've got to put your hand in your pocket, old man. You'll have to make everything, including a map of the countryside.'

'I know,' he said; 'that's where the fun comes. Hang it all, why shouldn't I indulge my fancy? I'm uncommonly well off, and I haven't chick or child to leave it to. Supposing I'm a hundred miles from rail-head, what about it? I'll make a motor-road and fix up a telephone. I'll grow most of my supplies, and start a colony to provide labour. When you come and stay with me, you'll get the best food and drink on earth, and sport that will make your mouth water. I'll put Lochleven trout in these streams – at 6000 feet you can do anything. We'll have a pack of hounds, too, and we can drive pig in the woods, and if we want big game there are the Mangwe flats at our feet. I tell you I'll make such a country-house as nobody ever dreamed of. A man will come plumb out of stark savagery into lawns and rose-gardens.' Lawson flung himself into his chair again and smiled dreamily at the fire.

'But why here, of all places?' I persisted. I was not feeling very well and did not care for the country.

'I can't quite explain. I think it's the sort of land I have always been looking for. I always fancied a house on a green plateau in a decent climate looking down on the tropics. I like heat and colour, you know, but I like hills too, and greenery, and the things that bring back Scotland. Give me a cross between Teviotdale and the Orinoco, and, by Gad! I think I've got it here.'

I watched my friend curiously, as with bright eyes and eager voice he talked of his new fad. The two races were very clear in him – the one desiring gorgeousness, and other athirst for the soothing spaces of the North. He began to plan out the house. He would get Adamson to design it, and it was to grow out of the landscape like a stone on the hillside. There would be wide verandas and cool halls, but great fireplaces against winter time. It would all be very simple and fresh – 'clean as morning' was his odd phrase; but then another idea supervened, and he talked of bringing the Tintorets from Hill Street. 'I want it to be a civilised house, you know. No silly luxury, but the best pictures and china and books . . . I'll have all the furniture made after the old plain English models out of native woods. I don't want second-hand sticks in a new country. Yes, by Jove, the Tintorets are a great idea, and all those Ming pots I bought. I had meant to sell them, but I'll have them out here.'

He talked for a good hour of what he would do, and his dream grew richer as he talked, till by the time he went to bed he had sketched something more like a palace than a country-house. Lawson was by no means a luxurious man. At present he was well content with a Wolseley valise, and shaved cheerfully out of a tin mug. It struck me as odd that a man so simple in his habits should have so sumptuous a taste in bric-à-brac. I told myself, as I turned in, that the Saxon mother from the Midlands had done little to dilute the strong wine of the East.

It drizzled next morning when we inspanned, and I mounted my horse in a bad temper. I had some fever on me, I think, and I hated this lush yet frigid tableland, where all the winds on earth lay in wait for one's marrow. Lawson was, as usual, in great spirits. We were not hunting, but shifting our hunting ground, so all morning we travelled fast to the north along the rim of the uplands.

At midday it cleared, and the afternoon was a pageant of pure colour. The wind sank to a low breeze; the sun lit the infinite green spaces, and kindled the wet forest to a jewelled coronal. Lawson gaspingly admired it all, as he cantered bareheaded up a bracken-clad slope. 'God's country,' he said twenty times. 'I've found it.' Take a piece of Sussex downland; put a stream in every hollow and a patch of wood; and at the edge, where the cliffs at home would fall to the sea, put a cloak of forest muffling the scarp and dropping thousands of feet to the blue plains. Take the diamond air of the Gornergrat, and the riot of colour which you get by a West Highland lochside in late September. Put flowers everywhere, the things we grow in hothouses, geraniums like sun-shades and arums like trumpets. That will give you a notion of the countryside we were in. I began to see that after all it was out of the common.

And just before sunset we came over a ridge and found something better. It was a shallow glen, half a mile wide, down which ran a blue-grey stream in linns like the Spean, till at the edge of the plateau it leaped into the dim forest in a snowy cascade. The opposite side ran up in gentle slopes to a rocky knoll, from which the eye had a noble prospect of the plains. All down the glen were little copses, half-moons of green edging some silvery shore of the burn, or delicate clusters of tall trees nodding on the hill-brow. The place so satisfied the eye that for the sheer wonder of its perfection we stopped and stared in silence for many minutes.

Then 'The House,' I said, and Lawson replied softly, 'The House!'

We rode slowly into the glen in the mulberry gloaming. Our transport wagons were half an hour behind, so we had time to explore. Lawson dismounted and plucked handfuls of flowers from the water-meadows. He was singing to himself all the time – an old French catch about *Cadet Rousselle* and his *trois maisons*.

'Who owns it?' I asked.

'My firm, as like as not. We have miles of land about here. But whoever the man is, he has got to sell. Here I build my tabernacle, old man. Here, and nowhere else!'

In the very centre of the glen, in a loop of the stream, was one copse which even in that half light struck me as different from the others. It was of tall, slim, fairy-like trees, the kind of wood the monks painted in old missals. No, I rejected the thought. It was no Christian wood. It was not a copse, but a 'grove' – one such as Artemis may have flitted through in the moonlight. It was small, forty or fifty yards in diameter, and there was a dark something at the heart of it which for a second I thought was a house.

We turned between the slender trees, and – was it fancy? – an odd tremor went through me. I felt as if I were penetrating the *temenos* of some strange and lovely divinity, the goddess of this pleasant vale. There was a spell in the air, it seemed, and an odd dead silence.

Suddenly my horse started at a flutter of light wings. A flock of doves rose from the branches, and I saw the burnished green of their plumes against the opal sky. Lawson did not seem to notice them. I saw his keen eyes staring at the centre of the grove and what stood there.

It was a little conical tower, ancient and lichened, but, so far as I could judge, quite flawless. You know the famous Conical Temple at Zimbabwe, of which prints are in every guide-book. This was of the same type, but a thousandfold more perfect. It stood about thirty feet high, of solid masonry, without door or window or cranny, as shapely as when it first came from the hands of the old builders. Again I had the sense of breaking in on a sanctuary. What right had I, a common vulgar modern, to be looking at this fair thing, among these delicate trees, which some white goddess had once taken for her shrine?

Lawson broke in on my absorption. 'Let's get out of this,' he said hoarsely, and he took my horse's bridle (he had left his own beast at the edge) and led him back to the open. But I noticed that his eyes were always turning back, and that his hand trembled.

'That settles it,' I said after supper. 'What do you want with your mediaeval Venetians and your Chinese pots now? You will have the finest antique in the world in your garden — a temple as old as time, and in a land which they say has no history. You had the right inspiration this time.'

I think I have said that Lawson had hungry eyes. In his enthusiasm they used to glow and brighten; but now, as he sat looking down at the olive shades of the glen, they seemed ravenous in their fire. He had hardly spoken a word since we left the wood.

'Where can I read about these things?' he asked, and I gave him the names of books.

Then, an hour later, he asked me who were the builders. I told him the little I knew about Phoenician and Sabæan wanderings*, and the ritual of Sidon and Tyre*. He repeated some names to himself and went soon to bed.

As I turned in, I had one last look over the glen, which lay ivory and black in the moon. I seemed to hear a faint echo of wings, and to see over the little grove a cloud of light visitants. 'The Doves of Ashtaroth have come back,' I said to myself. 'It is a good omen. They accept the new tenant.' But as I fell asleep I had a sudden thought that I was saying something rather terrible.

II

Three years later, pretty nearly to a day, I came back to see what Lawson had made of his hobby. He had bidden me often to Welgevonden, as he chose to call it — though I do not know why he should have fixed a Dutch name to a countryside where Boer never trod. At the last there had been some confusion about dates, and I wired the time of my arrival, and set off without an answer. A motor met me at the queer little wayside station of Taqui, and after many miles on a doubtful highway I came to the gates of the park, and a road on which it was a delight to move. Three years had wrought little difference in the land-scape. Lawson had done some planting — conifers and flowering shrubs and such-like — but wisely he had resolved that Nature had for the most part forestalled him. All the same, he must have spent a mint of money. The drive could not have been beaten in England, and fringes of mown turf on either hand had been pared out of the lush meadows. When we came over the edge of the hill and looked down on the secret glen, I could not repress a cry of pleasure. The house stood on the farther ridge, the view-point of the whole neighbourhood; and its dark timbers and white rough-cast walls melted into the hillside as if it had been there from the beginning of things. The vale below was ordered in lawns and gardens. A blue lake received the rapids of the stream, and its banks were a maze of green shades and glorious masses of blossom. I noticed, too, that the little grove we had explored on our first visit stood alone in a big stretch of lawn, so that its perfection might be clearly seen. Lawson had excellent taste, or he had had the best advice.

The butler told me that his master was expected home shortly, and took me into the library for tea. Lawson had left his Tintorets and Ming pots at home after all. It was a long, low room, panelled in teak half-way up the walls, and the shelves held a multitude of fine bindings. There were good rugs on the parquet floor, but no ornaments anywhere, save three. On the carved mantelpiece stood two of the old soapstone birds which they used to find at Zimbabwe, and between, on an ebony stand, a half moon of alabaster, curiously carved with zodiacal figures. My host had altered his scheme of furnishing, but I approved the change.

He came in about half-past six, after I had consumed two
cigars and all but fallen asleep. Three years make a difference in
most men, but I was not prepared for the change in Lawson. For
one thing, he had grown fat. In place of the lean young man I
had known, I saw a heavy, flaccid being, who shuffled in his
gait, and seemed tired and listless. His sunburn had gone, and
his face was as pasty as a city clerk's. He had been walking, and
wore shapeless flannel clothes, which hung loose even on his
enlarged figure. And the worst of it was, that he did not seem
over-pleased to see me. He murmured something about my
journey, and then flung himself into an arm-chair and looked
out of the window.

I asked him if he had been ill.

'Ill! No!' he said crossly. 'Nothing of the kind. I'm perfectly
well.'

'You don't look as fit as this place should make you. What do
you do with yourself? Is the shooting as good as you hoped?'

He did not answer, but I thought I heard him mutter
something like 'shooting be damned.'

Then I tried the subject of the house. I praised it extrava-
gantly, but with conviction. 'There can be no place like it in
the world,' I said.

He turned his eyes on me at last, and I saw that they were as
deep and restless as ever. With his pallid face they made him
look curiously Semitic. I had been right in my view about his
ancestry.

'Yes,' he said slowly, 'there is no place like it – in the world.'

Then he pulled himself to his feet. 'I'm going to change,' he
said. 'Dinner is at eight. Ring for Travers, and he'll show you
your room.'

I dressed in a noble bedroom, with an outlook over the
garden-vale and the escarpment to the far line of the plains, now
blue and saffron in the sunset. I dressed in an ill temper, for I
was seriously offended with Lawson, and also seriously alarmed.
He was either very unwell or going out of his mind, and it was

clear, too, that he would resent any anxiety on his account. I ransacked my memory for rumours, but found none. I had heard nothing of him except that he had been extraordinarily successful in his speculations, and that from his hill-top he directed his firm's operations with uncommon skill. If Lawson was sick or mad, nobody knew of it.

Dinner was a trying ceremony. Lawson, who used to be rather particular in his dress, appeared in a kind of smoking suit and a flannel collar. He spoke scarcely a word to me, but cursed the servants with a brutality which left me aghast. A wretched footman in his nervousness spilt some sauce over his sleeve. Lawson dashed the dish from his hand, and volleyed abuse with a sort of epileptic fury. Also he, who had been the most abstemious of men, swallowed disgusting quantities of champagne and old brandy.

He had given up smoking, and half an hour after we left the dining-room he announced his intention of going to bed. I watched him as he waddled upstairs with a feeling of angry bewilderment. Then I went to the library and lit a pipe. I would leave first thing in the morning – on that I was determined. But as I sat gazing at the moon of alabaster and the soapstone birds my anger evaporated, and concern took its place. I remembered what a fine fellow Lawson had been, what good times we had had together. I remembered especially that evening when we had found this valley and given rein to our fancies. What horrid alchemy in the place had turned a gentleman into a brute? I thought of drink and drugs and madness and insomnia, but I could fit none of them into my conception of my friend. I did not consciously rescind my resolve to depart, but I had a notion that I would not act on it.

The sleepy butler met me as I went to bed. 'Mr Lawson's room is at the end of your corridor, sir,' he said. 'He don't sleep over well, so you may hear him stirring in the night. At what hour would you like breakfast, sir? Mr Lawson mostly has his in bed.'

My room opened from the great corridor, which ran the full length of the front of the house. So far as I could make out, Lawson was three rooms off, a vacant bedroom and his servant's room being between us. I felt tired and cross, and tumbled into bed as fast as possible. Usually I sleep well, but now I was soon conscious that my drowsiness was wearing off and that I was in for a restless night. I got up and laved my face, turned the pillows, thought of sheep coming over a hill and clouds crossing the sky; but none of the old devices were of any use. After about an hour of make-believe I surrendered myself to facts, and, lying on my back, stared at the white ceiling and the patches of moonshine on the walls.

It certainly was an amazing night. I got up, put on a dressing-gown, and drew a chair to the window. The moon was almost at its full, and the whole plateau swam in a radiance of ivory and silver. The banks of the stream were black, but the lake had a great belt of light athwart it, which made it seem like a horizon, and the rim of land beyond like a contorted cloud. Far to the right I saw the delicate outlines of the little wood which I had come to think of as the Grove of Ashtaroth. I listened. There was not a sound in the air. The land seemed to sleep peacefully beneath the moon, and yet I had a sense that the peace was an illusion. The place was feverishly restless.

I could have given no reason for my impression, but there it was. Something was stirring in the wide moonlit landscape under its deep mask of silence. I felt as I had felt on the evening three years ago when I had ridden into the grove. I did not think that the influence, whatever it was, was maleficent. I only knew that it was very strange, and kept me wakeful.

By and by I bethought me of a book. There was no lamp in the corridor save the moon, but the whole house was bright as I slipped down the great staircase and across the hall to the library. I switched on the lights and then switched them off. They seemed a profanation, and I did not need them.

I found a French novel, but the place held me and I stayed. I sat down in an armchair before the fireplace and the stone birds. Very odd those gawky things, like prehistoric Great Auks, looked in the moonlight. I remember that the alabaster moon shimmered like translucent pearl, and I fell to wondering about its history. Had the old Sabæans used such a jewel in their rites in the Grove of Ashtaroth?

Then I heard footsteps pass the window. A great house like this would have a watchman, but these quick shuffling footsteps were surely not the dull plod of a servant. They passed on to the grass and died away. I began to think of getting back to my room.

In the corridor, I noticed that Lawson's door was ajar, and that a light had been left burning. I had the unpardonable curiosity to peep in. The room was empty, and the bed had not been slept in. Now I knew whose were the footsteps outside the library window.

I lit a reading-lamp and tried to interest myself in *Cruelle Enigme**. But my wits were restless, and I could not keep my eyes on the page. I flung the book aside and sat down again by the window. The feeling came over me that I was sitting in a box at some play. The glen was a huge stage, and at any moment the players might appear on it. My attention was strung as high as if I had been waiting for the advent of some world-famous actress. But nothing came. Only the shadows shifted and lengthened as the moon moved across the sky.

Then quite suddenly the restlessness left me, and at the same moment the silence was broken by the crow of a cock and the rustling of trees in a light wind. I felt very sleepy, and was turning to bed when again I heard footsteps without. From the window I could see a figure moving across the garden towards the house. It was Lawson, got up in the sort of towel dressing-gown that one wears on board ship. He was walking slowly and painfully, as if very weary. I did not see his face, but the man's whole air was that of extreme fatigue and dejection.

I tumbled into bed and slept profoundly till long after daylight.

III

The man who valeted me was Lawson's own servant. As he was laying out my clothes I asked after the health of his master, and was told that he had slept ill and would not rise till late. Then the man, an anxious-faced Englishman, gave me some information on his own account. Mr Lawson was having one of his bad turns. It would pass away in a day or two, but till it had gone he was fit for nothing. He advised me to see Mr Jobson, the factor, who would look to my entertainment in his master's absence.

Jobson arrived before luncheon, and the sight of him was the first satisfactory thing about Welgevonden. He was a big, gruff Scot from Roxburghshire, engaged, no doubt, by Lawson as a duty to his Border ancestry. He had short grizzled whiskers, a weather-worn face, and a shrewd, calm blue eye. I knew now why the place was in such perfect order.

We began with sport, and Jobson explained what I could have in the way of fishing and shooting. His exposition was brief and business-like, and all the while I could see his eye searching me. It was clear that he had much to say on other matters than sport.

I told him that I had come here with Lawson three years before, when he chose the site. Jobson continued to regard me curiously. 'I've heard tell of ye from Mr Lawson. Ye're an old friend of his, I understand.'

'The oldest,' I said. 'And I am sorry to find that the place does not agree with him. Why it doesn't I cannot imagine, for you look fit enough. Has he been seedy for long?'

'It comes and goes,' said Mr Jobson. 'Maybe once a month he has a bad turn. But on the whole it agrees with him badly. He's no' the man he was when I first came here.'

Jobson was looking at me very seriously and frankly. I risked a question.

'What do you suppose is the matter?'

He did not reply at once, but leaned forward and tapped my knee.

"I think it's something that doctors canna cure. Look at me, sir. I've always been counted a sensible man, but if I told you what was in my head you would think me daft. But I have one word for you. Bide till tonight is past and then speir your question. Maybe you and me will be agreed.'

The factor rose to go. As he left the room he flung me back a remark over his shoulder — 'Read the eleventh chapter of the First Book of Kings.'

After luncheon I went for a walk. First I mounted to the crown of the hill and feasted my eyes on the unequalled loveliness of the view. I saw the far hills in Portuguese territory, a hundred miles away, lifting up thin blue fingers into the sky. The wind blew light and fresh, and the place was fragrant with a thousand delicate scents. Then I descended to the vale, and followed the stream up through the garden. Poinsettias and oleanders were blazing in coverts, and there was a paradise of tinted water-lilies in the slacker reaches. I saw good trout rise at the fly, but I did not think about fishing. I was searching my memory for a recollection which would not come. By and by I found myself beyond the garden, where the lawns ran to the fringe of Ashtaroth's Grove.

It was like something I remembered in an old Italian picture. Only, as my memory drew it, it should have been peopled with strange figures — nymphs dancing on the sward, and a prick-eared faun peeping from the covert. In the warm afternoon sunlight it stood, ineffably gracious and beautiful, tantalising with a sense of some deep hidden loveliness. Very reverently I walked between the slim trees, to where the little conical tower stood half in the sun and half in shadow. Then I noticed something new. Round the tower ran a narrow path, worn in the grass by human feet. There had been no such path on my first visit, for I remembered the grass growing tall to the edge of the stone. Had the Kaffirs made a shrine of it, or were there other and stranger votaries?

When I returned to the house I found Travers with a message for me. Mr Lawson was still in bed, but he would like me to go to him. I found my friend sitting up and drinking strong tea – a bad thing, I should have thought, for a man in his condition. I remember that I looked about the room for some sign of the pernicious habit of which I believed him a victim. But the place was fresh and clean, with the windows wide open, and, though I could not have given my reasons, I was convinced that drugs or drink had nothing to do with the sickness.

He received me more civilly, but I was shocked by his looks. There were great bags below his eyes, and his skin had the wrinkled puffy appearance of a man in dropsy. His voice, too, was reedy and thin. Only his great eyes burned with some feverish life.

'I am a shocking bad host,' he said, 'but I'm going to be still more inhospitable. I want you to go away. I hate anybody here when I'm off colour.'

'Nonsense,' I said; 'you want looking after. I want to know about this sickness. Have you had a doctor?'

He smiled wearily. 'Doctors are no earthly use to me. There's nothing much the matter, I tell you. I'll be all right in a day or two, and then you can come back. I want you to go off with Jobson and hunt in the plains till the end of the week. It will be better fun for you, and I'll feel less guilty.'

Of course I pooh-poohed the idea, and Lawson got angry. 'Damn it, man,' he cried, 'why do you force yourself on me when I don't want you? I tell you your presence here makes me worse. In a week I'll be as right as the mail, and then I'll be thankful for you. But get away now; get away, I tell you.'

I saw that he was fretting himself into a passion. 'All right,' I said soothingly; 'Jobson and I will go off hunting. But I am horribly anxious about you, old man.'

He lay back on his pillows. 'You needn't trouble. I only want a little rest. Jobson will make all arrangements, and Travers will get you anything you want. Good-bye.'

I saw it was useless to stay longer, so I left the room. Outside I found the anxious-faced servant. 'Look here,' I said, 'Mr Lawson thinks I ought to go, but I mean to stay. Tell him I'm gone if he asks·you. And for Heaven's sake keep him in bed.'

The man promised, and I thought I saw some relief in his face.

I went to the library, and on the way remembered Jobson's remark about First Kings. With some searching I found a Bible and turned up the passage. It was a long screed about the misdeeds of Solomon, and I read it through without enlightenment. I began to re-read it, and a word suddenly caught my attention —

For Solomon went after Ashtaroth, the goddess of the Zidonians.

That was all, but it was like a key to a cipher. Instantly there flashed over my mind all that I had heard or read of that strange ritual which seduced Israel to sin. I saw a sunburnt land and a people vowed to the stern service of Jehovah. But I saw, too, eyes turning from the austere sacrifice to lonely hill-top groves and towers and images, where dwelt some subtle and evil mystery. I saw the fierce prophets, scourging the votaries with rods, and a nation penitent before the Lord; but always the backsliding again, and the hankering after forbidden joys. Ashtaroth was the old goddess of the East. Was it not possible that in all Semitic blood there remained, transmitted through the dim generations, some craving for her spell? I thought of the grandfather in the back street at Brighton and of those burning eyes upstairs.

As I sat and mused my glance fell on the inscrutable stone birds. They knew those old secrets of joy and terror. And that moon of alabaster! Some dark priest had worn it on his forehead when he worshipped, like Ahab, 'all the host of Heaven'. And then I honestly began to be afraid. I, a prosaic, modern Christian gentleman, a half-believer in casual faiths, was in the presence of some hoary mystery of sin far older than creeds or Christendom. There was fear in my heart − a kind of uneasy disgust, and above all a nervous eerie disquiet. Now I wanted to go away, and yet I was ashamed of the cowardly thought. I pictured Ashtaroth's Grove with sheer horror. What tragedy was in the air? What secret awaited twilight? For the night was coming, the night of the Full Moon, the season of ecstasy and sacrifice.

I do not know how I got through that evening. I was disinclined for dinner, so I had a cutlet in the library, and sat smoking till my tongue ached. But as the hours passed a more manly resolution grew up in my mind. I owed it to old friendship to stand by Lawson in this extremity. I could not interfere − God knows, his reason seemed already rocking − but I could be at hand in case my chance came. I determined not to undress, but to watch through the night. I had a bath, and changed into light flannels and slippers. Then I took up my position in a corner of the library close to the window, so that I could not fail to hear Lawson's footsteps if he passed.

Fortunately I left the lights unlit, for as I waited I grew drowsy, and fell asleep. When I woke the moon had risen, and I knew from the feel of the air that the hour was late. I sat very still, straining my ears, and as I listened I caught the sound of steps. They were crossing the hall stealthily, and nearing the library door. I huddled into my corner as Lawson entered.

He wore the same towel dressing-gown, and he moved swiftly and silently as if in a trance. I watched him take the alabaster moon from the mantelpiece and drop it in his pocket. A glimpse of white skin showed that the gown was his only clothing. Then he moved past me to the window, opened it, and went out.

Without any conscious purpose I rose and followed, kicking off my slippers that I might go quietly. He was running, running fast, across the lawns in the direction of the Grove – an odd shapeless antic in the moonlight. I stopped, for there was no cover, and I feared for his reason if he saw me. When I looked again he had disappeared among the trees.

I saw nothing for it but to crawl, so on my belly I wormed my way over the dripping sward. There was a ridiculous suggestion of deer-stalking about the game which tickled me and dispelled my uneasiness. Almost I persuaded myself I was tracking an ordinary sleep-walker. The lawns were broader than I imagined, and it seemed an age before I reached the edge of the Grove. The world was so still that I appeared to be making a most ghastly amount of noise. I remember that once I heard a rustling in the air, and looked up to see the green doves circling about the tree-tops.

There was no sign of Lawson. On the edge of the Grove I think that all my assurance vanished. I could see between the trunks to the little tower, but it was quiet as the grave, save for the wings above. Once more there came over me the unbearable sense of anticipation I had felt the night before. My nerves tingled with mingled expectation and dread. I did not think that any harm would come to me, for the powers of the air seemed not malignant. But I knew them for powers, and felt awed and abased. I was in the presence of the 'host of Heaven', and I was no stern Israelitish prophet to prevail against them.

I must have lain for hours waiting in that spectral place, my eyes riveted on the tower and its golden cap of moonshine. I remember that my head felt void and light, as if my spirit were becoming disembodied and leaving its dew-drenched sheath far below. But the most curious sensation was of something drawing me to the tower, something mild and kindly and rather feeble, for there was some other and stronger force keeping me back. I yearned to move nearer, but I could not drag my limbs an inch. There was a spell somewhere which I could not break. I do not think I was in any way frightened now. The starry influence was playing tricks with me, but my mind was half asleep. Only I never took my eyes from the little tower. I think I could not, if I had wanted to.

Then suddenly from the shadows came Lawson. He was stark-naked, and he wore, bound across his brow, the half-moon of alabaster. He had something, too, in his hand – something which glittered.

He ran round the tower, crooning to himself, and flinging wild arms to the skies. Sometimes the crooning changed to a shrill cry of passion, such as a mænad may have uttered in the train of Bacchus. I could make out no words, but the sound told its own tale. He was absorbed in some infernal ecstasy. And as he ran, he drew his right hand across his breast and arms, and I saw that it held a knife.

I grew sick with disgust – not terror, but honest physical loathing. Lawson, gashing his fat body, affected me with an overpowering repugnance. I wanted to go forward and stop him, and I wanted, too, to be a hundred miles away. And the result was that I stayed still. I believe my own will held me there, but I doubt if in any case I could have moved my legs.

The dance grew swifter and fiercer. I saw the blood dripping from Lawson's body, and his face ghastly white above his scarred breast. And then suddenly the horror left me; my head swam; and for one second – one brief second – I peered into a new world. A strange passion surged up in my heart. I seemed to see the earth peopled with forms not human, scarcely divine, but more desirable than man or god. The calm face of Nature broke up for me into wrinkles of wild knowledge. I saw the things which brush against the soul in dreams, and found them lovely. There seemed no cruelty in the knife or the blood. It was a delicate mystery of worship, as wholesome as the morning song of birds. I do not know how the Semites found Ashtaroth's ritual; to them it may well have been more rapt and passionate than it seemed to me. For I saw in it only the sweet simplicity of

Nature, and all riddles of lust and terror soothed away as a child's nightmares are calmed by a mother. I found my legs able to move, and I think I took two steps through the dusk towards the tower.

And then it all ended. A cock crew, and the homely noises of earth were renewed. While I stood dazed and shivering Lawson plunged through the Grove towards me. The impetus carried him to the edge, and he fell fainting just outside the shade.

My wits and common-sense came back to me with my bodily strength. I got my friend on my back, and staggered with him towards the house. I was afraid in real earnest now, and what frightened me most was the thought that I had not been afraid sooner. I had come very near the 'abomination of the Zidonians'.

At the door I found the scared valet waiting. He had apparently done this sort of thing before.

'Your master has been sleep-walking, and has had a fall,' I said. 'We must get him to bed at once.'

We bathed the wounds as he lay in a deep stupor, and I dressed them as well as I could. The only danger lay in his utter exhaustion, for happily the gashes were not serious, and no artery had been touched. Sleep and rest would make him well, for he had the constitution of a strong man. I was leaving the room when he opened his eyes and spoke. He did not recognise me, but I noticed that his face had lost its strangeness, and was once more that of the friend I had known. Then I suddenly bethought me of an old hunting remedy which he and I always carried on our expeditions. It is a pill made up from an ancient Portuguese prescription. One is an excellent specific for fever. Two are invaluable if you are lost in the bush, for they send a man for many hours into a deep sleep, which prevents suffering and madness, till help comes. Three give a painless death. I went to my room and found the little box in my jewel-case. Lawson swallowed two, and turned wearily on his side. I bade his man let him sleep till he woke, and went off in search of food.

IV

I had business on hand which would not wait. By seven, Jobson, who had been sent for, was waiting for me in the library. I knew by his grim face that here I had a very good substitute for a prophet of the Lord.

'You were right,' I said. 'I have read the 11th chapter of First Kings, and I have spent such a night as I pray God I shall never spend again.'

'I thought you would,' he replied. 'I've had the same experience myself.'

'The Grove?' I said.

'Ay, the wud,' was the answer in broad Scots.

I wanted to see how much he understood.

'Mr Lawson's family is from the Scottish Border?'

'Ay. I understand they come off Borthwick Water side,' he replied, but I saw by his eyes that he knew what I meant.

'Mr Lawson is my oldest friend,' I went on, 'and I am going to take measures to cure him. For what I am going to do I take the sole responsibility. I will make that plain to your master. But if I am to succeed I want your help. Will you give it me? It sounds like madness, and you are a sensible man and may like to keep out of it. I leave it to your discretion.'

Jobson looked me straight in the face. 'Have no fear for me,' he said; 'there is an unholy thing in that place, and if I have the strength in me I will destroy it. He has been a good master to me, and, forbye, I am a believing Christian. So say on, sir.'

There was no mistaking the air. I had found my Tishbite*.

'I want men,' I said – 'as many as we can get.'

Jobson mused. 'The Kaffirs will no' gang near the place, but there's some thirty white men on the tobacco farm. They'll do your will, if you give them an indemnity in writing.'

'Good,' said I. 'Then we will take our instructions from the only authority which meets the case. We will follow the

example of King Josiah.' I turned up the 23rd chapter of Second
Kings, and read —

*And the high places that were before Jerusalem, which were on the right hand of the
Mount of Corruption, which Solomon the king of Israel had builded for Ashtaroth
the abomination of the Zidonians . . . did the king defile.*

    *And he brake in pieces the images, and cut down the groves, and filled their
places with the bones of men.*

    *Moreover the altar that was at Beth-el, and the high place which Jeroboam the
son of Nebat, who made Israel to sin, had made, both that altar and the high place
he brake down, and burned the high place, and stamped it small to powder, and
burned the grove.*

Jobson nodded. 'It'll need dinnymite. But I've plenty of yon
down at the workshops. I'll be off to collect the lads.'

Before nine the men had assembled at Jobson's house. They
were a hardy lot of young farmers from home, who took their
instructions docilely from the masterful factor. On my orders
they had brought their shot-guns. We armed them with spades
and woodmen's axes, and one man wheeled some coils of rope in
a handcart.

In the clear, windless air of morning the Grove, set amid its
lawns, looked too innocent and exquisite for evil. I had a pang of
regret that a thing so fair should suffer; nay, if I had come alone,
I think I might have repented. But the men were there, and the
grim-faced Jobson was waiting for orders. I placed the guns,
and sent beaters to the far side. I told them that every dove must
be shot.

It was only a small flock, and we killed fifteen at the first
drive. The poor birds flew over the glen to another spinney, but
we brought them back over the guns and seven fell. Four more
were got in the trees, and the last I killed myself with a long
shot. In half an hour there was a pile of little green bodies on the
sward.

Then we went to work to cut down the trees. The slim stems
were an easy task to a good woodman, and one after another they

toppled to the ground. And meantime, as I watched, I became conscious of a strange emotion.

It was as if some one were pleading with me. A gentle voice, not threatening, but pleading — something too fine for the sensual ear, but touching inner chords of the spirit. So tenuous it was and distant that I could think of no personality behind it. Rather it was the viewless, bodiless grace of this delectable vale, some old exquisite divinity of the groves. There was the heart of all sorrow in it, and the soul of all loveliness. It seemed a woman's voice, some lost lady who had brought nothing but goodness unrepaid to the world. And what the voice told me was, that I was destroying her last shelter.

That was the pathos of it — the voice was homeless. As the axes flashed in the sunlight and the wood grew thin, that gentle spirit was pleading with me for mercy and a brief respite. It seemed to be telling of a world for centuries grown coarse and pitiless, of long sad wanderings, of hardly-won shelter, and a peace which was the little all she sought from men. There was nothing terrible in it. No thought of wrongdoing. The spell, which to Semitic blood held the mystery of evil, was to me, of a different race, only delicate and rare and beautiful. Jobson and the rest did not feel it, I with my finer senses caught nothing but the hopeless sadness of it. That which had stirred the passion in Lawson was only wringing my heart. It was almost too pitiful to bear. As the trees crashed down and the men wiped the sweat from their brows, I seemed to myself like the murderer of fair women and innocent children. I remember that the tears were running over my cheeks. More than once I opened my mouth to countermand the work, but the face of Jobson, that grim Tishbite, held me back.

I knew now what gave the Prophets of the Lord their mastery, and I knew also why the people sometimes stoned them.

The last tree fell, and the little tower stood like a ravished shrine, stripped of all defences against the world. I heard Jobson's voice speaking. 'We'd better blast that stane thing

now. We'll trench on four sides and lay the dinnymite. Ye're no'
looking weel, sir. Ye'd better go and sit down on the brae-face.'

I went up the hillside and lay down. Below me, in the waste
of shorn trunks, men were running about, and I saw the mining
begin. It all seemed like an aimless dream in which I had no
part. The voice of that homeless goddess was still pleading. It
was the innocence of it that tortured me. Even so must a
merciful Inquisitor have suffered from the plea of some fair girl
with the aureole of death on her hair. I knew I was killing rare
and unrecoverable beauty. As I sat dazed and heartsick, the
whole loveliness of Nature seemed to plead for its divinity. The
sun in the heavens, the mellow lines of upland, the blue mystery
of the far plains, were all part of that soft voice. I felt bitter scorn
for myself. I was guilty of blood; nay, I was guilty of the sin
against light which knows no forgiveness. I was murdering
innocent gentleness, and there would be no peace on earth for
me. Yet I sat helpless. The power of a sterner will constrained
me. And all the while the voice was growing fainter and dying
away into unutterable sorrow.

Suddenly a great flame sprang to heaven, and a pall of smoke.
I heard men crying out, and fragments of stone fell around the
ruins of the grove. When the air cleared, the little tower had
gone out of sight.

The voice had ceased, and there seemed to me to be a bereaved
silence in the world. The shock moved me to my feet, and I ran
down the slope to where Jobson stood rubbing his eyes.

'That's done the job. Now we maun get up the tree roots.
We've no time to howk. We'll just blast the feck o' them.'

The work of destruction went on, but I was coming back to
my senses. I forced myself to be practical and reasonable. I
thought of the night's experience and Lawson's haggard eyes,
and I screwed myself into a determination to see the thing
through. I had done the deed; it was my business to make it
complete. A text in Jeremiah came into my head: *Their children
remember their altars and their groves by the green trees upon the*

high hills.' I would see to it that this grove should be utterly forgotten.

We blasted the tree roots, and, yoking oxen, dragged the débris into a great heap. Then the men set to work with their spades, and roughly levelled the ground. I was getting back to my old self, and Jobson's spirit was becoming mine.

'There is one thing more,' I told him. 'Get ready a couple of ploughs. We will improve upon King Josiah.' My brain was a medley of Scripture precedents, and I was determined that no safeguard should be wanting.

We yoked the oxen again and drove the ploughs over the site of the grove. It was rough ploughing, for the place was thick with bits of stone from the tower, but the slow Afrikander oxen plodded on, and sometime in the afternoon the work was finished. Then I sent down to the farm for bags of rock-salt, such as they use for cattle. Jobson and I took a sack apiece, and walked up and down the furrows, sowing them with salt.

The last act was to set fire to the pile of tree trunks. They burned well, and on the top we flung the bodies of the green doves. The birds of Ashtaroth had an honourable pyre.

Then I dismissed the much-perplexed men, and gravely shook hands with Jobson. Black with dust and smoke I went back to the house, where I bade Travers pack my bags and order the motor. I found Lawson's servant, and heard from him that his master was sleeping peacefully. I gave him some directions, and then went to wash and change.

Before I left I wrote a line to Lawson. I began by transcribing the verses from the 23rd chapter of Second Kings. I told him what I had done, and my reason. 'I take the whole responsibility upon myself,' I wrote. 'No man in the place had anything to do with it but me. I acted as I did for the sake of our old friendship, and you will believe it was no easy task for me. I hope you will understand. Whenever you are able to see me send me word, and I will come back and settle with you. But I think you will realise that I have saved your soul.'

The afternoon was merging into twilight as I left the house on the road to Taqui. The great fire, where the grove had been, was still blazing fiercely, and the smoke made a cloud over the upper glen, and filled all the air with a soft violet haze. I knew that I had done well for my friend, and that he would come to his senses and be grateful . . . But as the car reached the ridge I looked back to the vale I had outraged. The moon was rising and silvering the smoke, and through the gaps I could see the tongues of fire. Somehow, I know not why, the lake, the stream, the garden-coverts, even the green slopes of hill, wore an air of loneliness and desecration.

And then my heartache returned, and I knew that I had driven something lovely and adorable from its last refuge on earth.

At the Article of Death

Another undergraduate piece, written probably in his first year at Brasenose,
and the third of his stories to appear in twelve months in The Yellow Book,
Aubrey Beardsley's new, rather precious, avant-garde *quarterly: it came in*
the penultimate number for January 1897 just after Far Above Rubies *by*
Netta Syrett. One modern image of Buchan does not fit at all with his
companions in that volume, Henry James, E. Nesbitt, Kenneth Grahame,
Richard Garnett, Richard le Gallienne – and he is taken to be the polar
opposite of Beardsley with his 'decadent decorations'. Yet finding this exercise
in rural realism there is a reminder that Buchan, even from his earliest days,
is more unexpected than several recent stereotypes of him have allowed.

Buchan, son of the Manse, later High Commissioner to the General
Assembly of the Church of Scotland, brought up on Bible and Catechism,
wrote with a fine, affirming understanding of the true powers of religion,
whether that religion was Christian (for example in Salute to Adventurers)
or Jewish (for example in A Prince of the Captivity). *He was no sentimen-*
talist, unlike some of the 'Kailyard' school of Scottish writers of the time,
including Barrie and 'Ian Maclaren'. He hated both comfortable shallowness
and that commercial religiosity which traded automatic salvation for bigotry.
His villains, in his longer fiction, are often in the mould of swollen Coven-
anters, overreaching themselves in spiritual arrogance.

In this tale, again, the slight youthful over-writing does not hinder the
sympathy: Buchan always wrote well of an absolute aloneness.

First published in Grey Weather, *it has not been in print again until*
now.

At the Article of Death

Nullum
Sacra caput Proserpina fugit. *

A noiseless evening fell chill and dank on the moorlands. The Dreichil was mist to the very rim of its precipitous face, and the long, dun sides of the Little Muneraw faded into grey vapour. Underfoot were plashy moss and dripping heather, and all the air was choked with autumnal heaviness. The herd of the Lanely Bield stumbled wearily homeward in this, the late afternoon, with the roof-tree of his cottage to guide him over the waste.

For weeks, months, he had been ill, fighting the battle of a lonely sickness. Two years agone his wife had died, and as there had been no child, he was left to fend for himself. He had no need for any woman, he declared, for his wants were few and his means of the scantiest, so he had cooked his own meals and done his own household work since the day he had stood by the grave in the Gledsmuir kirkyard. And for a little he did well; and then, inch by inch, trouble crept upon him. He would come home late in the winter nights, soaked to the skin, and sit in the peat-reek till his clothes dried on his body. The countless little ways in which a woman's hand makes a place healthy and habitable were unknown to him, and soon he began to pay the price of his folly. For he was not a strong man, though a careless onlooker might have guessed the opposite from his mighty frame. His folk had all been short-lived, and already his was the age of his father at his death. Such a fact might have warned him to circumspection; but he took little heed till that night in the March before, when, coming up the Little Muneraw and breathing hard, a chill wind on the summit cut him to the bone. He rose the next morn, shaking like a leaf, and then for weeks he lay ill in bed, while a young shepherd from the next sheep-farm did his work on the hill. In the early summer he rose a broken man, without strength or nerve, and always oppressed with an ominous sinking in the chest; but he toiled through his duties, and told no man his sorrow. The summer was parchingly hot, and the hillsides grew brown and dry as ashes. Often as he laboured up the interminable ridges, he found himself sickening at heart with a poignant regret. These were the places where once he had strode so freely with the crisp air cool on his forehead. Now he had no eye for the pastoral loveliness, no ear for the witch-song of the desert. When he reached a summit, it was only to fall panting, and when he came home at nightfall he sank wearily on a seat.

And so through the lingering summer the year waned to an autumn of storm. Now his malady seemed nearing its end. He had seen no man's face for a week, for long miles of moor severed him from a homestead. He could scarce struggle from his bed by mid-day, and his daily round of the hill was gone through with tottering feet. The time would soon come for drawing the ewes and driving them to the Gledsmuir market. If he could but hold on till the word came, he might yet have speech of a fellow man and bequeath his duties to another. But if he died first, the charge would wander uncared for, while he himself would lie in that lonely cot till such time as the lowland farmer sent the messenger. With anxious care he tended his flickering spark of life – he had long ceased to hope – and with something like heroism looked blankly towards his end.

But on this afternoon all things had changed. At the edge of the water-meadow he had found blood dripping from his lips, and half-swooned under an agonising pain at his heart. With burning eyes he turned his face to home, and fought his way inch by inch through the desert. He counted the steps crazily, and with pitiful sobs looked upon mist and moorland. A faint bleat of a sheep came to his ear; he heard it clearly, and the hearing wrung his soul. Not for him any more the hills of sheep and a shepherd's free and wholesome life. He was creeping, stricken, to his homestead to die, like a wounded fox crawling to its earth. And the loneliness of it all, the pity, choked him more than the fell grip of his sickness.

Inside the house a great banked fire of peats was smouldering. Unwashed dishes stood on the table, and the bed in the corner was unmade, for such things were of little moment in the extremity of his days. As he dragged his leaden foot over the threshold, the autumn dusk thickened through the white fog, and shadows awaited him, lurking in every corner. He dropped carelessly on the bed's edge, and lay back in deadly weakness. No sound broke the stillness, for the clock had long ago stopped for lack of winding. Only the shaggy collie which had lain down by the fire looked to the bed and whined mournfully.

In a little he raised his eyes and saw that the place was filled with darkness, save where the red eye of the fire glowed hot and silent. His strength was too far gone to light the lamp, but he could make a crackling fire. Some power other than himself made him heap bog-sticks on the peat and poke it feebly, for he shuddered at the ominous long shades which peopled floor and ceiling. If he had but a leaping blaze he might yet die in a less gross mockery of comfort.

Long he lay in the firelight, sunk in the lethargy of illimitable feebleness. Then the strong spirit of the man began to flicker within him and rise to sight ere it sank in death. He had always been a godly liver, one who had no youth of folly to look back upon, but a well-spent life of toil lit by the lamp of a half-understood devotion. He it was who at his wife's death-bed had administered words of comfort and hope; and had passed all his days with the thought of his own end fixed like a bull's eye in the target of his meditations. In his lonely hill-watches, in the weariful lambing days, and on droving journeys to faraway towns, he had whiled the hours with self-communing, and self-examination, by the help of a rigid Word. Nay, there had been far more than the mere punctilios of obedience to the letter; there had been the living fire of love, the heroical altitude of self-denial, to be the halo of his solitary life. And now God had sent him the last fiery trial, and he was left alone to put off the garments of mortality.

He dragged himself to a cupboard where all the appurtenances of the religious life lay to his hands. There were Spurgeon's sermons in torn covers, and a dozen musty 'Christian Treasuries'. Some antiquated theology, which he had got from his father, lay lowest, and on the top was the gaudy Bible, which he had once received from a grateful Sabbath class while he yet sojourned in the lowlands. It was lined and re-lined, and there he had often found consolation. Now in the last faltering of mind he had braced himself to the thought that he must die as became his possession, with the Word of God in his hand, and his thoughts fixed on that better country, which is an heavenly.

The thin leaves mocked his hands, and he could not turn to any well-remembered text. In vain he struggled to reach the gospels; the obstinate leaves blew ever back to a dismal psalm or a prophet's lamentation. A word caught his eye and he read vaguely: 'The shepherds slumber, O King, . . . the people is scattered upon the mountains . . . and no man gathereth them . . . there is no healing of the hurt, for the wound is grievous.' Something in the poignant sorrow of the phrase caught his attention for one second, and then he was back in a fantasy of pain and impotence. He could not fix his mind, and even as he strove he remembered the warning he had so often given to others against death-bed repentance. Then, he had often said, a man has no time to make his peace with his Maker, when he is wrestling with death. Now the adage came back to him; and gleams of comfort shot for one moment through his soul. He at any rate had long since chosen for God, and the good Lord would see and pity His servant's weakness.

A sheep bleated near the window, and then another. The flocks were huddling down, and wind and wet must be coming. Then a long dreary wind sighed round the dwelling, and at the same moment a bright tongue of flame shot up from the fire, and queer crooked shadows flickered over the ceiling. The sight caught his eyes, and he shuddered in nameless terror. He had never been a coward, but like all religious folk he had imagination and emotion. Now his fancy was perturbed, and he shrank from these uncanny shapes. In the failure of all else he had fallen to the repetition of bare phrases, telling of the fragrance and glory of the city of God. 'River of the water of Life,' he said to himself, . . . 'the glory and honour of the nations . . . and the street of the city was pure gold . . . and the saved shall walk in the light of it . . . and God shall wipe away all tears from their eyes.'

Again a sound without, the cry of sheep and the sough of a lone wind. He was sinking fast, but the noise gave him a spasm of strength. The dog rose and sniffed uneasily at the door, a trickle of rain dripped from the roofing, and all the while the silent heart of the fire glowed and hissed at his side. It seemed an uncanny thing that now in the moment of his anguish the sheep should bleat as they had done in the old strong days of herding.

Again the sound, and again the morris-dance of shadows among the rafters. The thing was too much for his failing mind. Some words of hope — 'streams in the desert, and' — died on his lips, and he crawled from the bed to a cupboard. He had not tasted strong drink for a score of years, for to the true saint in the uplands abstinence is a primary virtue; but he kept brandy in the house for illness or wintry weather. Now it would give him strength, and it was no sin to cherish the spark of life.

He found the spirits and gulped down a mouthful — one, two, till the little flask was drained, and the raw fluid spilled over beard and coat. In his days of health it would have made him drunk, but now all the fibres of his being were relaxed, and it merely stung him to a fantasmal vigour. More, it maddened his brain, already tottering under the assaults of death. Before he had thought feebly and greyly, now his mind surged in an ecstasy.

The pain that lay heavy on his chest, that clutched his throat, that tugged at his heart, was as fierce as ever, but for one short second the utter weariness of spirit was gone. The old fair words of Scripture came back to him, and he murmured promises and hopes till his strength failed him for all but thought, and with closed eyes he fell back to dream.

But only for one moment; the next he was staring blankly in a mysterious terror. Again the voices of the wind, again the shapes on floor and wall and the relentless eye of the fire. He was too helpless to move and too crazy to pray; he could only lie and stare, numb with expectancy. The liquor seemed to have driven all memory from him, and left him with a child's heritage of dreams and stories.

Crazily he pattered to himself a child's charm against evil fairies, which the little folk of the moors still speak at their play, —

> Wearie, Ovie, gang awa',
> Dinna show your face at a',
> Ower the muir and down the burn,
> Wearie, Ovie, ne'er return.

The black crook of the chimney was the object of his spells, for the kindly ingle was no less than a malignant twisted devil, with an awful red eye glowering through smoke.

His breath was winnowing through his worn chest like an autumn blast in bare rafters. The horror of the black night without, all filled with the wail of sheep, and the deeper fear of the red light within, stirred his brain, not with the far-reaching fanciful terror of men, but with the crude homely fright of a little child. He would have sought, had his strength suffered him, to cower one moment in the light as a refuge from the other, and the next to hide in the darkest corner to shun the maddening glow. And with it all he was acutely conscious of the last pangs of mortality. He felt the grating of cheekbones on skin, and the sighing, which did duty for breath, rocked him with agony.

Then a great shadow rose out of the gloom and stood shaggy

in the firelight. The man's mind was tottering, and once more he was back at his Scripture memories and vague repetitions. Aforetime his fancy had toyed with green fields, now it held to the darker places. 'It was the day when Evil Merodach was king in Babylon,' came the quaint recollection, and some lingering ray of thought made him link the odd name with the amorphous presence before him. The thing moved and came nearer, touched him, and brooded by his side. He made to shriek, but no sound came, only a dry rasp in the throat and a convulsive twitch of the limbs.

For a second he lay in the agony of a terror worse than the extremes of death. It was only his dog, returned from his watch by the door, and seeking his master. He, poor beast, knew of some sorrow vaguely and afar, and nuzzled into his side with dumb affection.

Then from the chaos of faculties a shred of will survived. For an instant his brain cleared, for to most there comes a lull at the very article of death. He saw the bare moorland room, he felt the dissolution of his members, the palpable ebb of life. His religion had been swept from him like a rotten garment. His mind was vacant of memories, for all were driven forth by purging terror. Only some relic of manliness, the heritage of cleanly and honest days, was with him to the uttermost. With blank thoughts, without hope or vision, with naught save an aimless resolution and a causeless bravery, he passed into the short anguish which is death.

Comedy in the Full Moon

All his life, Buchan loved in his stories to assemble diverse people together in a special countryside on some sort of romantic quest that was half-serious, half in play: Comedy in the Full Moon *is only one of a dozen stories where this happens;* John Macnab *is another.*

Here, in another undergraduate story, the texture is of a good soufflé. It is of its period (Victoria still had several years on the throne), though the Earl and Miss Phyllis have touches of self-parody. But the characters and the incidents are lightly touched with a splendid lunacy: normality, with an implicit hint of unscrupulous social climbing, has been left behind with the absent Mr Eden, the Countess, and the older men playing billiards. Everyone else is gathered to one spot to be suspended in air between a strange and beautiful earth and that insistent full moon.

This story also first appeared in Grey Weather.

Comedy in the Full Moon

'I dislike that man,' said Miss Phyllis, with energy.

'I have liked others better,' said the Earl.

There was silence for a little as they walked up the laurelled path, which wound by hazel thicket and fir-wood to the low ridges of moor.

'I call him Charles Surface,' said Miss Phyllis again, with a meditative air. 'I am no dabbler in the water-colours of character, but I think I could describe him.'

'Try,' said the Earl.

'Mr Charles Eden,' began the girl, 'is a man of talent. He has edged his way to fortune by dint of the proper enthusiasms and a seductive manner. He is a politician of repute and a lawyer of some practice, but his enemies say that like necessity he knows no law, and even his friends shrink from insisting upon his knowledge of politics. But he believes in all honest enthusiasms, temperance, land reform, and democracy with a capital D; he is, however, violently opposed to woman suffrage.'

'Every man has his good points,' murmured the Earl.

'You are interrupting me,' said Miss Phyllis, severely. 'To continue, his wife was the daughter of a baronet of ancient family and scanty means. Her husband supplied the element which she missed in her father's household, and today she is popular and her parties famous. Their house is commonly known as the Wilderness, because there the mixed multitude which came out of Egypt mingle with the chosen people. In character he is persuasive and good-natured; but then good-nature is really a vice which is called a virtue because it only annoys a man's enemies.'

'I am learning a great deal tonight,' said the man.

'You are,' said Miss Phyllis. 'But there, I have done. What I dislike in him is that one feels that he is the sort of man that has always lived in a house and is out of place anywhere but on a pavement.'

'And you call this a sketch in water-colours?'

'No, indeed. In oils,' said the girl, and they walked through a gate on to the short bent grass and the bouldered face of a hill. Something in the place seemed to strike her, for she dropped her voice and spoke simply.

'You know I am town-bred, but I am not urban in nature. I must chatter daily, but every now and then I grow tired of myself, and I hate people like Charles Eden who remind me of my weakness.'

'Life,' said the Earl, 'may be roughly divided into — But there, it is foolish to be splitting up life by hairs on such a night.'

Now they stood on the ridge's crest in the silver-grey light of a midsummer moon. Far up the long Gled valley they looked to the towering hills whence it springs; then to the left, where the sinuous Callowa wound its way beneath green and birk-clad mountains to the larger stream. In such a flood of brightness the far-distant peaks and shoulders stood out clear as day, but full of that hint of subtle and imperishable mystery with which the moon endows the great uplands in the height of summer. The air was still, save for the falling of streams and the twitter of nesting birds.

The girl stared wide-eyed at the scene, and her breath came softly with utter admiration.

'Oh, such a land!' she cried, 'and I have never seen it before. Do you know I would give anything to explore these solitudes, and feel that I had made them mine. Will you take me with you?'

'But these things are not for you, little woman,' he said. 'You are too clever and smart and learned in the minutiae of human conduct. You would never learn their secret. You are too complex for simple, old-world life.'

'Please don't say that,' said Miss Phyllis, with pleading eyes. 'Don't think so hardly of me. I am not all for show.' Then with fresh wonder she looked over the wide landscape.

'Do you know these places?' she asked.

'I have wandered over them for ten years and more,' said the Earl, 'and I am beginning to love them. In other ten, perhaps, I shall have gone some distance on the road to knowledge. The best things in life take time and labour to reach.'

The girl made no answer. She had found a little knoll in the opposite glen, clothed in a tangle of fern and hazels, and she eagerly asked its name.

'The folk here call it the Fairy Knowe,' he said. 'There is a queer story about it. They say that if any two people at midsummer in the full moon walk from the east and west so as to meet at the top, they will find a third there, who will tell them all the future. The old men speak of it carefully, but none believe it.'

'Oh, let us go and try,' said the girl, in glee. 'It is quite early in the evening, and they will never miss us at home.'

'But the others,' said he.

'Oh, the others,' with a gesture of amusement. 'We left Mr Eden talking ideals to your mother, and the other men preparing for billiards. They won't mind.'

'But it's more than half a mile, and you'll be very tired.'

'No, indeed,' said the girl, 'I could walk to the top of the farthest hills tonight. I feel as light as a feather, and I do so want to know the future. It will be such a score to speak to my aunt with the prophetic accent of the things to be.'

'Then come on,' said the Earl, and the two went off through the heather.

II

If you walk into the inn-kitchen at Callowa on a winter night, you will find it all but deserted, save for a chance traveller who is storm-stayed among the uncertain hills. Then men stay in their homes, for the place is little, and the dwellers in the remoter parts have no errand to town or village. But in the long nights of summer, when the moon is up and the hills dry underfoot, there are many folk down of an evening from the glens, and you may chance on men drinking a friendly glass with half a score of miles of journey before them. It is a cheerful scene – the wide room, with the twilight struggling with the new-lit lamp, the brown faces gathered around the table, and the rise and fall of the soft southern talk.

On this night you might have chanced on a special gathering, for it was the evening of the fair-day in Gled-foot, and many shepherds from the moors were eating their suppers and making ready for the road. It was then that Jock Rorison of the Red-swirehead – known to all the world as Lang Jock to distinguish him from his cousin little Jock of the Nick o' the Hurlstanes – met his most ancient friend, the tailor of Callowa. They had been at school together, together they had suffered the pains of learning; and now the one's lot was cast at the back of Creation, and the other's in a little dark room in the straggling street of Callowa. A bottle celebrated their meeting, and there and then in the half-light of the gloaming they fell into talk. They spoke of friends and kin, and the toils of their life; of village gossip and market prices. Thence they drifted into vague moralisings and muttered exhortation in the odour of whisky. Soon they were amiable beyond their wont, praising each other's merit, and prophesying of good fortune. And then – alas for human nature! – there came the natural transition to argument and reviling.

'I wadna be you, Jock, for a thousand pounds', said the tailor. 'Na, I wadna venture up that lang mirk glen o' yours for a' the wealth o' the warld.'

'Useless body,' said the shepherd, 'and what for that?'

'Bide a' nicht here,' said the tailor, 'and step on in the mornin'. Man, ye're an auld freend, and I'm wae to think that aucht ill should befa' ye.'

'Will ye no speak sense for yince, ye doited cratur?' was the ungracious answer, as the tall man rose to unhook his staff from the chimney corner. 'I'm for stertin' if I'm to win hame afore mornin'.'

'Weel,' said the tailor, with the choked voice of the maudlin, 'a' I've to say is that I wis the Lord may protect ye, for there's evil lurks i' the dens o' the way, saith the prophet.'

'Stop, John Rorison, stop,' again the tailor groaned. 'O man, bethink ye o' your end.'

'I wis ye wad bethink o' yin yoursel'.'

The tailor heeded not the rudeness . . . 'for ye ken a' the auld queer owercomes about the Gled Water. Yin Thomas the Rhymer made a word on 't. Quoth he,

> By the Gled side
> The guid folk bide.

'Dodsake, Robin, ye're a man o' learnin' wi' your poetry,' said the shepherd, with scorn. 'Rhymin' about auld wives' havers, sic wark for a grown man!'

A vague recollection of wrath rose to the tailor's mind. But he answered with the laborious dignity of argument, —

'I'm no sayin' that a' things are true that the body said. But I say this — that there's a heap o' queer things in the warld, mair nor you nor me nor onybody kens. Now, it's weel ken't that nane o' the folk about here like to gang to the Fairy Knowe . . .'

'It's weel ken't nae siccan thing,' said the shepherd, rudely. 'I wonder at you, a kirk member and an honest man's son, crakin' siccan blethers.'

'I'm affirmin' naething,' said the other, sententiously. 'What I say is that nae man, woman, or child in this parish, which is weel ken't for an intelligent yin, wad like to gang at the rising o' the mune up the side o' the Fairy Knowe. And it's weel ken't, tae, that when the twae daft lads frae the Rochan tried it in my faither's day and gaed up frae opposite airts, they met at the tap that which telled them a' that they ever did and a' that was ever like to befa' them, and put the fear o' death on them for ever and ever. Mind, I'm affirmin' naething; but what think ye o' that?'

'I think this o' 't — that either the folk were mair fou than the Baltic or they were weak i' the heid afore ever they set out. But I'm tired o' hearin' a sensible man bletherin', so I'm awa' to the Redswirehead.'

But the tailor was swollen with pride and romance, and filled with the audacity which comes from glasses replenished.

'Then I'll gang a bit o' the road wi' ye.'

'And what for sae?' said the shepherd, darkly suspicious. Whisky drove care to his head, and made him the most irritable of friends.

'I want the air, and it's graund munelicht. Your road gangs by the Knowe, and we micht as weel mak the experiment. Mind ye, I'm affirmin' naething.'

'Will ye no haud your tongue about what ye're affirmin'?'

'But I hold that it is a wise man's pairt to try all things, and whae kens but there micht be some queer sicht on that Knowe-tap? The auld folk were nane sae ready to be inventin' havers.'

'I think the man's mad,' was the shepherd's loud soliloquy. 'You want me to gang and play daft-like pranks late at nicht among birks and stanes on a muckle knowe. Weel, let it be. It lies on my road hame, but ye'd be weel serv't if some auld Druid cam out and grippit ye.'

'Whae's bletherin' now,' cried the tailor, triumphantly. 'I dinna gang wi' only supersteetions. I gang to get the fresh air and admire the wonderfu' works o' God. Hech, but they're bonny.' And he waved a patronising finger to the moon.

The shepherd took him by the shoulder and marched him down the road. 'Listen,' said he, 'I maun be hame afore the morn, and if ye're comin' wi' me ye'll hae to look smerter.' So down the white path and over Gled bridge they took their way, two argumentative figures, clamouring in the silent, amber spaces of the night.

III

The farmer of the Lowe Moss was a choleric man at all times, but every now and again his temper failed him utterly. He was florid and full-blooded, and the hot weather drove him wild with discomfort. Then came the torments of a dusty market and completed the task; so it fell out that on that evening in June he drove home at a speed which bade fair to hurry him to a premature grave, and ate his supper with little thankfulness.

Then he reflected upon his manifold labours. The next day was the clipping, and the hill sheep would have to be brought down in the early morning. The shepherds would be at the folds by seven, and it would mean rising in the small hours to have the flocks in the low fields in time. Now his own shepherd was gone on an errand and would not be back till the morrow's breakfast. This meant that he, the wearied, the sorely tried, must be up with the lark and tramping the high pastures. The thought was too much for him. He could not face it. There would be no night's rest for his wearied legs, though the Lord knew how he needed it.

But as he looked through the window a thought grew upon his mind. He was tired and sore, but he might yet manage an hour or two of toil, if a sure prospect of rest lay at the end. The moon was up and bright, and he might gather the sheep to the low meadows as easily as in the morning. This would suffer him to sleep in peace to the hour of seven, which was indulgence indeed to one who habitually rose at five. He was a man of imagination and hope, who valued a prospect. Far better, he held, the present discomfort, if the certainty of ease lay before him. So he gathered his aching members, reached for his stick, whistled on his dogs, and set out.

It was a long climb up the ridges of the Lowe Burn to the stell of fir-trees which marked his boundaries. Then began the gathering of the sheep, and a great scurry of dogs, — black dots on the sleepy, moon-lit hill. With much crying of master and barking of man the flocks were massed and turned athwart the slopes in the direction of the steading. All the while he limped grumblingly behind, thinking on bed, and leaving everything to his shaggy lieutenants. Then they crossed the Lowe Burn, skirted the bog, and came in a little to the lower meadows, while afar off over the rough crest of the Fairy Knowe twinkled the lights of the farm.

Meanwhile from another point of the hill there came another wayfarer to the same goal. The Sentimentalist* was a pictur-esque figure on holiday, enjoying the summer in the way that still remains the best. Three weeks before he had flung the burden of work from his shoulders, and gone with his rod to the Callowa foot, whence he fished far and near even to the utmost recesses of the hills. On this evening the soft airs and the triumphant moon had brought him out of doors. He had a dim memory of a fragrant hazelled knoll above the rocky Gled, which looked up and down three valleys. The place drew him, as it lived in his memory, and he must needs get his plaid and cross the miles of heather to the wished-for sleeping-place. There he would bide the night and see the sunrise, and haply the next morning make a raid into the near village to receive letters delayed for weeks.

He crossed the hill when the full white glory of the moon was already apparent in the valleys. The air was so still and mild that one might have slept there and then on the bare hillside and been no penny the worse. The heart of the Sentimentalist was cheered, and he scanned the prospect with a glad thankfulness. To think that three weeks ago he had been living in sultriness and dreary over-work, with a head as dazed as a spinning-top and a ruin of nerves. Now every faculty was alive and keen, he had no thought of nerves, and his old Norfolk jacket, torn and easy, now stained with peat-water and now bleached with weather, was an index to his immediate past. In a little it would be all over, and then once more the dust and worry and heat. But meantime he was in fairyland, where there was little need for dreary prognostication.

And in truth it was a fairyland which dawned on his sight at the crest of the hill. A valley filled with hazy light, and in the middle darkly banded by the stream. All things, village, knoll, bog, and coppice, bright with a duskiness which revealed nought in detail, but only hints of form and colour. A noise of distant sheep rose from the sleeping place, and the single, solitary note of a night-bird far over the glen. At his foot were crushed thickets of little hill-flowers, thyme and pansies and the odorous bog-myrtle. Beneath him, not half a mile distant, was a mound with two lone birches on its summit, and he knew the place of his quest. This was the far-famed Fairy Knowe, where at midsummer the little folk danced, and where, so ran the tale, lay the mystic entrance, of which True Thomas spake, to the kingdom of dreams and shadows. Twenty-five miles distant a railway ran, but here there were still simplicity and antique tales. So in a fine spirit he set himself to the tangled meadow-land which intervened.

IV

Miss Phyllis looked long and wonderingly at the tangled, moonlit hill. 'Is this the place?' she asked.

The Earl nodded. 'Do you feel devout, madam,' said he, 'and will you make the experiment?'

Miss Phyllis looked at him gravely. 'Have I not scrambled over miles of bog, and do you think that I have risked my ankles for nothing? Besides I was always a devout believer.'

'Then this is the way of it. You wait here and walk slowly up, while I will get to the other side. There is always a wonderful view at least on the top.'

'But I am rather afraid that I . . .'

'Oh, very well,' said the Earl. 'If we don't perform our part, how can we expect a hard-worked goblin to do his?'

'Then,' said Miss Phyllis, with tight lips and a sigh of melodrama, 'lead on, my lord.' And she watched his figure disappear with some misgiving.

For a little she scanned the patched shadow of birk and fern, and listened uneasily to the rustle of grasses. She heard the footsteps cease, and then rise again in the silence. Suddenly it seemed as if the place had come to life. A crackling, the noise of something in lumbering motion, càme from every quarter. Then there would be a sound of scampering, and again the echo of heavy breathing. Now Miss Phyllis was not superstitious, and very little of a coward. Moreover, she was a young woman of the world, with a smattering of most things in heaven and earth, and the airs of an infinite experience. But this moonlit knoll, this wide-stretching, fantastic landscape, and the lucid glamour of the night, cast a spell on her, and for once she forgot everything. Miss Phyllis grew undeniably afraid.

She glanced timorously to the left, whence came the sounds, and then with commendable spirit began to climb the slope. If things were so queer she might reasonably carry out the letter of her injunctions, and in any case the Earl would be there to meet her. But the noise grew stranger, the sound of rustling and scrambling and breathing as if in the chase. Then to her amazement a crackle of twigs rose from her right, and as she hastily turned her head to meet the new alarum, she found herself face to face with a tall man in a plaid.

For one moment both stared in frank discomfiture. Miss Phyllis was horribly alarmed and in deepest mystery. But, she began to reflect, spirits have never yet been known to wear Norfolk jackets and knickerbockers, or take the guise of stalwart, brown-faced men. The Sentimentalist, too, after the natural surprise, recovered himself and held out his hand.

'How do you do, Miss Phyllis?' said he.

The girl gasped, and then a light of recognition came into her eyes.

'What are you doing here, Mr Grey?' she asked.

'Surely I have the first right to the question,' the man said, smiling.

'Then, if you must know, I am looking for the customary spirit to tell the future. I thought you were the thing, and was fearfully scared.'

'But who told you that story, Miss Phyllis? I did not think you would have been so credulous. Your part was always the acute critic's.'

'Then you were wrong,' said the girl, with emphasis. 'Besides, it was Charlie Erskine's doing. He brought me here, and is faithfully keeping his compact at the other side of the hill.'

'Well, well, Callowa had always a queer way of entertaining his guests. But there, Miss Phyllis, I have not seen civilisation for weeks, and am half inclined to believe in things myself. Never again shall you taunt me with "boyish enthusiasm". Was not that your phrase?'

'I have sinned,' said the girl, 'but don't talk of it. Henceforth I belong to the sentimentalists. But you must not spoil my plans. I must get to the top and wait devoutly on the tertium quid. You can wait here or go round the foot and meet us at the other side. You have made me feel sceptical already.'

'I am at your service, my lady, and I hope you will get good news from the fairy-folk when . . .'

But at this juncture something held the speech and eyes of both. A figure came wildly over the brow of the hill, as if running for dear life, and took the slope in great bounds through brake and bramble and heather-tussock. Onward it came with frantic arms and ineffectual cries. Suddenly it caught sight of the two as they stood at the hill-foot, the girl in white which showed dimly beneath her cloak, and the square figure of the man. It drew itself up in a spasm, stood one moment in uncomprehending terror, and then flung itself whimpering at their feet.

V

The full history of the events of these minutes has yet to be written. But such is the rough outline of the process of disaster.

It appears that the farmer of the Lowe Moss was driving his sheep in comfort with the aid of his collies, and had just crossed the meadowland and come to the edge of the Knowe. He was not more than half a mile from home, and he was wearied utterly. There still remained the maze of tree-roots and heaps of stones known as the Broken Dykes, and here it was hard to drive beasts even in the clear moonlight. So as he looked to the far lights of his home his temper began to break, and he vehemently abused his dogs.

Just at the foot of the slope there is a nick in the dyke, and far on either side stretches the hazel tangle. If once sheep get there it is hard for the best of collies to recover them in short time. But the flock was heading right, narrow in front, marshalled by vigilant four-footed watchmen, with the leaders making straight for the narrow pass. Then suddenly something happened beyond human expectation. In front of the drove the figure of a man arose as if from the ground. It was enough for the wild hill-sheep. To right and left they scattered, flanked in their race by the worn-out dogs, and in two minutes were far and wide among the bushes.

For a moment in the extremity of his disgust the farmer's power of thought and speech forsook him. Then he looked at the cause of all the trouble. He knew the figure for that of a wandering dealer with whom he had long fought bitter warfare. Doubtless the man had come there by night to spy out the nakedness of his flock and report accordingly. In any case he had been warned off the land before, and the farmer had many old grudges against him. The memory of all overtook him at the moment and turned his brain. He rubbed his eyes. No, there could be no mistaking that yellow top-coat and that scraggy figure. So with stick upraised he ran for the intruder.

When the Earl saw the sheep fleeing wide and an irate man rushing toward him, his first impulse was to run. What possible cause could lead a man to drive sheep at night among rough meadows? But the next instant all hope of escape was at an end, for the foe was upon him. He had just time to leap aside and escape a great blow from a stick, and then he found himself in a fierce grapple with a thick-set, murderous ruffian.

Meanwhile the shepherd of the Redswirehead and the tailor of Callowa had left the high-road and tramped over the moss to the Knowe-foot. The tailor's wine-begotten bravery was somewhat lessened by the still spaces of country and the silent eye of night. His companion had no thought in the matter save to get home, and if his way lay over the crest of the Fairy Knowe it mattered little to him. But when they left the high-road it became necessary to separate, if the correct fashion of the thing were to be observed. The shepherd must slacken pace and make for the near side of the hill, while the tailor would hasten to the other, and the twain would meet at the top.

The shepherd had no objection to going slowly. He lit his pipe and marched with measured tread over the bracken-covered meadows. The tailor set out gaily for the farther side, but ere he had gone far his spirits sank. Fairy tales and old wives' fables had still a measure of credence with him, and this was the sort of errand on which he had never before embarked. He was flying straight in the face of all his most cherished traditions in company with a godless shepherd who believed in nothing but his own worthiness. He began to grow nervous and wish that he were safe in the Callowa Inn instead of scrambling on a desert hill. Yet the man had a vestige of pluck which kept him from turning back, and a fragment of the sceptical which gave him hope.

At the Broken Dykes he halted and listened. Some noise came floating over the tangle other than the fitful bleat of sheep or the twitter of birds. He listened again, and there it came, a crashing and swaying, and a confused sound as of a man muttering. Every several hair bristled on his unhappy head, till he reflected that it must be merely a bullock astray among the bushes, and with some perturbation hastened on his way. He fought through the clinging hazels, knee-deep in bracken, and stumbling ever and again over a rock of heather. The excitement of the climb for a moment drove out his terrors, and with purple face and short-ened breath he gained the open. And there he was rooted still, for in the middle a desperate fight was being fought by two unearthly combatants.

He had the power left to recognise that both had the sem-blance of men and the dress of mortals. But never for a moment was he deceived. He knew of tales without end which told of unearthly visitants meeting at midnight on the lone hillside to settle their ghostly feuds. And even as he looked the mantle of one blew apart, and a glimpse of something strange and white appeared beneath. This was sufficient for the tailor. With a gasp he turned to the hill and climbed it like a deer, moaning to himself in his terror. Over the crest he went and down the other slope, flying wildly over little craigs, diving headlong every now and again into tussocks of bent, or struggling in a maze of birches. Then, or ever he knew, he was again among horrors. A woman with a fluttering white robe stood before him, and by her a man of strange appearance and uncanny height. He had no time to think, but his vague impression was of sheeted ghosts and awful terrors. His legs failed, his breath gave out at last, and he was floundering helplessly at Miss Phyllis' feet.

Meantime, as the young man and the girl gazed mutely at this new visitant, there entered from the left another intruder, clad in home-spun, with a mighty crook in his hand and a short black pipe between his teeth. He raised his eyes slightly at the vision of the two, but heaven and earth did not contain what might disturb his composure. But at the sight of the prostrate tailor he stopped short, and stared. Slowly the thing dawned upon his brain. The sense of the ludicrous, which dwelled far down in his heart, was stirred to liveliness, and with legs apart he woke the echoes in boisterous mirth.

'God, but it's guid,' and he wiped his eyes on his sleeve. 'That man,' and again the humour of the situation shook him, 'that man thocht to frichten me wi' his ghaists and bogles, and look at him!'

The tailor raised his scared eyes to the newcomer. 'Dinna blaspheme, Jock Rorison,' he moaned with solemn unction. 'I hae seen it, the awfu' thing — twae men fechtin' a ghaistly battle, and yin o' them wi' the licht shinin' through his breist-bane.'

'Hearken to him,' said the shepherd, jocularly. 'The wicked have digged a pit,' he began with dignity, and then farcically ended with 'and tumbled in 't themsel'.'

But Miss Phyllis thought fit to seek a clue to the mystery.

'Please tell me what is the meaning of all this,' she asked her companion.

'Why, the man has seen Callowa, and fled.'

'But he speaks of two and a "ghaistly combat".'

'Then Callowa with his usual luck has met the spirit of the place and fallen out with him. I think we had better go and see.'

But the tailor only shivered at the thought, till the long shepherd forcibly pulled him to his feet, and dragged his reluctant steps up the side of the hill.

The combat at the back of the knowe had gone on merrily enough till the advent of the tailor. Both were men of muscle, well-matched in height and years, and they wrestled with vigour and skill. The farmer was weary at the start, but his weariness was less fatigue than drowsiness, and as he warmed to his work he felt his strength returning. The Earl knew nothing of the game; he had not wrestled in his youth with strong out-of-door labourers, and his only resources were a vigorous frame and uncommon agility. But as the minutes passed and both breathed hard, the younger man began to feel that he was losing ground. He could scarce stand out against the strain on his arms, and his ankles ached with the weight which pressed on them.

Now it fell out that just as the tailor arrived on the scene the farmer made a mighty effort and all but swung his opponent from his feet. In the wrench that followed, the buttons of the Earl's light overcoat gave way, and to the farmer's astonished gaze an expanse of white shirt-front was displayed. For a second he relaxed his hold, while the other freed himself and leaped back to recover breath.

Slowly it dawned upon the farmer's intelligence that this was no cattle-dealer with whom he contended. Cattle-dealers do not habitually wear evening clothes when they have any work of guile on hand. And then gradually the flushed features before him awoke recognition. The next moment he could have sunk beneath the ground with confusion, for in this nightly marauder who had turned his sheep he saw no other than the figure of his master, the laird of all the countryside.

For a little the power of speech was denied him, and he stared blankly and shamefacedly while the Earl recovered his scattered wits. Then he murmured hoarsely, —

'I hope your lordship will forgi'e me. I never thocht it was yoursel', for I wad dae onything rather than lift up my hand against ye. I thocht it was an ill-daein' dealer frae east the country, whae has cheated me often, and I was vexed at his turnin' the sheep, seein' that I've had a lang day's wander.' Then he stopped, for he was a man of few words and he could go no further in apology.

Then the Earl, who had entered into the fight in a haphazard spirit, without troubling to enquire its cause, put the fitting end to the strained relations. He was convulsed with laughter, deep and overpowering. Little by little the farmer's grieved face relaxed, and he joined in the mirth, till these two made the silent place echo with unwonted sounds.

To them thus engaged entered a company of four, Miss Phyllis, the Sentimentalist, the shepherd, and the tailor. Six astonished human beings stood exchanging scrutinies under the soft moon. With the tailor the mood was still terror, with the shepherd careless amazement, and with the other two unquenchable mirth. For the one recognised the irate, and now apologetic, farmer of the Lowe Moss and the straggling sheep which told a tale to the observant; while both saw in the other of the dishevelled and ruddy combatants the once respectable form of a friend.

Then spoke the farmer: —

'What's ta'en a' the folk? This knowe's like a kirk skailin'. And, dod, there's Jock Rorison. Is this your best road to the Redswirehead, Jock?'

But the shepherd and his friend were speechless for they had recognised their laird, and the whole matter was beyond their understanding.

'Now,' said Miss Phyllis, 'here's a merry meeting. I have seen more wonders tonight than I can quite comprehend. First, there comes Mr Grey from nowhere in particular with a plaid on his shoulders; then a man with a scared face tumbles at our feet; then another comes to look for him; and now here you are, and you seem to have been fighting. These hills of yours are worse than any fairyland, and, do you know, they are rather exhausting.'

Meantime the Earl was solemnly mopping his brow and smiling on the assembly. 'By George,' he muttered, and then his breath failed him and he could only chuckle. He looked at the tailor, and the sight of that care-ridden face again choked him with laughter.

'I think we have all come across too many spirits tonight,' he said, 'and they have been of rather substantial flesh and bone. At least so I found it. Have you learned much about the future, Miss Phyllis?'

The girl looked shyly at her side. 'Mr Grey has been trying to teach me,' said she.

The Earl laughed with great good-nature. 'Midsummer madness,' he said. 'The moon has touched us all.' And he glanced respectfully upward, where the White Huntress urged her course over the steeps of heaven.

'Divus' Johnston

This story, which first appeared in a literary journal called The Golden Hynde* *in December 1913, was given to Lord Lamancha on its reprinting in the volume* The Runagates Club *in 1928. This politician, named after a spot eight miles northwest of the Tweeddale town of Peebles, most famously appears in* John Macnab, *three years before, where it is said of him that 'people trusted him because . . . he was believed to have that combination of candour and intelligence which England desires in her public men.' Here, such candour is given a touch of irony by the device of interior narrators: Buchan introduces Lamancha who introduces Thomson who introduces Johnston who is – well, in an unusual position.*

'Divus' Johnston

Lord Lamancha's Story

In deorum numerum relatus est non ore modo decernentium sed et persuasione vulgi.

SUETONIUS*

We were discussing the vagaries of ambition, and decided that most of the old prizes that humanity contended for had had their gilt rubbed off. Kingdoms, for example, which younger sons used to set out to conquer. It was agreed that nowadays there was a great deal of drudgery and very little fun in being a king.

'Besides, it can't be done,' Leithen put in. 'The Sarawak case. Sovereignty over territory can only be acquired by a British subject on behalf of His Majesty.'

There was far more real power, someone argued, in the profession of prophet. Mass-persuasion was never such a force as today. Sandy Arbuthnot, who had known Gandhi and admired him, gave us a picture of that strange popular leader – ascetic, genius, dreamer, child. 'For a little,' he said, 'Gandhi had more absolute sway over a bigger lump of humanity than anybody except Lenin.'

'I once knew Lenin,' said Fulleylove, the traveller, and we all turned to him.

'It must have been more than twenty years ago,' he explained. 'I was working at the British Museum and lived in lodgings in Bloomsbury, and he had a room at the top of the house. Ilyitch was the name we knew him by. He was a little, beetle-browed chap, with a pale face and the most amazing sleepy black eyes, which would suddenly twinkle and blaze as some thought passed through his mind. He was very pleasant and good-humoured, and would spend hours playing with the landlady's children. I remember I once took him down with me for a day into the country, and he was the merriest little grig . . . Did I realise how big he was? No, I cannot say I did. He was the ordinary Marxist, and he wanted to resurrect Russia by hydraulics and electrification. He seemed to be a funny compound of visionary and *terre-à-terre* scientist. But I realised that he could lay a spell on his countrymen. I have been to Russian meetings with him – I talk Russian, you know – and it was astounding the way he could make his audience look at him like hungry sheep. He gave me the impression of utter courage and candour, and a king of demoniac simplicity. . . . No, I never met him again, but oddly enough I was in Moscow during his funeral. Russian geographers were interesting themselves in the line of the old silk-route to Cathay, and I was there by request to advise them. I had not a very comfortable time, but everybody was very civil to me. So I saw Lenin's funeral, and unless you saw that you can have no notion of his power. A great black bier like an altar, and hundreds and thousands of people weeping and worshipping – yes, worshipping.'

'The successful prophet becomes a kind of god,' said Lamancha. 'Have you ever known a god, Sandy? . . . No more have I. But there is one living today somewhere in Scotland. Johnston is his name. I once met a very particular friend of his. I will tell you the story, and you can believe it or not as you like.'

I had this narrative – he said – from my friend Mr Peter Thomson of 'Jessieville', Maxwell Avenue, Strathbungo, whom I believe to be a man incapable of mendacity, or, indeed, of imagination. He is a prosperous and retired ship's captain, dwelling in the suburbs of Glasgow, who plays two rounds of golf every day of the week, and goes twice every Sunday to a pink, new church. You may often see his ample figure, splendidly habited in broadcloth and finished off with one of those square felt hats which are the Scottish emblem of respectability, moving sedately by Mrs Thomson's side down the avenue of

'Balmorals' and 'Bellevues' where dwell the aristocracy of
Strathbungo. It was not there that I met him, however, but in a
Clyde steamboat going round the Mull, where I spent a com-
fortless night on my way to a Highland fishing. It was blowing
what he called 'a wee bit o' wind', and I could not face the
odorous bunks which opened on the dining-room. Seated abaft
the funnel, in an atmosphere of ham-and-eggs, bilge and fresh
western breezes, he revealed his heart to me, and this I found in it.

'About the age of forty' – said Mr Thomson – 'I was captain of
the steamer *Archibald McKelvie*, 1,700 tons burthen, belonging
to Brock, Rattray, and Linklater of Greenock. We were principally engaged in the China trade, but made odd trips into the
Malay Archipelago and once or twice to Australia. She was a
handy bit boat, and I'll not deny that I had many mercies
vouchsafed to me when I was her skipper. I raked in a bit of
salvage now and then, and my trading commission, paid regularly into the British Linen Bank at Maryhill, was mounting up
to a fairsh sum. I had no objection to Eastern parts, for I had a
good constitution and had outgrown the daftnesses of youth.
The berth suited me well, I had a decent lot for ship's company,
and I would gladly have looked forward to spending the rest of
my days by the *Archibald McKelvie*.

'Providence, however, thought otherwise, for He was preparing a judgment against that ship like the kind you read about in
books. We were five days out from Singapore, shaping our
course for the Philippines, where the Americans were then
fighting, when we ran into a queer lown sea. Not a breath of air
came out of the sky; if you kindled a match the flame wouldna
leap, but smouldered like touchwood; and every man's body ran
with sweat like a mill-lade. I kenned fine we were in for the
terrors of hell, but I hadna any kind of notion how terrible hell
could be. First came a wind that whipped away my funnel, like a
potato-peeling. We ran before it, and it was like the swee-gee
we used to play at when we were laddies. One moment the

muckle sea would get up on its hinder end and look at you, and the next you were looking at it as if you were on top of Ben Lomond looking down on Luss. Presently I saw land in a gap of the waters, a land with great blood-red mountains, and, thinks I to myself, if we keep up the pace this boat of mine will not be hindered from ending two or three miles inland in somebody's kail-yard. I was just wondering how we would get the *Archibald McKelvie* back to her native element when she saved me the trouble; for she ran dunt on some kind of a rock, and went straight to the bottom.

'I was the only man saved alive, and if you ask me how it happened I don't know. I felt myself choking in a whirlpool; then I was flung through the air and brought down with a smack into deep waters; then I was in the air again, and this time I landed amongst sand and tree-trunks and got a bash on the head which dozened my senses.

'When I came to it was morning, and the storm had abated. I was lying about half-way up a beach of fine white sand, for the wave that had carried me landwards in its flow had brought me some of the road back in its ebb. All round me was a sort of free-coup – trees knocked to matchwood, dead fish, and birds and beasts, and some boards which I jaloused came from the *Archibald McKelvie*. I had a big bump on my head, but otherwise I was well and clear in my wits, though empty in the stomach and very dowie in the heart. For I knew something about the islands, of which I supposed this to be one. They were either barren wastes, with neither food nor water, or else they were inhabited by the bloodiest cannibals of the archipelago. It looked as if my choice lay between having nothing to eat and being eaten myself.

'I got up, and, after returning thanks to my Maker, went for a walk in the woods. They were full of queer painted birds, and it was an awful job climbing in and out of the fallen trees. By and by I came into an open bit with a burn where I slockened my thirst. It cheered me up, and I was just beginning to think that this was not such a bad island, and looking to see if I could find anything in the nature of coconuts, when I heard a whistle like a steam-siren. It was some sort of signal, for the next I knew I was in the grip of a dozen savages, my arms and feet were lashed together, and I was being carried swiftly through the forest.

'It was a rough journey, and the discomfort of that heathen handling kept me from reflecting upon my desperate position. After nearly three hours we stopped, and I saw that we had come to a city. The streets were not much to look at, and the houses were mud and thatch, but on a hillock in the middle stood a muckle temple not unlike a Chinese pagoda. There was a man blowing a horn, and a lot of folk shouting, but I paid no attention, for I was sore troubled with the cramp in my left leg. They took me into one of the huts and made signs that I was to have it for my lodging. They brought me water to wash, and a very respectable dinner, which included a hen and a vegetable not unlike greens. Then they left me to myself, and I lay down and slept for a round of the clock.

'I was three days in that hut. I had plenty to eat and the folk were very civil, but they wouldna let me outbye and there was no window to look out of. I couldna make up my mind what they wanted with me. I was a prisoner, but they did not behave as if they bore any malice, and I might have thought I was an honoured guest, but for the guards at the door. Time hung heavy on my hands, for I had nothing to read and no light to read by. I said over all the chapters of the Bible and all the Scots songs I could remember, and I tried to make a poem about my adventures, but I stuck at the fifth line, for I couldna find a rhyme to McKelvie.

'On the fourth morning I was awakened by the most deafening din. I saw through the door that the streets were full of folk in holiday clothes, most of them with flowers in their hair and carrying palm branches in their hands. It was like something out of a Bible picture book. After I had my breakfast four lads in long white gowns arrived, and in spite of all my protests they made a bonny spectacle of me. They took off my clothes, me blushing with shame, and rubbed me with a kind of oil that smelt of cinnamon. Then they shaved my chin, and painted on my forehead a mark like a freemason's. Then they put on me a kind of white nightgown with a red sash round the middle, and they wouldna be hindered from clapping on my head a great wreath of hothouse flowers, as if I was a funeral.

'And then like a thunder-clap I realised my horrible position. *I was a funeral*. I was to be offered up as a sacrifice to some heathen god – an awful fate for a Free-kirk elder in the prime of life.

'I was so paralytic with terror that I never tried to resist. Indeed, it would have done me little good, for outside there were, maybe, two hundred savages, armed and drilled like soldiers. I was put into a sort of palanquin, and my bearers started at a trot with me up the hill to the temple, the whole population of the city running alongside, and singing songs about their god. I was sick with fear, and I durstna look up, for I did not know what awesome sight awaited me.

'At last I got my courage back. "Peter," I says to myself, "be a man. Remember your sainted Covenanting forefathers. You have been chosen to testify for your religion, though it's no likely that yon savages will understand what you say." So I shut my jaw and resolved before I died to make a declaration of my religious principles, and to loosen some of the heathens' teeth with my fists.

'We stopped at the temple door and I was led through a court and into a muckle great place like a barn, with bats flying about the ceiling. Here there were nearly three thousand heathens sitting on their hunkers. They sang a hymn when they saw me, and I was just getting ready for action when my bearers carried me into another place, which I took to be the Holy of Holies. It was about half the size of the first, and at the end of it was a great curtain of leopards' skins hanging from roof to floor. My bearers set me in the middle of the room, and then rolled about on their stomachs in adoration before the curtain. After a bit they finished their prayers and crawled out backwards, and I was left alone in that fearsome place.

'It was the worst experience of my life. I believed that behind the skins there was a horrible idol, and that at any moment a priest with a knife would slip in to cut my throat. You may crack about courage, but I tell you that a man who can wait without a quiver on his murderers in the middle of a gloomy kirk is more than human. I am not ashamed to confess that the sweat ran over my brow, and my teeth were knocking in my head.

'But nothing happened. Nothing, except that as I sat there I began to notice a most remarkable smell. At first I thought the place was on fire. Then I thought it was the kind of stink called incense that they make in Popish kirks, for I once wandered into a cathedral in Santiago. But neither guess was right, and then I put my thumb on the proper description. It was nothing but the smell of the third-class carriages on the Coatbridge train on a Saturday night after a football match – the smell of plug tobacco smoked in clay pipes that were no just very clean. My eyes were getting accustomed to the light, and I found the place no that dark; and as I looked round to see what caused the smell; I spied something like smoke coming from beyond the top of the curtain.

'I noticed another thing. There was a hole in the curtain, about six feet from the floor, and at that hole as I watched I saw an eye. My heart stood still, for, thinks I, that'll be the priest of Baal who presently will stick a knife into me. It was long ere I could screw up courage to look again, but I did it. And then I saw that the eye was not that of a savage, which would be black and blood-shot. It was a blue eye, and, as I looked, it winked at me.

'And then a voice spoke out from behind the curtain, and this was what it said. It said, "God-sake, Peter, is that you? And how did ye leave them a' at Maryhill?"

'And from behind the curtain walked a muckle man, dressed in a pink blanket, a great red-headed man, with a clay pipe in his mouth. It was the god of the savages, and who do ye think it was? A man Johnston, who used to bide in the same close as me in Glasgow . . .'

Mr Thomson's emotion overcame him, and he accepted a stiff drink from my flask. Wiping away a tear, which may have been of sentiment or of mirth, he continued:

'You may imagine that I was joyful and surprised to see him, and he, so to speak, fell on my neck like the father of the Prodigal Son. He hadna seen a Scotch face for four years. He raked up one or two high priests and gave instructions, and soon I was comfortably lodged in a part of the temple close to his own rooms. Eh, man, it was a noble sight to see Johnston and the priests. He was a big, red-haired fellow, six feet four, and as strong as a stot, with a voice like a north-easter, and yon natives fair crawled like caterpillars in his presence. I never saw a man with such a natural talent for being a god. You would have thought he had been bred to the job all his days, and yet I minded him keeping a grocer's shop in the Dalmarnock Road.

'That night he told me his story. It seemed that he had got a post at Shanghai in a trading house, and was coming out to it in one of those God-forgotten German tramps that defile the China seas. Like me, he fell in with a hurricane, and, like me, his ship was doomed. He was a powerful swimmer, and managed to keep afloat until he found some drifting wreckage, and after the wind had gone down he paddled ashore. There he was captured by the savages, and taken, like me, to their city. They were going to sacrifice him, but one chief, wiser than the rest, called attention to his size and strength, and pointed out that they were at war with their neighbours, and that a big man would be of more use in the fighting line than on an altar in the temple.

'So off went Johnston to the wars. He was a bonny fighter, and very soon they made him captain of the royal bodyguard, and a fortnight later the general commanding-in-chief over the whole army. He said he had never enjoyed himself so much in his life, and when he got back from his battles the whole population of the city used to meet him with songs and flowers. Then an old priest found an ancient prophecy about a Red God who would come out of the sea and lead the people to victory. Very soon there was a strong party for making Johnston a god, and when, with the help of a few sticks of trade dynamite, he had blown up the capital of the other side and brought back his army in triumph with a prisoner apiece, popular feeling could not be restrained. Johnston was hailed as divine. He hadna much grip of the language, and couldna explain the situation, so he thought it best to submit.

'"Mind you," he said to me, "I've been a good god to these poor blind ignorant folk." He had stopped the worst of their habits and put down human sacrifices, and got a sort of town council appointed to keep the city clean, and he had made the army the most efficient thing ever heard of in the islands. And now he was preparing to leave. This was what they expected, for the prophecy had said that the Red God, after being the saviour of his people, would depart as he had come across the sea. So, under his directions, they had built him a kind of boat with which he hoped to reach Singapore. He had got together a considerable fortune, too, chiefly in rubies, for as a god he had plenty of opportunities of acquiring wealth honestly. He said there was a sort of greengrocer's and butcher's shop before his altar every morning, and he got one of the priests, who had some business notions, to sell off the goods for him.

'There was just one thing that bothered Mr Johnston. He was a good Christian man and had been an elder in a kirk in the Cowcaddens, and he was much in doubt whether he had not committed a mortal sin in accepting the worship of these heathen islanders. Often I argued it out with him, but I did not seem able to comfort him rightly. "Ye see," he used to say to me, "if I have broken anything, it's the spirit and no the letter of the commandment. I havena set up a graven image, for ye canna call me a graven image."

'I mind that I quoted to him the conduct of Naaman, who was allowed to bow in the house of Rimmon, but he would not have it. "No, no," he cried "that has nothing to do with the point. It's no a question of my bowing in the house of Rimmon. I'm auld Rimmon himself."'

'That's a strange story, Mr Thomson,' I said. 'Is it true?'

'True as death. But you havena heard the end of it. We got away, and by-and-by we reached Singapore, and in course of time our native land. Johnston, he was a very rich man now, and I didna go without my portion; so the loss of the *Archibald McKelvie* turned out the best piece of luck in my life. I bought a share in Brock's Line, but nothing would content Johnston but that he must be a gentleman. He got a big estate in Annandale, where all the Johnstons came from long ago, and one way and another he has spent an awful siller on it. Land will swallow up money quicker than the sea.'

'And what about his conscience?' I asked.

'It's keeping quieter,' said Mr Thomson. 'He takes a great interest in Foreign Missions, to which he subscribes largely, and they tell me that he has given the funds to build several new kirks. Oh yes, and he's just been adopted as a prospective Liberal candidate. I had a letter from him no further back than yesterday. It's about his political career, as he calls it. He told me, what didna need telling, that I must never mention a word about his past. "If discretion was necessary before," he says, "it's far more necessary now, for how could the Party of Progress have any confidence in a man if they heard he had once been a god?"'*

Politics and the Mayfly

One of the difficulties in evaluating Buchan is that he often feels so fresh that it is a shock to realise that when an early story like this was written Tennyson had only just died. So the intrusion of a word or attitude from that time can feel as exaggerated, and even possibly as offensive, as it might be in the work of a recent writer. This story, again from Buchan's first year at Oxford, illustrates why Buchan is still read with delight when so many of his contemporaries are totally forgotten. Buchan was a famous fisherman from his boyhood, and here the pull of the water is simply framed, and as in fly-fishing the balance of great forces most delicately poised.

It first appeared in Chambers' Journal *for 9 May 1896, and was reprinted in the Boston, Massachusetts,* Living Age *five weeks later, and then in* Grey Weather. *The Tweeddale village which Buchan was later to fix so firmly as Gledsmuir appears in the earlier version as Marchthorn.*

Politics and the Mayfly

The farmer of Clachlands was a Tory, stern and unbending. It was the tradition of his family, from his grandfather, who had been land-steward to Lord Manorwater, down to his father, who had once seconded a vote of confidence in the sitting member. Such traditions, he felt, were not to be lightly despised; things might change, empires might wax and wane, but his obligation continued; a sort of perverted *noblesse oblige* was the farmer's watchword in life; and by dint of much energy and bad language, he lived up to it.

As fate would have it, the Clachlands ploughman was a Radical of Radicals. He had imbibed his opinions early in life from a speaker on the green of Gledsmuir, and ever since, by the help of a weekly penny paper and an odd volume of Gladstone's speeches, had continued his education. Such opinions in a conservative countryside carry with them a reputation for either abnormal cleverness or abnormal folly. The fact that he was a keen fisher, a famed singer of songs, and the best judge of horses in the place, caused the verdict of his neighbours to incline to the former, and he passed for something of an oracle among his fellows. The blacksmith, who was the critic of the neighbourhood, summed up his character in a few words. 'Him,' said he, in a tone of mingled dislike and admiration, 'him! He would sweer white was black the morn, and dod! he would prove it tae.'

It so happened in the early summer, when the land was green and the trout plashed in the river, that Her Majesty's Government saw fit to appeal to an intelligent country. Among a people whose politics fight hard with their religion for a monopoly of their interests, feeling ran high and brotherly kindness departed. Houses were divided against themselves. Men for-

merly of no consideration found themselves suddenly important, and discovered that their intellects and conscience, which
they had hitherto valued at little, were things of serious interest
to their betters. The lurid light of publicity was shed upon the
lives of the rival candidates; men formerly accounted worthy
and respectable were proved no better than white sepulchres;
and each man was filled with a morbid concern for his fellow's
character and beliefs.

The farmer of Clachlands called a meeting of his labourers in
the great dusty barn, which had been the scene of many similar
gatherings. His speech on the occasion was vigorous and to the
point. 'Ye are a' my men,' he said, 'an' I'll see that ye vote richt.
Y're uneddicated folk, and ken naething aboot the matter, sae
ye just tak' my word for't, that the Tories are in the richt and
vote accordingly. I've been a guid maister to ye, and it's shurely
better to pleesure me, than a wheen leein' scoondrels whae
tramp the country wi' leather bags and printit trash.'

Then arose from the back the ploughman, strong in his
convictions. 'Listen to me, you men,' says he; 'just vote as ye
think best. The maister's a guid maister, as he says, but he's
nocht to dae wi' your votin'. It's what they ca' inteemedation to
interfere wi' onybody in this matter. So mind that, an' vote for
the workin'-man an' his richts.'

Then ensued a war of violent words.

'Is this a meetin' in my barn, or a pennywaddin?'

'Ca 't what ye please. I canna let ye mislead the men.'

'Whae talks about misleadin'? Is 't misleadin' to lead them
richt?'

'The question,' said the ploughman, solemnly, 'is what you
ca' richt.'

'William Laverhope, if ye werena a guid plooman, ye wad
gang post-haste oot o' here the morn.'

'I carena what ye say. I'll stand up for the richts o' thae men.'

'Men!' – this with deep scorn. 'I could mak' better men than
thae wi' a stick oot o' the plantin'.'

'Ay, ye say that noo, an' the morn ye'll be ca'in' ilka yin o' them *Mister*, a' for their votes.'

The farmer left in dignified disgust, vanquished but still dangerous; the ploughman in triumph mingled with despair. For he knew that his fellow-labourers cared not a whit for politics, but would follow to the letter their master's bidding.

The next morning rose clear and fine. There had been a great rain for the past few days, and the burns were coming down broad and surly. The Clachlands Water was chafing by bank and bridge and threatening to enter the hay-field, and every little ditch and sheep-drain was carrying its tribute of peaty water to the greater flood. The farmer of Clachlands, as he looked over the landscape from the doorstep of his dwelling, marked the state of the weather and pondered over it.

He was not in a pleasant frame of mind that morning. He had been crossed by a ploughman, his servant. He liked the man, and so the obvious way of dealing with him – by making things uncomfortable or turning him off – was shut against him. But he burned to get the upper hand of him, and discomfit once for all one who had dared to question his wisdom and good sense. If only he could get him to vote on the other side – but that was out of the question. If only he could keep him from voting – that was possible but unlikely. He might forcibly detain him, in which case he would lay himself open to the penalties of the law, and be nothing the gainer. For the victory which he desired was a moral one, not a triumph of force. He would like to circumvent him by cleverness, to score against him fairly and honourably on his own ground. But the thing was hard, and, as it seemed to him at the moment, impossible.

Suddenly, as he looked over the morning landscape, a thought struck him and made him slap his legs and chuckle hugely. He walked quickly up and down the gravelled walk. 'Losh, it's guid. I'll dae't. I'll dae't, if the weather juist hauds.'

His unseemly mirth was checked by the approach of someone who found the farmer engaged in the minute examination of gooseberry leaves. 'I'm concerned aboot thae busses,' he was saying; 'they've been ill lookit to, an' we'll no hae half a crop.' And he went off, still smiling, and spent a restless forenoon in the Gledsmuir market.

In the evening he met the ploughman, as he returned from the turnip-singling, with his hoe on his shoulder. The two men looked at one another with the air of those who know that all is not well between them. Then the farmer spoke with much humility.

'I maybe spoke rayther severe yestreen,' he said. 'I hope I didna hurt your feelings.'

'Na, na! No me!' said the ploughman, airily.

'Because I've been thinking ower the matter, an' I admit that a man has a richt to his ain thochts. A'body should hae principles an' stick to them,' said the farmer, with the manner of one making a recondite quotation.

'Ay,' he went on, 'I respect ye, William, for your consistency. Ye're an example to us a'.'

The other shuffled and looked unhappy. He and his master were on the best of terms, but these unnecessary compliments were not usual in their intercourse. He began to suspect, and the farmer, who saw his mistake, hastened to change the subject.

'Graund weather for the fishin',' said he.

'Oh, is it no?' said the other, roused to excited interest by this home topic. 'I tell ye by the morn they'll be takin' as they've never ta'en this 'ear. Doon in the big pool in the Clachlands Water, at the turn o' the turnip-field, there are twae or three pounders, and aiblins yin o' twae pund. I saw them mysel' when the water was low. It's ower big the noo, but when it gangs doon the morn, and gets the colour o' porter, I'se warrant I could whup them oot o' there wi' the flee.'

'D' ye say sae?' said the farmer, sweetly. 'Weel, it's a lang time since I tried the fishin', but I yince was keen on 't. Come in bye, William; I've something ye micht like to see.'

From a corner he produced a rod, and handed it to the other.

It was a very fine rod indeed, one which the owner had gained in a fishing competition many years before, and treasured accordingly. The ploughman examined it long and critically. Then he gave his verdict. 'It's the brawest rod I ever saw, wi' a fine hickory butt, an' guid greenhert tap and middle. It wad cast the sma'est flee, and haud the biggest troot.'

'Weel,' said the farmer, genially smiling, 'ye have a half-holiday the morn when ye gang to the poll. There'll be plenty o' time in the evening to try a cast wi' 't. I'll lend it ye for the day.'

The man's face brightened. 'I wad tak' it verra kindly,' he said, 'if ye wad. My ain yin is no muckle worth, and, as ye say, I'll hae time for a cast the morn's nicht.'

'Dinna mention it. Did I ever let ye see my flee-book? Here it is,' and he produced a thick flannel book from a drawer. 'There's a maist miscellaneous collection, for a' waters an' a' weathers. I got a heap o' them frae auld Lord Manorwater, when I was a laddie, and used to cairry his basket.'

But the ploughman heeded him not, being deep in the examination of its mysteries. Very gingerly he handled the tiny spiders and hackles, surveying them with the eye of a connoisseur.

'If there's anything there ye think at a' like the water, I'll be verra pleased if ye'll try 't.'

The other was somewhat put out by this extreme friendliness. At another time he would have refused shamefacedly, but now the love of sport was too strong in him. 'Ye're far ower guid,' he said; 'thae twae paitrick wings are the verra things I want, an' I dinna think I've ony at hame. I'm awfu' gratefu' to ye, an' I'll bring them back the morn's nicht.'

'Guid-e'en,' said the farmer, as he opened the door, 'an' I wish ye may hae a guid catch.' And he turned in again, smiling sardonically.

The next morning was like the last, save that a little wind had risen, which blew freshly from the west. White cloudlets drifted across the blue, and the air was as clear as spring-water.

Down in the hollow the roaring torrent had sunk to a full, lipping stream, and the colour had changed from a turbid yellow to a clear, delicate brown. In the town of Gledsmuir, it was a day of wild excitement, and the quiet Clachlands road bustled with horses and men. The labourers in the fields scarce stopped to look at the passers, for in the afternoon they too would have their chance, when they might journey to the town in all importance, and record their opinions of the late Government.

The ploughman of Clachlands spent a troubled forenoon. His nightly dreams had been of landing great fish, and now his waking thoughts were of the same. Politics for the time were forgotten. This was the day which he had looked forward to for so long, when he was to have been busied in deciding doubtful voters, and breathing activity into the ranks of his cause. And lo! the day had come and found his thoughts elsewhere. For all such things are, at the best, of fleeting interest, and do not stir men otherwise than sentimentally; but the old kindly love of field-sports, the joy in the smell of the earth and the living air, lie very close to a man's heart. So this apostate, as he cleaned his turnip rows, was filled with the excitement of the sport, and had no thoughts above the memory of past exploits and the anticipation of greater to come.

Mid-day came, and with it his release. He roughly calculated that he could go to the town, vote, and be back in two hours, and so have the evening clear for his fishing. There had never been such a day for the trout in his memory, so cool and breezy and soft, nor had he ever seen so glorious a water. 'If ye dinna get a fou basket the nicht, an' a feed the morn, William Laverhope, your richt hand has forgot its cunning,' said he to himself.

He took the rod carefully out, put it together, and made trial casts on the green. He tied the flies on a cast and put it ready for use in his own primitive fly-book, and then bestowed the whole in the breast-pocket of his coat. He had arrayed himself in his best, with a white rose in his button-hole, for it behoved a man to be well dressed on such an occasion as voting. But yet he did not start. Some fascination in the rod made him linger and try it again and again.

Then he resolutely laid it down and made to go. But something caught his eye — the swirl of the stream as it left the great pool at the hay-field, or the glimpse of still, gleaming water. The impulse was too strong to be resisted. There was time enough and to spare. The pool was on his way to the town, he would try one cast ere he started, just to see if the water was good. So, with rod on his shoulder, he set off.

Somewhere in the background a man, who had been watching his movements, turned away, laughing silently, and filling his pipe.

A great trout rose to the fly in the hay-field pool, and ran the line up-stream till he broke it. The ploughman swore deeply, and stamped on the ground with irritation. His blood was up, and he prepared for battle. Carefully, skillfully he fished, with every nerve on tension and ever-watchful eyes. Meanwhile, miles off in the town the bustle went on, but the eager fisherman by the river heeded it not.

Late in the evening, just at the darkening, a figure arrayed in Sunday clothes, but all wet and mud-stained, came up the road to the farm. Over his shoulder he carried a rod, and in one hand a long string of noble trout. But the expression on his face was not triumphant; a settled melancholy overspread his countenance, and he groaned as he walked.

Mephistopheles stood by the garden-gate, smoking and surveying his fields. A well-satisfied smile hovered about his mouth, and his air was the air of one well at ease with the world.

'Weel, I see ye've had guid sport,' said he to the melancholy Faust. 'By-the-bye, I didna notice ye in the toun. And losh! man, what in the warld have ye dune to your guid claes?'

The other made no answer. Slowly he took the rod to pieces and strapped it up; he took the fly-book from his pocket; he selected two fish from the heap; and laid the whole before the farmer.

'There ye are,' said he, 'and I'm verra much obleeged to ye for your kindness.' But his tone was of desperation and not of gratitude; and his face, as he went onward, was a study in eloquence repressed.

The Wife of Flanders

In The Path of the King, *Buchan tells in fourteen quite disparate episodes a narrative that begins with a small, very lonely Viking boy and ends with the death of Abraham Lincoln, 'the last of the kings'. The link, beautifully worked out, is the unseen transmission of royal blood.*

This book, the first fruits of Buchan's new and deeply happy life at Elsfield after the War, is widely and justly admired: G. M. Trevelyan praised it strongly. It was first serialised in Outward Bound* *in 1920 and 1921, and published in book form in 1921: like most of Buchan's books it ran rapidly through many editions, including translations, in this case into Czech. Susan Buchan prepared a dramatised version of this story for a French's Acting Edition in 1936*

Throughout the book, the outward sign of the kingly strain is a gold ring: the inner, a special independence, shown for example as a quite unexpected heroic act, or as a sudden twist of fate, but generally worked obliquely by the narrator — the episodes demonstrate effectively fourteen methods of narrative obliquity. This is the third.

The Wife of Flanders

From the bed set high on a dais came eerie spasms of laughter, a harsh cackle like fowls at feeding time.

'Is that the last of them, Anton?' said a voice.

A little serving-man with an apple-hued face bowed in reply. He bowed with difficulty, for in his arms he held a huge grey cat, which still mewed with the excitement of the chase. Rats had been turned loose on the floor, and it had accounted for them to the accompaniment of a shrill urging from the bed. Now the sport was over, and the domestics who had crowded round the door to see it had slipped away, leaving only Anton and the cat.

'Give Tib a full meal of offal,' came the order, 'and away with yourself. Your rats are a weak breed. Get me the stout grey monsters like Tuesday se'ennight.'

The room was empty now save for two figures both wearing the habit of the religious. Near the bed sat a man in the full black robe and hood of the monks of Cluny. He warmed plump hands at the brazier and seemed at ease and at home. By the door stood a different figure in the shabby clothes of a parish priest, a curate from the kirk of St Martin's who had been a scandalised spectator of the rat hunt. He shuffled his feet as if uncertain of his next step — a thin, pale man with a pinched mouth and timid earnest eyes.

The glance from the bed fell on him. 'What will the fellow be at?' said the voice testily. 'He stands there like a sow about to litter, and stares and grunts. Good e'en to you, friend. When you are wanted you will be sent for. Jesu's name, what have I done to have that howlet glowering at me?'

The priest at the words crossed himself and turned to go, with a tinge of red in his sallow cheeks. He was faithful to his duties and had come to console a deathbed, though he was well aware that his consolations would be spurned.

As he left there came again the eerie laughter from the bed. 'Ugh, I am weary of that incomparable holiness. He hovers about to give me the St John's Cup, and would fain speed my passing. But I do not die yet, good father. There's life still in the old wolf.'

The monk in a bland voice spoke some Latin to the effect that mortal times and seasons were ordained of God. The other stretched out a skinny hand from the fur coverings and rang a silver bell. When Anton appeared she gave the order 'Bring supper for the reverend father', at which the Cluniac's face mellowed into complacence.

It was a Friday evening in a hard February. Out-of-doors the snow lay deep in the streets of Bruges, and every canal was frozen solid so that carts rumbled along them as on a street. A wind had risen which drifted the powdery snow and blew icy draughts through every chink. The small-paned windows of the great upper-room were filled with oiled vellum, but they did not keep out the weather, and currents of cold air passed through them to the doorway, making the smoke of the four charcoal braziers eddy and swirl. The place was warm, yet shot with bitter gusts, and the smell of burning herbs gave it the heaviness of a chapel at high mass. Hanging silver lamps, which blazed blue and smoky, lit it in patches, sufficient to show the cleanness of the rush-strewn floor, the glory of the hangings of cloth-of-gold and damask, and the burnished sheen of the metal-work. There was no costlier chamber in that rich city.

It was a strange staging for death, for the woman on the high bed was dying. Slowly fighting every inch of the way with a grim tenacity, but indubitably dying. Her vital ardour had sunk below the mark from which it could rise again, and was now ebbing as water runs from a little crack in a pitcher. The best leeches in all Flanders and Artois had come to doctor her. They had prescribed the horrid potions of the age: tinctures of earth-worms; confections of spiders and wood-lice and viper's flesh; broth of human skulls, oil, wine, ants' eggs, and crabs' claws; the *bufo preparatus*, which was a live toad roasted in a pot and ground to a powder; and innumerable plaisters and electuaries. She had begun by submitting meekly, for she longed to live, and had ended, for she was a shrewd woman, by throwing the stuff at the apothecaries' heads. Now she ordained her own diet, which was of lamb's flesh lightly boiled, and woman's milk, got from a wench in the purlieus of St Sauveur. The one medicine which she retained was powdered elk's horn, which had been taken from the beast between two festivals of the Virgin. This she had from the foresters in the Houthulst woods, and swallowed it in white wine an hour after every dawn.

The bed was a noble thing of ebony, brought by the Rhine road from Venice, and carved with fantastic hunting scenes by Hainault craftsmen. Its hangings were stiff brocaded silver, and above the pillows a great unicorn's horn, to protect against poisoning, stood out like the beak of a ship. The horn cast an odd shadow athwart the bed, so that a big claw seemed to lie on the coverlet curving towards the throat of her who lay there. The parish priest had noticed this at his first coming that evening, and had muttered fearful prayers.

The face on the pillows was hard to discern in the gloom, but when Anton laid the table for the Cluniac's meal and set a lamp on it, he lit up the cavernous interior of the bed, so that it became the main thing in the chamber. It was the face of a woman who still retained the lines and the colouring of youth. The voice had harshened with age, and the hair was white as wool, but the cheeks were still rosy and the grey eyes still had fire. Notable beauty had once been there. The finely arched brows, the oval of the face which the years had scarcely sharpened, the proud, delicate nose, all spoke of it. It was as if their possessor recognised those things and would not part with them, for her attire had none of the dishevelment of a sick-room. Her coif of fine silk was neatly adjusted, and the great

robe of marten's fur which cloaked her shoulders was fastened
with a jewel of rubies which glowed in the lamplight like a star.

Something chattered beside her. It was a little brown monkey
which had made a nest in the warm bedclothes.

She watched with sharp eyes the setting of the table. It was a
Friday's meal and the guest was a monk, so it followed a fashion,
but in that house of wealth, which had links with the ends of the
earth, the monotony was cunningly varied. There were oysters
from the Boulogne coast, and lampreys from the Loire, and
pickled salmon from England. There was a dish of liver dressed
with rice and herbs in the manner of the Turk, for liver, though
contained in flesh, was not reckoned as flesh by liberal church-
men. There was a roast goose from the shore marshes, that
barnacle bird which pious epicures classed as shell-fish and
thought fit for fast days. A silver basket held a store of thin
toasted rye-cakes, and by the monk's hand stood a flagon of that
drink most dear to holy palates, the rich syrupy hippocras.

The woman looked on the table with approval, for her house
had always prided itself upon its good fare. The Cluniac's
urbane composure was stirred to enthusiasm. He said a *Confiteor
tibi Domine*, rolling the words on his tongue as if in anticipation
of the solider mouthfuls awaiting him. The keen weather had
whetted his appetite and he thanked God that his northern
peregrinations had brought him to a house where the Church
was thus honoured. He had liked the cavalier treatment of the
lean parish priest, a sour dog who brought his calling into
disfavour with the rich and godly. He tucked back his sleeves,
adjusted the linen napkin comfortably about his neck, and fell
to with a will. He raised his first glass of hippocras and gave
thanks to his hostess. A true mother in Israel!

She was looking at him with favour. He was the breed of
monk that she liked, suave, well-mannered, observant of men
and cities. Already he had told her entertaining matter about
the French King's court, and the new Burgrave of Ghent, and
the escapades of Count Baldwin. He had lived much among

gentlefolk and kept his ears open . . . She felt stronger and cheerfuller than she had been for days. That rat-hunt had warmed her blood. She was a long way from death in spite of the cackle of idiot chirurgeons, and there was much savour still in the world. There was her son, too, the young Philip . . . Her eye saw clearer, and she noted the sombre magnificence of the great room, the glory of the brocade, the gleam of silver. Was she not the richest woman in all Bruges, aye and in all Hainault and Guelderland? And the credit was her own. After the fashion of age in such moods her mind flew backward, and she saw very plain a narrow street in a wind-swept town looking out on a bleak sea. She had been cold, then, and hungry, and deathly poor. Well, she had travelled some way from that hovel. She watched the thick carved stems of the candlesticks and felt a spacious ease and power.

The Cluniac was speaking. He had supped so well that he was in love with the world.

'Your house and board, my lady, are queen-like. I have seen worse in palaces.'

Her laugh was only half pleased. 'Too fine, you would add, for a burgher wife. Maybe, but rank is but as man makes it. The Kings of England are sprung of a tanner. Hark you, father! I made a vow to God when I was a maid, and I have fulfilled my side of the bargain. I am come of a nobler race than any Markgrave, aye, than the Emperor himself, and I swore to set the seed of my body, which the Lord might grant me, again among the great ones. Have I not done it? Is not Philip, my son, affianced to that pale girl of Avesnes, and with more acres of pleasant land to his name than any knightlet in Artois?'

The Cluniac bowed a courtly head. 'It is a great alliance – but not above the dignity of your house.'

'House you call it, and I have had the making of it. What was Willebald but a plain merchant-man, one of many scores at the Friday Market? Willebald was clay that I moulded and gilded till God put him to bed under a noble lid in the New Kirk. A worthy man, but loutish and slow like one of his own hookers. Yet when I saw him on the plainstones by the English harbour I knew that he was a weapon made for my hand.'

Her voice had become even and gentle as of one who remembers far-away things. The Cluniac, having dipped his hands in a silver basin, was drying them in the brazier's heat. Presently he set to picking his teeth daintily with a quill, and fell into the listener's pose. From long experience he knew the atmosphere which heralds confidences, and was willing to humour the provider of such royal fare.

'You have never journeyed to King's Lynn?' said the voice from the bed. 'There is little to see there but mudbars and fens and a noisy sea. There I dwelt when I was fifteen years of age, a maid hungry in soul and body. I knew I was of the seed of Forester John and through him the child of a motley of ancient kings, but war and famine had stripped our house to the bone. And now I, the last of the stock, dwelt with a miserly mother's uncle who did shipwright's work for the foreign captains. The mirror told me that I was fair to look on, though ill-nourished, and my soul assured me that I had no fear. Therefore I had hope, but I ate my heart out waiting on fortune.'

She was looking at the monk with unseeing eyes, her head half turned towards him.

'Then came Willebald one March morning. I saw him walk up the jetty in a new red cloak, a personable man with a broad beard and a jolly laugh. I knew him by repute as the luckiest of the Flemish venturers. In him I saw my fortune. That night he supped at my uncle's house and a week later he sought me in marriage. My uncle would have bargained, but I had become a grown woman and silenced him. With Willebald I did not chaffer, for I read his heart and knew that in a little he would be wax to me. So we were wed, and I took to him no dowry but a ring which came to me from my forebears, and a brain that gold does not buy.'

The monkey by her side broke into a chattering. 'Peace,

Peterkin,' she said. 'You mind me of the babbling of the merchant-folk, when I spurred Willebald into new roads. He had done as his father before him, and bought wool and salted fish from the English, paying with the stuffs of our Flemish looms. A good trade of small and sure profits, but I sought bigger quarries. For, mark you, there was much in England that had a value in this country of ours which no Englishman guessed.'

'Of what nature?' the monk asked with curiosity in his voice.

'Roman things. Once in that land of bogs and forests there were bustling Roman towns and rich Roman houses, which disappeared as every tide brought in new robbers from the sea. Yes, but not all. Much of the preciousness was hidden and the place of its hiding forgotten. Bit by bit the churls found the treasure-trove, but they did not tell their lords. They melted down jewels and sold them piecemeal to Jews for Jews' prices, and what they did not recognise as precious they wantonly destroyed. I have seen the marble heads of heathen gods broken with the hammer to make mortar of, and great cups of onyx and alabaster used as water troughs for a thrall's mongrels . . . Knowing the land, I sent pedlars north and west to collect such stuff, and what I bought for pence I sold for much gold in the Germanies and throughout the French cities. Thus Willebald amassed wealth, till it was no longer worth his while to travel the seas. We lived snug in Flanders, and our servants throughout the broad earth were busy getting us gear.'

The Cluniac was all interest. The making of money lay very near the heart of his Order. 'I have heard wondrous tales of your enterprise,' he told her. 'I would fain know the truth.'

'Packman's tricks,' she laughed. 'Nevertheless it is a good story. For I turned my eyes to the East, whence come those things that make the pride of life. The merchants of Venice were princes, and it was in my head to make those of Bruges no worse. What did it profit that the wind turned daily the sails of our three hundred mills if we limited ourselves to common

burgher wares and the narrow northern markets? We sent
emissaries up the Rhine and beyond the Alps to the Venice
princes, and brought hither the spices and confections of Egypt
and the fruits and wines of Greece, and the woven stuffs of Asia
till the marts of Flanders had the savour of Araby. Presently in
our booths could be seen silks of Italy, and choice metals from
Innsbruck, and furs from Muscovy, and strange birds and beasts
from Prester John's country, and at our fairs such a concourse of
outlandish traders as put Venice to shame. 'Twas a long fight
and a bitter for Willebald and me, since, mark you, we had to
make a new road over icy mountains, with a horde of freebooters
hanging on the skirts of our merchant trains and every little
burg on the way jealous to hamper us. Yet if the heart be
resolute, barriers will fall. Many times we were on the edge of
beggary, and grievous were our losses, but in the end we
triumphed. There came a day when we had so many bands of the
Free Companions in our pay that the progress of our merchan-
dise was like that of a great army, and from rivals we made the
roadside burgs our allies, sharing modestly in our ventures.
Also there were other ways. A pilgrim travels unsuspect, for
who dare rob a holy man? and he is free from burgal dues; but
if the goods be small and very precious, pilgrims may carry
them.'

The monk, as in duty bound, shook a disapproving head.

'Sin, doubtless,' said the woman, 'but I have made ample
atonement. Did I not buy with a bushel of gold a leg of the
blessed St George for the New Kirk, and give to St Martin's a
diamond as big as a thumb nail and so bright that on a dark day
it is a candle to the shrine? Did not I give to our Lady at Aix
a crown of ostrich feathers the marrow of which is not in
Christendom?'

'A mother in Israel, in truth,' murmured the cleric.

'Yea, in Israel,' said the old wife with a chuckle. 'Israel was
the kernel of our perplexities. The good Flemings saw no farther
than their noses, and laughed at Willebald when he began his

ventures. When success came, it was easy to win them over, and by admitting them to a share in our profits get them to fling their caps in the air and huzza for their benefactors. But the Jews were a tougher stock. Mark you, father, when God blinded their eyes to the coming of the Lord Christ, He opened them very wide to all lower matters. Their imagination is quick to kindle, and they are as bold in merchant-craft as Charlemagne in war. They saw what I was after before I had been a month at it, and were quick to profit by my foresight. There are but two ways to deal with Israelites — root them from the face of the earth or make them partners with you. Willebald would have fought them; I, more wise, bought them at a price. For two score years they have wrought faithfully for me. You say well, a mother in Israel!'

'I could wish that a Christian lady had no dealings with the accursed race,' said the Cluniac.

'You could wish folly', was the tart answer. 'I am not as your burgher folk, and on my own affairs I take no man's guiding, be he monk or merchant. Willebald is long dead; may he sleep in peace. He was no mate for me, but for what he gave me I repaid him in the coin he loved best. He was a proud man when he walked through the Friday Market with every cap doffed. He was ever the burgher, like the child I bore him.'

'I had thought the marriage more fruitful. They spoke of two children, a daughter and a son.'

The woman turned round in her bed so that she faced him. The monkey whimpered and she cuffed its ears. Her face was sharp and exultant, and for a sick person her eyes were oddly bright.

'The girl was Willebald's. A poor slip of vulgar stock with the spirit of a house cat. I would have married her well, for she was handsome after a fashion, but she thwarted me and chose to wed a lout of a huckster in the Bredestreet. She shall have her portion from Willebald's gold, but none from me. But Philip is true child of mine, and sprung on both sides of high race. Nay, I name no names, and before men he is of my husband's getting. But to you at the end of my days I speak the truth. That son of wrath has rare blood in him. Philip . . .'

The old face had grown kind. She was looking through the monk to some happy country of vision. Her thoughts were retracing the roads of time, and after the war of age she spoke them aloud. Imperiously she had forgotten her company.

'So long ago,' came the tender voice. 'It is years since they told me he was dead among the heathen, fighting by the Lord Baldwin's side. But I can see him as if it were yesterday, when he rode into these streets in spring with April blooms at his saddle-bow. They called him Phoebus in jest, for his face was like the sun . . . Willebald, good dull man, was never jealous, and was glad that his wife should be seen in brave company. Ah, the afternoons at the baths when we sported like sea-nymphs and sang merry ballads! And the proud days of Carnival where men and women consorted freely and without guile like the blessed in Paradise! Such a tide for lovers! . . . Did I not lead the dance with him at the Burgrave's festival, the twain of us braver than morning? Sat I not with him in the garden of St Vaast, his head in my lap, while he sang me virelays of the south? What was Willebald to me or his lean grey wife to him? He made me his queen, me the burgher wife, at the jousting at Courtrai, when the horses squealed like pigs in the mellay and I wept in fear for him. Ah, the lost sweet days! Philip, my darling, you make a grave gentleman, but you will not equal him who loved your mother.'

The Cluniac was a man of the world whom no confidences could scandalise. But he had business of his own to speak of that night, and he thought it wise to break into this mood of reminiscence.

'The young lord, Philip, your son, madam? You have great plans for him? What does he at the moment?'

The softness went out of the voice and the woman's gaze came back to the chamber. 'That I know not. Travelling the ways of

the world and plucking roadside fruits, for he is no home-bred
and womanish stripling. Wearing his lusty youth on the maids,
I fear. Nay, I forget. He is about to wed the girl of Avesnes and
is already choosing his bridal train. It seems he loves her. He
writes me she has a skin of snow and eyes of vair. I have not seen
here. A green girl, doubtless with a white face and cat's eyes.
But she is of Avesnes, and that blood comes pure from Clovis,
and there is none prouder in Hainault. He will husband her
well, but she will be a clever woman if she tethers to her side a
man of my bearing. He will be for the high road and the
battle-front.'

'A puissant and peaceable knight, I have heard tell,' said the
Cluniac.

'Puissant beyond doubt, and peaceable — when his will is
served. He will play boldly for great things and will win them.
Ah, monk! What knows a childless religious of a mother's
certainty? 'Twas not for nothing that I found Willebald and
changed the cobbles of King's Lynn for this fat country. It is
gold that brings power, and the stiffest royal neck must bend to
him who has the deep coffers. It is gold and his high hand that
will set my Philip by the side of kings. Lord Jesus, what a
fortune I have made for him! There is coined money at the
goldsmiths' and in my cellars, and the ships at the ports, and a
hundred busy looms, and lands in Hainault and Artois, and fair
houses in Bruges and Ghent. Boats on the Rhine and many
pack-trains between Antwerp and Venice are his, and a wealth
of preciousness lies in his name with the Italian merchants.
Likewise there is this dwelling of mine, with plenishing which
few kings could buy. My sands sink in the glass, but as I lie
a-bed I hear the bustle of wains and horses in the streets, and the
talk of shipfolk, and the clatter of my serving men beneath, and
I know that daily, hourly, more riches flow hither to furnish my
son's kingdom.'

The monk's eyes sparkled at this vision of wealth, and he
remembered his errand.

'A most noble heritage. But if the Sire God in His inscrutable providence should call your son to His holy side, what provision have you made for so mighty a fortune? Does your daughter then share?'

The face on the pillows became suddenly wicked and very old. The eyes were lit with hate.

'Not a bezant of which I have the bequeathing. She has something from Willebald, and her dull husband makes a livelihood. 'Twill suffice for the female brats, of whom she has brought three into the world to cumber it . . . By the Gospels, she will lie on the bed she has made. I did not scheme and toil to make gold for such leaden souls.'

'But if your most worthy son should die ere he has begot children, have you made no disposition?' The monk's voice was pointed with anxiety, for was not certainty on this point the object of his journey? The woman perceived it and laughed maliciously.

'I have made dispositions. Such a chapel will be builded in the New Kirk as Rome cannot equal. Likewise there will be benefactions for the poor and a great endowment for the monks at St Sauveur. If my seed is not to continue on earth I will make favour in Paradise.'

'And we of Cluny, madam?' The voice trembled in spite of its training.

'Nay, I have not forgotten Cluny. Its Abbot shall have the gold flagons from Jerusalem and some wherewithal in money. But what is this talk? Philip will not die, and like his mother he loves Holy Church and will befriend her in all her works . . . Listen, father, it is long past the hour when men cease from labour, and yet my provident folk are busy. Hark to the bustle below. That will be the convoy from the Vermandois. Jesu, what a night!'

Flurries of snow beat on the windows, and draughts stirred the hot ashes in the braziers and sent the smoke from them in odd spirals about the chamber. It had become perishing cold, and the monkey among the bedclothes whimpered and snuggled closer into his nest. There seemed to be a great stir about the house-door. Loud voices were heard in gusts, and a sound like a woman's cry. The head on the pillow was raised to listen.

'A murrain on those folk. There has been bungling among the pack-riders. That new man Derek is an oaf of oafs.'

She rang her silver bell sharply and waited on the ready footsteps. But none came. There was silence now below, an ominous silence.

'God's curse upon this household,' the woman cried. The monkey whimpered again, and she took it by the scruff and tossed it to the floor. 'Peace, ape, or I will have you strangled. Bestir yourself, father, and call Anton. There is a blight of deafness in this place.'

The room had suddenly lost its comfort and become cold and desolate. The lamps were burning low and the coloured hangings were in deep shadow. The storm was knocking fiercely at the lattice.

The monk rose with a shiver to do her bidding, but he was forestalled. Steps sounded on the stairs and the steward entered. The woman in the bed had opened her mouth to upbraid, when something in his dim figure struck her silent.

The old man stumbled forward and fell on his knees beside her.

'Madam, dear madam,' he stammered, 'ill news has come to this house . . . There is a post in from Avesnes . . . The young master . . .'

'Philip,' and the woman's voice rose to a scream. 'What of my son?'

'The Lord has taken away what He gave. He is dead, slain in a scuffle with highway robbers . . . Oh, the noble young lord! The fair young knight! Woe upon this stricken house!'

The woman lay very still, while the old man on his knees drifted into broken prayers. Then he observed her silence, scrambled to his feet in a panic, and lit two candles from the nearest brazier. She lay back on the pillows in a deathly faintness, her face drained of blood. Only her tortured eyes showed that life was still in her.

Her voice came at last, no louder than a whisper. It was soft now, but more terrible than the old harshness.

'I follow Philip,' it said. '*Sic transit gloria* . . . Call me Arnulf the goldsmith and Robert the scrivener . . . Quick, man, quick. I have much to do ere I die.'

As the steward hurried out, the Cluniac, remembering his office, sought to offer comfort, but in his bland worldling's voice the consolations sounded hollow. She lay motionless, while he quoted the Scriptures. Encouraged by her docility, he spoke of the certain reward promised by Heaven to the rich who remembered the Church at their death. He touched upon the high duties of his Order and the handicap of its poverty. He bade her remember her debt to the Abbot of Cluny.

She seemed about to speak and he bent eagerly to catch her words.

'Peace, you babbler,' she said. 'I am done with your God. When I meet him I will outface Him. He has broken His compact and betrayed me. My riches go to the Burgrave for the comfort of this city where they were won. Let your broken rush of a Church wither and rot!'

Scared out of all composure by this blasphemy, the Cluniac fell to crossing himself and mumbling invocations. The diplomat had vanished and only the frightened monk remained. He would fain have left the room had he dared, but the spell of her masterful spirit held him. After that she spoke nothing . . .

Again there was a noise on the stairs and she moved a little, as if mustering her failing strength for the ultimate business. But it was not Arnulf the goldsmith. It was Anton, and he shook like a man on his way to the gallows.

'Madam, dear madam,' he stammered, again on his knees.

'There is another message. One has come from the Bredestreet with word of your lady daughter. An hour ago she has borne a child . . . A lusty son, madam.'

The reply from the bed was laughter.

It began low and hoarse like a fit of coughing, and rose to the high cackling mirth of extreme age. At the sound both Anton and the monk took to praying. Presently it stopped, and her voice came full and strong as it had been of old.

'*Mea culpa*,' it said, '*mea maxima culpa*. I judged the Sire God over hastily. He is merry and has wrought a jest on me. He has kept His celestial promise in His own fashion. He takes my brave Philip and gives me instead a suckling . . . So be it. The infant has my blood, and the race of Forester John will not die. Arnulf will have an easy task. He need but set the name of this newborn in Philip's place. What manner of child is he, Anton? Lusty, you say, and well-formed? I would my arms could have held him . . . But I must be about my business of dying. I will take the news to Philip.'

Hope had risen again in the Cluniac's breast. It seemed that here was a penitent. He approached the bed with a raised crucifix, and stumbled over the whimpering monkey. The woman's eyes saw him and a last flicker woke in them.

'Begone, man,' she cried. 'I have done with the world. Anton, rid me of both these apes. And fetch the priest of St Martin's, for I would confess and be shriven. Yon curate is no doubt a fool, but he serves my jesting God.'

The Frying-pan and the Fire

Buchan has been accused of 'snobbery with violence', a shot that misses with both barrels. Rarely given to physical aggression, even in his 'shockers' (acquaintance with his contemporary thriller-writers illuminates this vividly), he is similarly not given to snobbery, though he enjoys including the upper crust among his characters.

That this, the Duke of Burminster's story from The Runagates Club, is rich with ironies as well as exuberance is shown by the epigraph, a mock-solemn quotation about 'degenerate patrician youth' from a non-existent book by a spoof authority. Letterbeck is the English version of a possible German word Letterbäck meaning one who bakes letters.

But ironies multiply. Apparently, on the third page the whole secret of the tale is sprung. All is explained (the end has already appeared at the beginning) by the upland chase — apparently. At accelerating speed, however, the chase turns into many different things in a series of episodes each shot and edited to work at a cracking pace like sequences in a wild film, with as epilogue a satirical cartoon about a mother-duck. The ultimate arrival, 'looking into the absolutely bewildered eyes of Tommy Deloraine', launches him back into his previous plane of existence.

The Frying-pan and the Fire

The Duke of Burminster's Story

From the Bath, in its most exotic form, degenerate patrician youth passed to the coarse delights of the Circus, and thence to that parody of public duties which it was still the fashion of their class to patronise.

VON LETTERBECK: *Imperial Rome**

PART I
The Frying-pan

Lamancha had been staying for the week-end at some country house, and had returned full of wrath at the way he had been made to spend his evenings. 'I thought I hated bridge,' he said, 'but I almost longed for it as a change from cracking my brain and my memory to find lines from poets I had forgotten to describe people I didn't know. I don't like games that make me feel a congenital idiot. But there was one that rather amused me. You invented a preposterous situation and the point was to explain naturally how it came about. Drink, lunacy and practical joking were barred as explanations. One problem given was the Bishop of London on a camel, with a string of sea-trout round his neck, playing on a penny whistle on the Hoe at Plymouth. There was a fellow there, a Chancery K.C., who provided a perfectly sensible explanation.'

'I have heard of stranger things,' said Sandy Arbuthnot, and he winked at Burminster, who flushed and looked uncomfortable. As the rest of our eyes took the same direction the flush deepened on that round cheerful face.

'It's no good, Mike,' said Arbuthnot. 'We've been waiting months for that story of yours, and this is the place and the hour for it. We'll take no denial.'

'Confound you, Sandy, I can't tell it. It's too dashed silly.'

'Not a bit of it. It's full of profound philosophical lessons, and it's sheer romance, as somebody has defined the thing – strangeness flowering from the commonplace. So pull up your socks and get going.'

'I don't know how to begin,' said Burminster.

'Well, I'll start it for you . . . The scene is the railway station of Langshiels on the Scottish Borders on a certain day last summer. On the platform are various gentlemen in their best clothes with rosettes in their buttonholes – all strictly sober, it being but the third hour of the afternoon. There are also the rudiments of a brass band. Clearly a distinguished visitor is expected. The train enters the station, and from a third-class carriage descends our only Mike with a muddy face and a scratched nose. He is habited in dirty white cord breeches, shocking old butcher boots, a purple knitted waistcoat, and what I believe is called a morning coat; over all this splendour a ticky ulster – clearly not his own since it does not meet – and on his head an unspeakable bowler hat. He is welcomed by the deputation and departs, attended by the band, to a political meeting in the Town Hall. But first – I quote from the local paper – "The Duke, who had arrived in sporting costume, proceeded to the Station Hotel, where he rapidly changed." We want to know the reason of these cantrips.'

Burminster took a long pull at his tankard, and looked round the company with more composure.

'It isn't much of a story, but it's true, and, like nearly every scrape I ever got into, Archie Roylance was at the bottom of it. It all started from a discussion I had with Archie. He was staying with me at Larristane, and we got talking about the old Border raiders and the way the face of the countryside had changed and that sort of thing. Archie said that, now the land was as bare as a marble-topped table and there was no cover on the hills to hide a tomtit, a man couldn't ride five miles anywhere between the Cheviots and the Clyde without being

seen by a dozen people. I said that there was still plenty of cover
if you knew how to use it – that you could hide yourself as well
on bent and heather as in a thick wood if you studied the
shadows and the lie of the land, same as an aeroplane can hide
itself in an empty sky. Well, we argued and argued, and the
upshot was that I backed myself to ride an agreed course,
without Archie spotting me. There wasn't much money on it –
only an even sovereign – but we both worked ourselves up into
considerable keenness. That was where I fell down. I might have
known that anything Archie was keen about would end in the
soup.

'The course we fixed was about fifteen miles long, from
Gledfoot bridge over the hills between Gled and Aller and the
Blae Moor to the Mains of Blae. That was close to Kirk Aller,
and we agreed, if we didn't meet before, to foregather at the
Cross Keys and have tea and motor home. Archie was to start
from a point about four miles north-east of Gledfoot and cut in
on my road at a tangent. I could shape any course I liked, but I
couldn't win unless I got to the Mains of Blae before five o'clock
without being spotted. The rule about that was that he must
get within speaking distance of me – say three hundred yards –
before he held me up. All the Larristane horses were at grass, so
we couldn't look for pace. I chose an old hunter of mine that was
very leery about bogs; Archie picked a young mare that I had
hunted the season before and that he had wanted to buy from
me. He said that by rights he ought to have the speedier steed,
since, if he spotted me, he had more or less to ride me down.

'We thought it was only a pleasant summer day's diversion. I
didn't want to give more than a day to it, for I had guests
arriving that evening, and on the Wednesday – this was a
Monday – I had to take the chair for Deloraine at a big Conservative meeting at Langshiels, and I meant to give a lot of time to
preparing a speech. I ought to say that neither of us knew the bit
of country beyond its general lines, and we were forbidden to
carry maps. The horses were sent on, and at 9.30 a.m. I was at

Gledfoot bridge ready to start. I was wearing khaki riding breeches, polo boots, an old shooting coat and a pretty old felt hat. I mention my costume, for later it became important.

'I may as well finish with Archie, for he doesn't come any more into this tale. He hadn't been half an hour in the saddle when he wandered into a bog, and it took him till three in the afternoon to get his horse out. Consequently he chucked in his hand, and went back to Larristane. So all the time I was riding cunning and watching out of my right eye to see him on the skyline he was sweating and blaspheming in a peat moss.

'I started from Gledfoot up the Rinks burn in very good spirits, for I had been studying the big Ordnance map and I believed I had a soft thing. Beyond the Rinks Hope I would cross the ridge to the top of the Skyre burn, which at its head is all split up into deep grassy gullies. I had guessed this from the map, and the people at Gledfoot had confirmed it. By one or other of these gullies I could ride in good cover till I reached a big wood of firs that stretched for a mile down the left bank of the burn. Archie, to cut in on me, had a pretty steep hill to cross, and I calculated that by the time he got on the skyline I would be in the shelter of one of the gullies or even behind the wood. Not seeing me on the upper Skyre, he would think that I had bustled a bit and would look for me lower down the glen. I would lie doggo and watch for him, and when I saw him properly started I meant to slip up a side burn and get into the parallel glen of the Hollin. Once there I would ride like blazes, and either get to the Blae Moor before him – in which case I would simply canter at ease up to the Mains of Blae – or, if I saw him ahead of me, fetch a circuit among the plantings and come in on the farm from the other side. That was the general layout, but I had other dodges in hand in case Archie tried to be clever.

'So I tittuped along the hill turf beside the Rinks burn, feeling happy and pretty certain I would win. My horse, considering he was fresh from the grass, behaved very well, and we travelled in good style. My head was full of what I was going to

say at Langshiels, and I thought of some rather fine things —
"Our opponents would wreck the old world in order to build a
new, but you cannot found any system on chaos, not even
Communism" — I rather fancied that. Well, to make a long
story short, I got to the Rinks Hope in thirty minutes, and there
I found the herd gathering his black-faced lambs.

'Curiously enough I knew the man — Prentice they called him
— for he had been one of the young shepherds at Larristane. So I
stopped to have a word with him, and watched him at work. He
was short-handed for the job, and he had a young collie only
half-trained, so I offered to give him a hand and show my form
as a mounted stockman. The top of that glen was splendid
going, and I volunteered to round up the west hirsel. I considered that I had plenty of time and could spare ten minutes to
help a pal.

'It was a dashed difficult job, and it took me a good half-hour,
and it was a mercy my horse didn't get an over-reach among the
mossy well-heads. However, I did it, and when I started off
again both I and my beast were in a lather of sweat. That must
have confused me, and the way I had been making circles round
the sheep, for I struck the wrong feeder, and instead of following the one that led to the top of the Skyre burn I kept too much
to my left. When I got to the watershed I looked down on a
country utterly different from what I had expected. There was
no delta of deep gullies, but a broad green cup seamed with
stone walls, and below it a short glen which presently ran out
into the broader vale of the Aller.

'The visibility was none too good, so I could not make out the
further prospect. I ought to have realised that this was not the
Skyre burn. But I only concluded that I had misread the map,
and besides, there was a big wood lower down which I thought
was the one I had remarked. There was no sign of Archie as yet
on the high hills to my right, so I decided I had better get off the
skyline and make my best speed across that bare green cup.

'It took me a long time, for I had a lot of trouble with the

stone dykes. The few gates were all fastened up with wire, and I
couldn't manage to undo them. So I had to scramble over the
first dyke, and half pull down the next, and what with one thing
and another I wasted a shocking amount of time. When I got to
the bottom I found that the burn was the merest trickle, not the
strong stream of the Skyre, which is a famous water for trout.
But there, just ahead of me, was the big wood, so I decided I
must be right after all.

'I had kept my eye lifting to the ridge on the right, and
suddenly I saw Archie. I know now that it wasn't he, but it was
a man on a horse and it looked his living image. He was well
down the hillside and he was moving fast. He didn't appear to
have seen me, but I realised that he would in a minute, unless I
found cover.

'I jogged my beast with the spur, and in three seconds was
under cover of the fir-wood. But here I found a track, and it
struck me that it was this track which Archie was following, and
that he would soon be up with me. The only thing to do seemed
to be to get inside the wood. But this was easier said than done,
for a great wall with broken bottles on the top ran round that
blessed place. I had to do something pretty quick, for I could
hear the sound of hoofs behind me, and on the left there was
nothing but the benty side of a hill.

'Just then I saw a gate, a massive thing of close-set oak
splints, and for a mercy it was open. I pushed through it and
slammed it behind me. It shut with a sharp click as if it was a
patent self-locking arrangement. A second later I heard the
noise of a horse outside and hands trying the gate. Plainly they
couldn't open it. The man I thought was Archie said "Damn"
and moved away.

'I had found sanctuary, but the question now was how to get
out of it. I dismounted and wrestled with the gate, but it was as
firm as a rock. About this time I began to realise that something
was wrong, for I couldn't think why Archie should have wanted
to get through the gate if he hadn't seen me, and, if he had seen

194 THE BEST SHORT STORIES OF JOHN BUCHAN

me, why he hadn't shouted, according to our rules. Besides, this wasn't a wood, it was the grounds of some house, and the map had shown no house in the Skyre glen . . . The only thing to do was to find somebody to let me out. I didn't like the notion of riding about in a stranger's policies, so I knotted my bridle and let my beast graze, while I proceeded on foot to prospect.

'The ground shelved steeply, and almost at once my feet went from under me and I slithered down a bank of raw earth. You see there was no grip in the smooth soles of my polo boots. The next I knew I had banged hard into the back of a little wooden shelter which stood on a sunny mantelpiece of turf above the stream. I picked myself up and limped round the erection, rubbing the dirt from my eyes, and came face to face with a group of people.

'They were all women, except one man, who was reading aloud to them, and they were all lying in long chairs. Pretty girls they seemed to be from the glimpse I had of them, but rather pale, and they all wore bright-coloured cloaks.

'I daresay I looked a bit of a ruffian, for I was very warm and had got rather dirty in slithering down, and had a rent in my breeches. At the sight of me the women gave one collective bleat like a snipe, and gathered up their skirts and ran. I could see their cloaks glimmering as they dodged like woodcock among the rhododendrons.

'The man dropped his book and got up and faced me. He was a young fellow with a cadaverous face and side-whiskers, and he seemed to be in a funk of something, for his lips twitched and his hands shook as if he had fever. I could see that he was struggling to keep calm.

'"So you've come back, Mr Brumby," he said. "I hope you had a g-good time?"

'For a moment I had a horrid suspicion that he knew me, for they used to call me "Brummy" at school. A second look convinced me that we had never met, and I realised that the word he had used was Brumby. I hadn't a notion what he meant, but the only thing seemed to be to brazen it out. That was where

I played the fool. I ought to have explained my mistake there and then, but I still had the notion that Archie was hanging about, and I wanted to dodge him. I dropped into a long chair, and said that I had come back and that it was a pleasant day. Then I got out my pipe.

'"Here, you mustn't do that," he said. "It isn't allowed."

'I put the pipe away, and wondered what lunatic asylum I had wandered into. I wasn't permitted to wonder long, for up the path from the rhododendrons came two people in a mighty hurry. One was an anxious-faced oldish man dressed like a valet, and the other a middle-aged woman in nurse's uniform. Both seemed to be excited, and both to be trying to preserve an air of coolness.

'"Ah, Schwester," said the fellow with the whiskers. "Here is Mr Brumby back again and none the worse."

'The woman, who had kind eyes and a nice gurgling voice, looked at me reproachfully.

'"I hope you haven't taken any harm, sir," she said. "We had better go back to the house, and Mr Grimpus will give you a nice bath and a change, and you'll lie down a bit before luncheon. You must be very tired, sir. You'd better take Mr Grimpus's arm."

'My head seemed to be spinning, but I thought it best to lie low and do what I was told till I got some light. Silly ass that I was, I was still on the tack of dodging Archie. I could easily have floored Grimpus, and the man with the whiskers wouldn't have troubled me much, but there was still the glass-topped wall to get over, and there might be heftier people about, grooms and gardeners and the like. Above all, I didn't want to make any more scenes, for I had already scared a lot of sick ladies into the rhododendrons.

'So I went off quite peaceably with Grimpus and the sister, and presently we came to a house like a small hydropathic, hideously ugly but beautifully placed, with a view south to the Aller Valley. There were more nurses in the hall and a porter with a jaw like a prize-fighter. Well, I went up in a lift to the second floor, and there was a bedroom and a balcony, and several trunks, and brushes on the dressing-table lettered H. B. They made me strip and get into a dressing-gown, and then a doctor arrived, a grim fellow with gold spectacles and a soft, bedside manner. He spoke to me soothingly about the beauty of the weather and how the heather would soon be in bloom on the hill; he also felt my pulse and took my blood pressure, and talked for a long time in a corner with the sister. If he said there was anything wrong with me he lied, for I had never felt fitter in my life except for the bewilderment of my brain.

'Then I was taken down in a lift to the basement, and Grimpus started out to give me a bath. My hat! That was a bath! I lay in six inches of scalding water, while a boiling cataract beat on my stomach; then it changed to hot hail and then to gouts that hit like a pickaxe; and then it all turned to ice. But it made me feel uncommonly frisky. After that they took me back to my bedroom and I had a gruelling massage, and what I believe they call violet rays. By this time I was fairly bursting with vim, but I thought it best to be quite passive, and when they told me I must try to sleep before luncheon, I only grinned and put my head on the pillow like a child. When they left me I badly wanted to smoke, but my pipe had gone with my clothes, and I found laid out for me a complete suit of the man Brumby's flannels.

'As I lay and reflected I began to get my bearings. I knew where I was. It was a place called Craigiedean, about six miles from Kirk Aller, which had been used as a shell-shock hospital during the War and had been kept on as a home for nervous cases. It wasn't a private asylum, as I had thought at first; it called itself a Kurhaus, and was supposed to be the last thing in science outside Germany. Now and then, however, it got some baddish cases, people who were almost off their rocker, and I fancied that Brumby was one. He was apparently my double, but I didn't believe in exact doubles, so I guessed that he had

just arrived, and hadn't given the staff time to know him well
before he went off on the bend. The horseman whom I had taken
for Archie must have been out scouring the hills for him.

'Well, I had dished Archie all right, but I had also dished
myself. At any moment the real Brumby might wander back,
and then there would be a nice show up. The one thing that
terrified me was that my identity should be discovered, for this
was more or less my own countryside, and I should look a proper
ass if it got about that I had been breaking into a nerve-cure
place, frightening women, and getting myself treated like a
gentle loony. Then I remembered that my horse was in the wood
and might be trusted to keep on grazing along the inside of the
wall where nobody went. My best plan seemed to be to wait my
chance, slip out of the house, recover my beast and find some
way out of the infernal park. The wall couldn't be everywhere,
for after all the place wasn't an asylum.

'A gong sounded for luncheon, so I nipped up, and got into
Brumby's flannels. They were all right for length, but a bit
roomy. My money and the odds and ends from my own pockets
were laid out on the dressing-table, but not my pipe and pouch,
which I judged had been confiscated.

'I wandered downstairs to a big dining-room, full of little
tables, with the most melancholy outfit seated at them that you
ever saw in all your days. The usual thing was to have a table to
oneself, but sometimes two people shared one – husband and
wife, no doubt, or mother and daughter. There were eight
males including me, and the rest were females of every age from
flappers to grandmothers. Some looked pretty sick, some quite
blooming, but all had a watchful air, as if they were holding
themselves in and pursuing some strict regime. There was no
conversation, and everybody had brought a book or a magazine
which they diligently studied. In the centre of each table, beside
the salt and pepper, stood a little fleet of medicine bottles. The
sister who led me to my place planted down two beside me.

'I soon saw the reason of the literary absorption. The food was simply bestial. I was hungry and thirsty enough to have eaten two beefsteaks and drunk a quart of beer, and all I got was three rusks, a plate of thin soup, a purée of vegetables and a milk pudding in a teacup. I envied the real Brumby, who at that moment, if he had any sense, was doing himself well in a public-house. I didn't dare to ask for more in case of inviting awkward questions, so I had plenty of leisure to observe the company. Nobody looked at anybody else, for it seemed to be the fashion to pretend you were alone in a wilderness, and even the couples did not talk to each other. I made a cautious preliminary survey to see if there was anyone I knew, but they were all strangers. After a time I felt so lonely that I wanted to howl.

'At last the company began to get up and straggle out. The sister whom I had seen first – the others called her Schwester and she seemed to be rather a boss – appeared with a bright smile and gave me my medicine. I had to take two pills and some horrid drops out of a brown bottle. I pretended to be very docile, and I thought that I'd take the chance to pave the way to getting to my horse. So I said that I felt completely rested, and would like a walk that afternoon. She shook her head.

'"No, Mr Brumby. Dr Miggle's orders are positive that you rest today."

'"But I'm feeling really very fit," I protested. "I'm the kind of man who needs a lot of exercise."

'"Not yet," she said with a patient smile. "At present your energy is morbid. It comes from an irregular nervous complex, and we must first cure that before you can lead a normal life. Soon you'll be having nice long walks. You promised your wife, you know, to do everything that you were told, and it was very wrong of you to slip out last night and make us all so anxious. Dr Miggle says that must *never* happen again." And she wagged a reproving finger.

'So I had a wife to add to my troubles. I began now to be really worried, for not only might Brumby turn up any moment, but his precious spouse, and I didn't see how I was to explain to her what I was doing in her husband's trousers. Also the last sentence disquieted me. Dr Miggle was determined that I should not bolt again, and he looked a resolute lad. That meant that I would be always under observation, and that at night my bedroom door would be locked.

'I made an errand to go up to my room, while Grimpus waited for me in the hall, and had a look at the window. There was a fine thick Virginia creeper which would make it easy to get to the floor beneath, but it was perfectly impossible to reach the ground, for below was a great chasm of a basement. There was nothing doing that way, unless I went through the room beneath, and that meant another outrage and probably an appalling row.

'I felt very dispirited as I descended the stairs, till I saw a woman coming out of that identical room . . . Blessed if it wasn't my Aunt Letitia!

'I needn't have been surprised, for she gave herself out as a martyr to nerves, and was always racing about the world looking for a cure. She saw me, took me for Brumby, and hurried away. Evidently Brumby's doings had got about, and there were suspicions of his sanity. The moment was not propitious for following her, since Grimpus was looking at me.

'I was escorted to the terrace by Grimpus, tucked up in a long chair, and told to stay there and bask in the sun. I must not read, but I could sleep if I liked. I never felt less like slumber, for I was getting to be a very good imitation of a mental case. I must get hold of Aunt Letitia. I could see her in her chair at the other end of the terrace, but if I got up and went to her she would take me for that loony Brumby and have a fit.

'I lay cogitating and baking in the sun for about two hours. Then I observed that sisters were bringing out tea or medicines to some of the patients and I thought I saw a chance of a move. I called one of them to me, and in a nice invalidish voice complained that the sun was too hot for me and that I wanted to be moved to the other end where there was more shade. The sister went off to find Grimpus and presently that sportsman appeared.

'"I've had enough of this sun-bath," I told him, "and I feel a headache coming. I want you to shift me to the shade of the beeches over there."

'"Very good, sir," he said, and helped me to rise, while he picked up chair and rugs. I tottered delicately after him, and indicated a vacant space next to Aunt Letitia. She was dozing, and mercifully did not see me. The chair on my other side was occupied by an old gentleman who was sound asleep.

'I waited for a few minutes and began to wriggle my chair a bit nearer. Then I made a pellet of earth from a crack in the paving stones and jerked it neatly on to her face.

'"Hist!" I whispered. "Wake up, Aunt Letty."

'She opened one indignant eye, and turned it on me, and I thought she was going to swoon.

'"Aunt Letty," I said in an agonised voice. "For Heaven's sake don't shout. I'm not Brumby. I'm your nephew Michael."

'Her nerves were better than I thought, for she managed to take a pull on herself and listen to me while I muttered my tale. I could see that she hated the whole affair, and had some kind of grievance against me for outraging the sanctity of her pet cure. However, after a bit of parleying, she behaved like a brick.

'"You are the head of our family, Michael," she said, "and I am bound to help you out of the position in which your own rashness has placed you. I agree with you that it is essential to have no disclosure of identity. It is the custom here for patients to retire to their rooms at eight-thirty. At nine o'clock I shall have my window open, and if you enter by it you can leave by the door. That is the most I can do for you. Now please be silent, for I am ordered to be very still for an hour before tea."

'You can imagine that after that the time went slowly. Grimpus brought me a cup of tea and a rusk, and I fell asleep and only woke when he came at half-past six to escort me

indoors. I would have given pounds for a pipe. Dinner was at
seven, and I said that I would not trouble to change, though
Brumby's dress-clothes were laid out on the bed. I had the
needle badly, for I had a horrid fear that Brumby might turn up
before I got away.

'Presently the doctor arrived, and after cooing over me a bit
and feeling my pulse, he started out to cross-examine me about
my past life. I suppose that was to find out the subconscious
complexes which were upsetting my wits. I decided to go jolly
carefully, for I suspected that he had either given Brumby the
once-over or had got some sort of report about his case. I was
right, for the first thing he asked me was about striking my
sister at the age of five. Well, I haven't got a sister, but I had to
admit to beating Brumby's, and I said the horrible affair still
came between me and my sleep. That seemed to puzzle him, for
apparently I oughtn't to have been thinking about it; it should
have been buried deep in my unconscious self, and worrying me
like a thorn in your finger which you can't find. He asked me a
lot about my nurse, and I said that she had a brother who went
to gaol for sheep stealing. He liked that, and said it was a
fruitful line of inquiry. Also he wanted to know about my
dreams, and said I should write them down. I said I had
dreamed that a mare called Nursemaid won the Oaks, but found
there was no such animal running. That cheered him up a bit,
and he said that he thought my nurse might be the clue. At that
I very nearly gave the show away by laughing, for my nurse was
old Alison Hyslop, who is now the housekeeper at Larristane,
and if anybody called her a clue she'd have their blood.

'Dinner was no better than luncheon – the same soup and
rusks and vegetables, with a bit of ill-nourished chicken added.
This time I had to take three kinds of medicine instead of two. I
told the sister that I was very tired, and Grimpus took me
upstairs at eight o'clock. He said that Dr Miggle proposed to
give me another go of violet rays, but I protested so strongly
that I was too sleepy for his ministrations that Grimpus, after

going off to consult him, announced that for that evening the rays would be omitted. You see I was afraid that they would put me to bed and remove my clothes, and I didn't see myself trapesing about the country in Brumby's pyjamas.

'As Grimpus left me I heard the key turn in the lock. It was as well that I had made a plan with Aunt Letitia.

'At nine o'clock I got out of my window. It was a fine night, with the sun just setting and a young moon. The Virginia creeper was sound, and in less than a minute I was outside Aunt Letitia's window. She was waiting in a dressing-gown to let me in, and I believe the old soul really enjoyed the escapade. She wanted to give me money for my travels, but I told her that I had plenty. I poked my nose out, saw that the staircase and hall were empty, and quietly closed the door behind me.

'The big hall door was shut, and I could hear the prize-fighting porter moving in his adjacent cubby hole. There was no road that way, so I turned to the drawing-room, which opened on the terrace. But that was all in darkness, and I guessed that the windows were shuttered. There was nothing for it but to try downstairs. I judged that the servants would be at supper, so I went through a green-baize swing-door and down a long flight of stone steps.

'Suddenly I blundered into a brightly lit kitchen. There was no one in it, and beyond was a door which looked as if it might lead to the open air. It actually led to a scullery, where a maid was busy at a tap. She was singing to herself a song called "When the kye come hame', so I knew she belonged to the countryside. So did I, and I resolved to play the bold game.

'"Hey, lassie," I said. "Whaur's the road out o' this hoose? I maun be back in Kirk Aller afore ten."

'The girl stopped her singing and stared at me. Then in response to my grin she laughed.

'"Are ye frae Kirk Aller?" she asked.

'"I've gotten a job there," I said. "I'm in the Cally station,

and I cam' up about a parcel for ane o' the leddies here. But I
come frae further up the water, Larristane way."

'"D'ye say sae? I'm frae Gledside mysel'. What gars ye be in
sic a hurry? It's a fine nicht and there's a mune."

'She was a flirtatious damsel, but I had no time for dalliance.

'"There's a lassie in Kirk Aller will take the heid off me if I
keep her waitin'."

'She tossed her head and laughed. "Haste ye then, my man-
nie. Is it Shanks' powny?"

'"Na, na, I've a bicycle ootbye."

'"Well, through the wash-hoose and up the steps and roond
by the roddydendrums and ye're in the yaird. Guid nicht to ye."

'I went up the steps like a lamplighter and dived into the
rhododendrons, coming out on the main avenue. It ran long and
straight to the lodge gates, and I didn't like the look of it. My
first business was to find my horse, and I had thought out more
or less the direction. The house stood on the right bank of the
burn, and if I kept to my left I would cross the said burn lower
down and could then walk up the other side. I did this without
trouble. I forded the burn in the meadow, and was soon climbing the pine-wood which clothed the gorge. In less than twenty
minutes I had reached the gate in the wall by which I had
entered.

'There was no sign of my horse anywhere. I followed the wall
on my left till it curved round and crossed the burn, but the
beast was not there, and it was too dark to look for hoof-marks. I
tried to my right and got back to the level of the park, but had
no better luck. If I had had any sense I would have given up the
quest, and trusted to getting as far as Gledfoot on my own feet.
The horse might be trusted to turn up in his own time. Instead I
went blundering on in the half-light of the park, and presently I
blundered into trouble.

'Grimpus must have paid another visit to my room, found me
gone, seen the open window, and started a hue-and-cry. They
would not suspect my Aunt Letitia, and must have thought that

I had dropped like a cat into the basement. The pursuit was coming down the avenue, thinking I had made for the lodge gates, and as ill-luck would have it, I had selected that moment to cross the drive, and they spotted me. I remember that out of a corner of one eye I saw the lights of a fly coming up the drive, and I wondered if Brumby had selected this inauspicious moment to return.

'I fled into the park with three fellows after me. Providence never meant me for a long-distance runner, and, besides, I was feeling weak from lack of nourishment. But I was so scared of what would happen if I was caught that I legged it like a miler, and the blighters certainly didn't gain on me.

'But what I came to was the same weary old wall with the bottle glass on the top of it. I was pretty desperate, and I thought I saw a way. A young horse-chestnut tree grew near the wall and one bough overhung it. I made a jump at the first branch, caught it, and with a bit of trouble swung myself up into the crutch. This took time, and one of the fellows came up and made a grab at my leg, but I let him have Brumby's rubber-soled heel in the jaw.

'I caught the bigger branch and wriggled along it till I was above and beyond the wall. Then the dashed thing broke with my twelve stone, and I descended heavily on what looked like a highroad.

'There was no time to spare, though I was a bit shaken, for the pursuit would not take long to follow me. I started off down that road looking for shelter, and I found it almost at once. There was a big covered horse-van moving ahead of me, with a light showing from the interior. I sprinted after it, mounted the step and stuck my head inside.

'"Can I come in?" I panted. "Hide me for ten minutes and I'll explain."

'I saw an old, spectacled, whiskered face. It was portentously solemn, but I thought I saw a twinkle in the eye.

'"Ay," said a toothless mouth, "ye can come in." A hand

grabbed my collar, and I was hauled inside. That must have been just when the first of my pursuers dropped over the wall.'

PART II
The Fire

'I had got into a caravan which was a sort of bedroom, and behind the driver's seat was a double curtain. There I made myself inconspicuous while the old man parleyed with the pursuit.

'"Hae ye seen a gentleman?" I could hear a panting voice. "Him that drappit ower the wa'? He was rinnin' hard."

'"What kind of a gentleman?"

'"He had on grey claithes – aboot the same height as mysel'." The speaker was not Grimpus.

'"Naebody passed me," was the strictly truthful answer. "Ye'd better seek the ither side o' the road among the bracken. There's plenty hidy-holes there. Wha's the man?"

'"Ane o' the doctor's folk." I knew, though I could not see, that the man had tapped his forehead significantly. "Aweel, I'll try back. Guid nicht to ye."

'I crept out of my refuge and found the old man regarding me solemnly under the swinging lamp.

'"I'm one of the auld-fashioned Radicals," he announced, "and I'm for the liberty o' the individual. I dinna hold wi' lockin' folks up because a pernicketty doctor says they're no wise. But I'd be glad to be assured, sir, that ye're no a dangerous lunattic. If ye are, Miggle has nae business to be workin' wi' lunattics. His hoose is no an asylum."

'"I'm as sane as you are," I said, and as shortly as I could I told him my story. I said I was a laird on Gledwater-side – which was true, and that my name was Brown – which wasn't. I told him about my bet with Archie and my ride and its disastrous ending. His face never moved a muscle; probably he didn't believe me, but because of his political principles he wasn't going to give me away.

'"Ye can bide the night with me," he said. "The morn we'll be busy and ye can gang wherever ye like. It's a free country in spite o' our God-forsaken Government."

'I blessed him, and asked to whom I was indebted for this hospitality.

'"I'm the Great McGowan," he said. "The feck o' the pawraphernalia is on ahead. We open the morn in Kirk Aller."

'He had spoken his name as if it were Mussolini or Dempsey, one which all the world should know. I knew it too, for it had been familiar to me from childhood. You could have seen it any time in the last twenty years flaming upon hoardings up and down the Lowlands – The Great McGowan's Marvellous Multitudinous Menagerie – McGowan's Colossal Circassian Circus – The Only Original McGowan.

'We rumbled on for another half-mile, and then turned from the road into a field. As we bumped over the grass I looked out of the door and saw about twenty big caravans and wagons at anchor. There was a strong smell of horses and of cooking food, and above it I seemed to detect the odour of unclean beasts. We took up our station apart from the rest, and after the proprietor had satisfied himself by a brief inspection that the whole outfit was there, he announced that it was time to retire. Mr McGowan had apparently dined, and he did not offer me food, which I would have welcomed, but he mixed me a rummer of hot toddy. I wondered if it would disagree with the various medicines I had been compelled to take, and make me very sick in the night. Then he pointed out my bunk, undressed himself as far as his shirt, pulled a nightcap over his venerable head, and in five minutes was asleep. I had had a wearing day, and in spite of the stuffiness of the place it wasn't long before I dropped off also.

'I awoke next morning to find myself alone in the caravan. I opened the window and saw that a fine old racket was going on. The show had started to move, and as the caravans bumped over

the turf various specimens inside were beginning to give
tongue. It was going to be a gorgeous day and very hot. I was a
little bit anxious about my next move, for Kirk Aller was
unpleasantly near Craigiedean and Dr Miggle. In the end I
decided that my best plan would be to take the train to Langshiels and there hire a car to Larristane, after sending a telegram
to say I was all right, in case my riderless steed should turn up
before me. I hadn't any headgear, but I thought I could buy
something in Kirk Aller, and trust to luck that nobody from the
Kurhaus spotted me in the street. I wanted a bath and a shave
and breakfast, but I concluded I had better postpone them till I
reached the hotel at Langshiels.

'Presently Mr McGowan appeared, and I could see by his face
that something had upset him. He was wearing an old check
dressing-gown, and he had been padding about in his bare feet
on the dewy grass.

'"Ye told me a story last night, Mr Brown," he began
solemnly, "which I didna altogether believe. I apologise for
being a doubting Thomas. I believe every word o't, for I've just
had confirmation."

'I mumbled something about being obliged to him, and he
went on.

'"Ay, for the pollis were here this morning – seeking you.
Yon man at Craigiedean is terrible ill-set against ye, Mr Brown.
The pollisman – his name's Tam Doig, I ken him fine – says
they're looking for a man that personated an inmate, and went
off wi' some o' the inmate's belongings. I'm quotin' Tam Doig.
I gave Tam an evasive answer, and he's off on his bicycle the
other road, but – I ask ye as a freend, Mr Brown – what is
precisely the facts o' the case?"

'"Good God!" I said. "It's perfectly true. These clothes I'm
wearing belong to the man Brumby, though they've got my
own duds in exchange. He must have come back after I left.
What an absolutely infernal mess! I suppose they could have me
up for theft."

'"Mair like obtaining goods on false pretences, though I think ye have a sound answer. But that's no the point, Mr Brown. The doctor is set on payin' off scores. Ye've entered his sawnatorium and gone through a' the cantrips he provides, and ye've made a gowk o' him. He wants to make an example o' *you*. Tam Doig was sayin' that he's been bleezin' half the night on the telephone, an' he'll no rest till ye're grippit. Now ye tell me that ye're a laird and a man o' some poseetion, and I believe ye. It wad be an ill job for you and your freends if ye was to appear before the Shirra."

'I did some rapid thinking. So far I was safe, for there was nothing about the clothes I had left behind to identify me. I was pretty certain that my horse had long ago made a bee-line for the Larristane stables. If I could only get home without being detected, I might regard the episode as closed.

'"Supposing I slip off now," I said. "I have a general notion of the land, and I might get over the hills without anybody seeing me."

'He shook his head. "Ye wouldn't travel a mile. Your description has been circulated and a' body's lookin' for ye — a man in a grey flannel suit and soft shoes wi' a red face and nae hat. Guid kens what the doctor has said about ye, but the countryside is on the look-out for a dangerous, and maybe lunattic, criminal. There's a reward offered of nae less than twenty pound."

'"Can you not take me with you to Kirk Aller?" I asked despairingly.

'"Ay, ye can stop wi' me. But what better wad ye be in Kirk Aller? That's where the Procurator Fiscal bides."

'Then he put on his spectacles and looked at me solemnly.

'"I've taken a fancy to ye, Mr Brown, and ye can tell the world that. I ask you, are ye acquaint wi' horses?"

'I answered that I had lived among them all my life, and had been in the cavalry before I went into the Air Force.

'"I guessed it by your face. Horses have a queer trick o' leavin' their mark on a body. Now, because I like ye, I'll make a proposeetion to ye that I would make to no other man . . . I'm without a ring-master. Joseph Japp, who for ten years has had the job with me, is lyin' wi' the influenzy at Berwick. I could make shift with Dublin Davie, but Davie has no more presence than a messan dog, and forbye Joseph's clothes wouldna fit him. When I cast my eyes on ye this mornin' after hearin' Tam Doig's news, I says to mysel', 'Thou art the man.'"

'Of course I jumped at the offer. I was as safe in Kirk Aller, as Joseph Japp's understudy, as I was in my own house. Besides, I liked the notion; it would be a good story to tell Archie. But I said it could only be for one night, and that I must leave tomorrow, and he agreed. "I want to make a good show for a start in Kirk Aller — forbye, Joseph will be ready to join me at Langshiels."

'I borrowed the old boy's razor and had a shave and a wash, while he was cooking breakfast. After we had fed he fetched my predecessor's kit. It fitted me well enough, but Lord! I looked a proper blackguard. The cord breeches had been recently cleaned, but the boots were like a pair of dilapidated buckets, and the coat would have made my tailor weep. Mr McGowan himself put on a frock-coat and a high collar and spruced himself up till he looked exactly like one of those high-up Irish dealers you see at the Horse Show — a cross between a Cabinet Minister and a Methodist parson. He said the ring-master should ride beside the chief exhibit, so we bustled out and I climbed up in front of a wagon which bore a cage containing two very low-spirited lions. I was given a long whip, and told to make myself conspicuous.

'I didn't know Kirk Aller well, so I had no fear of being recognised either as myself or as the pseudo-Brumby. The last time I had been there was when I had motored over from Larristane to dine with the Aller Shooting Club. My present entry was of a more sensational kind. I decided to enjoy myself and to attract all the notice I could, and I certainly succeeded.

Indeed, you might say I received an ovation. As it happened it was a public holiday, and the streets were pretty full. We rumbled up the cobbled Westgate, and down the long High Street, with the pavements on both sides lined with people and an attendant mob of several hundred children. The driver was a wizened little fellow in a jockey cap, but I was the principal figure on the box. I gave a fine exhibition with my whip, and when we slowed down I picked out conspicuous figures in the crowd and chaffed them. I thought I had better use Cockney patter, as being more in keeping with my job, and I made a happy blend of the table-talk of my stud-groom and my old batman in the regiment. It was rather a high-class performance and you'd be surprised how it went down. There was one young chap with a tremendous head of hair that I invited to join his friends in the cage, and just then one of the dejected lions let out a growl, and I said that Mamma was calling to her little Percy. And there was an old herd from the hills, who had been looking upon the wine-cup, and who, in a voice like a fog-horn, wanted to know what we fed the beasts on. Him I could not refrain from answering in his own tongue. "Braxy, my man," I cried, "The yowes ye lost when we were fou last Boswell's Fair." I must have got home somehow, for the crowd roared, and his friends thumped the old chap on the back and shouted: "That's a guid ane! He had you there, Tam."

'My triumphant procession came to an end on the Aller Green, where the show was to be held. A canvas palisade had been set up round a big stretch of ground, and the mob of children tailed off at the gate. Inside most of our truck had already arrived. The stadium for the circus had been marked off, and tiers of wooden seats were being hammered together. A big tent had been set up, which was to house the menagerie, and several smaller tents were in process of erection. I noticed that the members of the troupe looked at me curiously till Mr McGowan arrived and introduced me. "This is Mr Brown, a friend of mine," he said, "who will take on Joe Japp's job for the night." And, aside to me, "Man, I heard ye comin' down the High Street. Ye did fine. Ye're a great natural talent for the profession." After that we were all very friendly, and the whole company had a snack together in one of the tents – bread and cheese and bottled beer.

'The first thing I did was to make a bundle of Brumby's clothes, which Mr McGowan promised to send back to Craigie-dean when the coast was clear. Then I bribed a small boy to take a telegram to the Post Office – to Archie at Larristane, saying I had been detained and hoped to return next day. After that I took off my coat and worked like a beaver. It was nearly six o'clock before we had everything straight, and the show opened at seven, so we were all a bit the worse for wear when we sat down to high tea. It's a hard job an artiste's, as old McGowan observed.

'I never met a queerer, friendlier, more innocent company, for the proprietor seemed to have set out to collect originals, and most of them had been with him for years. The boss of the menagerie was an ex-sailor, who had a remarkable way with beasts; he rarely spoke a word, but just grinned and whistled through broken teeth. The clown, who said his name was Sammle Dreep, came from Paisley, and was fat enough not to need the conventional bolster. Dublin Davie, my second in command, was a small Irishman who had been an ostler, and limped owing to having been with the Dublin Fusiliers at Gallipoli. The clown had a wife who ran the commissariat, when she wasn't appearing in the ring as Zenobia, the Pride of the Sahara. Then there were the Sisters Wido – a young married couple with two children; and the wife of a man who played the clarionet – figured in the bill as Elise the Equestrienne. I had a look at the horses, which were the ordinary skinny, broad-backed, circus ponies. I found out later that they were so well trained that I daresay they could have done their turns in the dark.

'At a quarter to seven we lit the naphtha flares and our orchestra started in. McGowan told me to get inside Japp's dress clothes, and rather unwillingly I obeyed him, for I had got rather to fancy my morning's kit. I found there was only a coat and waistcoat, for I was allowed to retain the top-boots and cords. Happily the shirt was clean, but I had a solitaire with a sham diamond as big as a shilling, and the cut of the coat would have been considered out-of-date by a self-respecting waiter in Soho. I had also a scarlet silk handkerchief to stuff in my bosom, a pair of dirty white kid gloves, and an immense coach whip.

'The menagerie was open, but that night the chief attraction was the circus, and I don't mind saying that about the best bit of the circus was myself. In one of the intervals McGowan insisted on shaking hands and telling me that I was wasted in any other profession than a showman's. The fact is I was rather above myself, and entered into what you might call the spirit of the thing. We had the usual Dick Turpin's ride to York, and an escape of Dakota Dan (one of the Sisters Wido) from Red Indians (the other Wido, Zenobia and Elise, with about a ton of feathers on their heads). The Equestrienne equestered, and the Widos hopped through hoops, and all the while I kept up my patter and spouted all the rot I could remember.

'The clown was magnificent. He had a Paisley accent you could have cut like a knife, but he prided himself on talking aristocratic English. He had a lot of badinage with Zenobia about her life in the desert. One bit I remember. She kept on referring to bulbuls, and asked him if he had ever seen a bull-bull. He said he had, for he supposed it was a male coo-coo. But he was happiest at my expense. I never heard a chap with such a flow of back-chat. A funny thing – but when he wasn't calling me "Little Pansy-face", he addressed me as "Your Grace" and "Me Lord Dook", and hoped that the audience would forgive my négligé attire, seeing my coronet hadn't come back from the wash.

'Altogether the thing went with a snap from beginning to end, and when old McGowan, all dressed up with a white waistcoat, made a speech at the end and explained about the next performances he got a perfect hurricane of applause. After that we had to tidy up. There was the usual trouble with several procrastinating drunks, who wanted to make a night of it. One of them got into the ring and tried to have a row with me. He was a big loutish fellow with small eyes and red hair, and had the look of a betting tout. He stuck his face close to mine and bellowed at me:

'"I ken ye fine, ye ——! I seen ye at Lanerick last back-end . . . Ye ca'd yoursel' Gentleman Geordie, and ye went off wi' my siller. By God, I'll get it out o' ye, ye —— welsher."

'I told him that he was barking up the wrong tree, and that I was not a bookie and had never been near Lanerick, but he refused to be convinced. The upshot was that Davie and I had to chuck him out, blaspheming like a navvy and swearing that he was coming back with his pals to do me in.

'We were a very contented lot of mountebanks at supper that night. The takings were good and the menagerie also had been popular, and we all felt that we had been rather above our form. McGowan, for whom I was acquiring a profound affection, beamed on us, and produced a couple of bottles of blackstrap to drink the health of the Colossal Circassian Circus. That old fellow was a nonesuch. He kept me up late – for I stopped with him in his caravan – expounding his philosophy of life. It seemed he had been intended for the kirk, but had had too much *joie de vivre* for the pulpit. He was a born tramp, and liked waking up most days in a new place, and he loved his queer outfit and saw the comedy of it. "For three and thirty years I've travelled the country," he said, "and I've been a public benefactor, Mr Brown. I've put colour into many a dowie life, and I've been a godsend to the bairns. There's no vulgarity in my performances – they're a' as halesome as spring water." He quoted Burns a bit, and then he got on to politics, for he was a great Radical, and maintained that Scotland was about the only true democracy, because a man was valued precisely for what he was and no more. "Ye're a laird, Mr Brown, but ye're a guid fellow, and this night ye've shown yourself to be a man and a brither. What do you and me care for mawgnates? We take no stock in your Andra Carnegies and your Dukes o' Burminster." And as I dropped off to sleep he was obliging with a verse of "A man's man for a' that."

'I woke in excellent spirits, thinking what a good story I should have to tell when I returned to Larristane. My plan was to get off as soon as possible, take the train to Langshiels, and then hire. I could see that McGowan was sorry to part with me, but he agreed that it was too unhealthy a countryside for me to dally in. There was to be an afternoon performance, so everybody had to hustle, and there was no reason for me to linger. After breakfast I borrowed an old ulster from him, for I had to cover up my finery, and a still older brown bowler to replace the topper I had worn on the preceding day.

'Suddenly we heard a fracas, and the drunk appeared who had worried me the night before. He had forced his way in and was pushing on through an expostulating crowd. When he saw me he made for me with a trail of blasphemy. He was perfectly sober now and looked very ugly.

'"Gie me back my siller," he roared. "Gie me back the five-pund note I won at Lanerick when I backed Kettle o' Fish." If I hadn't warded him off he would have taken me by the throat.

'I protested again that he was mistaken, but I might as well have appealed to a post. He swore with every variety of oath that I was Gentleman Geordie, and that I had levanted with his winnings. As he raved I began to see a possible explanation of his madness. Some bookmaker, sporting my sort of kit, had swindled him. I had ridden several times in steeplechases at Lanerick and he had seen me and got my face in his head, and mixed me up with the fraudulent bookie.

'It was a confounded nuisance, and but for the principle of the thing I would have been inclined to pay up. As it was we had to fling him out, and he went unwillingly, doing all the damage he could. His parting words were that he and his pals weren't done with me, and that though he had to wait fifty years he would wring my neck.

'After that I thought I had better waste no time, so I said good-bye to McGowan and left the show-ground by the back entrance close to the Aller. I had a general notion of the place, and knew that if I kept down the river I could turn up a lane called the Water Wynd, and get to the station without traversing any of the main streets. I had ascertained that there was a train at 10.30 which would get me to Langshiels at 11.15, so that I could be at Larristane for luncheon.

'I had underrated the persistence of my enemy. He and his pals had picketed all the approaches to the show, and when I turned into the Water Wynd I found a fellow there, who at the sight of me blew a whistle. In a second or two he was joined by three others, among them my persecutor.

'"We've gotten ye noo," he shouted, and made to collar me.

'"If you touch me," I said, "it's assault, and a case for the police."

'"That's your game, is it?" he cried. "Na, na, we'll no trouble the pollis. They tell me the Law winna help me to recover a bet, so I'll just trust to my nieves. Will ye pay up, ye ——, or take the bloodiest bashin' ye ever seen?"

'I was in an uncommon nasty predicament. There was nobody in the Wynd but some children playing, and the odds were four to one. If I fought I'd get licked. The obvious course of safety was to run up the Wynd towards the High Street, where I might find help. But that would mean a street row and the intervention of the police, a case in court, and the disclosure of who I was. If I broke through and ran back to McGowan I would be no farther forward. What was perfectly clear was that I couldn't make the railway station without landing myself in the worst kind of mess.

'There wasn't much time to think, for the four men were upon me. I hit out at the nearest, saw him go down, and then doubled up the Wynd and into a side alley on the right.

'By the mercy of Providence this wasn't a cul-de-sac, but twisted below the old walls of the burgh, and then became a lane between gardens. The pursuit was fairly hot, and my accursed boots kept slipping on the cobbles and cramped my form. They were almost upon me before I reached the lane, but then I put on a spurt, and was twenty yards ahead when it ended in a wall with a gate. The gate was locked, but the wall was low, and I scrambled over it, and dropped into the rubbish heap of a garden.

'There was no going back, so I barged through some gooseberry bushes, skirted a lawn, squattered over a big square of gravel, and charged through the entrance gates of a suburban villa. My enemies plainly knew a better road, for when I passed the entrance they were only a dozen yards off on my left. That compelled me to turn to the right, the direction away from Kirk Aller. I was now on a highway where I could stretch myself, and it was not long before I shook off the pursuit. They were whiskyfied ruffians and not much good in a hunt. It was a warm morning, but I did not slacken till I had put a good quarter of a mile between us. I saw them come round a turn, lumbering along, cooked to the world, so I judged I could slow down to an easy trot.

'I was cut off from my lines of communication, and the only thing to do was to rejoin them by a detour. The Aller valley, which the railway to Langshiels followed, gave me a general direction. I remembered that about six miles off there was a station called Rubersdean, and that there was an afternoon train which got to Langshiels about three o'clock. I preferred to pick it up there, for I didn't mean to risk showing my face inside Kirk Aller again.

'By this time I had got heartily sick of my adventures. Being chased like a fox is amusing enough for an hour or two, but it soon palls. I was becoming a regular outlaw — wanted by the police for breaking into a nursing-home and stealing a suit, and very much wanted by various private gentlemen on the charge of bilking. Everybody's hand seemed to be against me, except old McGowan's, and I had had quite enough of it. I wanted nothing so much as to be back at Larristane, and I didn't believe I would tell Archie the story, for I was fed up with the whole business.

'I didn't dare go near a public-house, and the best I could do for luncheon was a bottle of ginger-beer and some biscuits which I bought at a sweetie-shop. To make a long story short, I reached Rubersdean in time, and as there were several people on the platform I waited till the train arrived before showing myself. I got into a third-class carriage at the very end of it.

'The only occupants were a woman and a child, and my appearance must have been pretty bad, for the woman looked as if she wanted to get out when she saw me. But I said it was a fine day and 'guid for the crops', and I suppose she was reassured by my Scotch tongue, for she quieted down. The child was very inquisitive, and they discussed me in whispers. "What's that man, Mamaw?" it asked. "Never mind, Jimmie." "But I want to ken, Mamaw." "Wheesht, dearie. He's a crool man. He kills the wee mawpies." At that the child set up a howl, but I felt rather flattered, for a rabbit-trapper was a respectable profession compared to those with which I had recently been credited.

'At the station before Langshiels they collect the tickets. I had none, so when the man came round I could only offer a Bank of England five-pound note. He looked at it very suspiciously, asked me rudely if I had nothing smaller, consulted the station-master, and finally with a very ill grace got me change out of the latter's office. This hung up the train for a good five minutes, and you could see by their looks that they thought I was a thief. The thing had got so badly on my nerves that I could have wept. I counted the minutes till we reached Langshiels, and I was not cheered by the behaviour of my travelling companion. She was clearly convinced of the worst, and when we came out of a tunnel she was jammed into the farthest corner, clutching her child and her bag, and looking as if she had escaped from death. I can tell you it was a thankful man that shot out on to the platform at Langshiels . . .

'I found myself looking into the absolutely bewildered eyes of Tommy Deloraine . . . I saw a lot of fellows behind him with rosettes and scared faces, and I saw what looked like a band . . .

'It took me about a hundredth part of a second to realise that I had dropped out of the frying-pan into the fire. You will scarcely believe it, but since I had rehearsed my speech going up the Rinks burn, the political meeting at Langshiels had gone clean out of my head. I suppose I had tumbled into such an utterly new world that no link remained with the old one. And as my foul luck would have it, I had hit on the very train by which I had told Deloraine I would travel.

'"For heaven's sake, Tommy, tell me where I can change," I hissed. "Lend me some clothes or I'll murder you."

'Well, that was the end of it. I got into a suit of Tommy's at the Station Hotel – luckily he was about my size – and we proceeded with the brass band and the rosetted committee to the Town Hall. I made a dashed good speech, though I say it who shouldn't, simply because I was past caring what I did. Life had been rather too much for me the last two days.'

Burminster finished his tankard, and a light of reminiscence came into his eye.

'Last week,' he said, 'I was passing Buckingham Palace. One of the mallards from St James's Park had laid away, and had hatched out a brood somewhere up Constitution Hill. The time had come when she wanted to get the ducklings back to the water. There was a big crowd, and through the midst of it marched two bobbies with the mother-duck between them, while the young ones waddled behind. I caught the look in her eye, and, if you believe me, it was the comicalest mixture of relief and embarrassment, shyness, self-consciousness and desperation.

'I would like to have shaken hands with that bird. I knew exactly how she felt.'

Notes

Occasional minor variations, mostly of punctuation and spelling, between magazine publication and first hardback edition, I have ignored – 'Saxon downland' for 'Sussex downland' in the sixth story, for example. Significant changes are recorded here.

The Company of the Marjolaine

14 The epigraph can be translated 'Who passes by so late, Companions of Sweet Marjoram?' From the old French ballad 'Les Chevaliers du Guet' (The Knights of the Watch). In it, a knight seeks a girl to marry, and is told there is none; he offers gold and jewels, and is told she is not interested: he offers his heart, and is told – 'in that case, choose'.

14 Buchan's narrator is intended as a member of the famous Whig family, and in particular as a relative of that Charles Townshend who features so brilliantly in Edmund Burke's speech on American Taxation in 1774.

30 Jacques-Auguste de Thou, a seventeenth-century French historian, famous for justice and tolerance.

31 A Joseph Galloway, a pro-English Philadelphia lawyer, was a leader in Anglo-American constitutional thinking of the time.

The Last Crusade

58 The epigraph is one of those splendidly familiar quotations which one knows exactly where to find until one needs to locate it, when it becomes impossible to trace. Buchan loved Burke, and not only produced a fine *Selection* of over four hundred pages for the Nelson Seven-pennies in 1925, but liked to use figures from Burke's voluminous works: we noted Charles Townshend in the first story. Lovers of *The Three Hostages* will be charmed to find the original Marquis de la Tour du Pin in Burke's great *French Revolution* pamphlet.

The Grove of Ashtaroth

93 *Ashtaroth*, from a Hebrew word for 'wife', was a goddess worshipped from ancient times by all Semitic nations, even deep into Africa. She was the Assyrian and Babylonian Ishtar; her biblical name as 'Ash-toreth' bore relation to a word for 'shameful thing'. A fertility-goddess with a double nature, in some ways parallel to the Greek Persephone, she was seductively both creative and destructive. The Old Testament

is not specific about the dangers of her cult, which was widespread, but in several references is absolute in condemning it. The reforms of Josiah, King of Judah, resulting from the discovery of the Book of Deuteronomy, included the destruction of the 'high places' of the cult. Buchan was to develop the Greek side of Persephone as Koré in *The Dancing Floor* in 1926.

93 τέμενος: a piece of land sacred to a god.

93 *locus amoenus*: a pleasant, delightful place.

94 The epigraph (which did not appear in the *Blackwood's* version), may be crudely translated 'It is what in the end, in the pupils of their eyes, both laughs and cries, to enervating excess – the love of things eternal, of the long dead and of the ancient gods'. It is from the last of the group of poems headed *Eaux-fortes* [*Etchings*] in Verlaine's early collection *Poèmes Saturniens (1865–7)*. The opening poem in the collection is about the belief that those born under the sign of Saturn have a dark side to their nature. This, the fifth poem of *Eaux-fortes*, is entitled *Grotesques*, and is virtually impossible to translate, being a series of sonorous impressionistic phrases describing frightening, shadowy figures. Buchan uses the fifth verse.

100 *Phoenician and Sabæan, Sidon and Tyre*. The Phoenicians, known in the Old Testament as Canaanites, occupied the Mediterranean coast of Palestine, two of their principal cities being the ports of Sidon and Tyre. The Sabæans lived in what is now the Yemen: and it was their ruler, the Queen of Sheba, who visited Solomon. All were great traders. In about 1000 B.C., the Sidonians and Tyrians were working far up the Nile, throughout the Middle East, the Mediterranean and even the coasts of the Atlantic; they were also mining tin in Cornwall, with depots on the Scillies and the Isle of Wight. A Tyrian princess, Jezebel, married the most wicked Israelite king, Ahab, who, under her influence, began to worship the Phoenician goddess Astarte, or Ashtoreth. (Another Tyrian princess, incidentally, is famous as the Dido of Virgil's *Aeneid*.)

105 *Cruelle Enigme*: a novel by Paul Bourget, dedicated in 1885 to Henry James, with the aim *'donner une impression personnelle de la Vie'*.

114 *Tishbite*: i.e. Elijah, the first and greatest of the Old Testament prophets, whose conflict with Ahab and Jezebel finally led to the driving of the Phoenician gods and goddesses from Israel.

At the Article of Death

122 The epigraph, (added for publication in *Grey Weather*), might be translated 'Honoured Proserpina leaves no head untouched'. The lines are from Horace's rather obscure *Ode*, Book I, XXVIII. The words

quoted contain considerable difficulty: a notorious textual crux has resulted in the more common reading 'saeva' for 'sacra', rendering the meaning 'cruel Proserpina avoids no head'. It was thought that the goddess (the Roman equivalent of Persephone) cut a lock of hair from those about to die, as was done with sacrificial victims. The first full line refers to old and young flocking together to the grove.

Comedy in the Full Moon

137 *The Sentimentalist*: a sharp revival in the word 'sentimental', itself only dating from the mid-eighteenth century, came in the 1890s to mean 'being above material interests'. Barrie, in 1896, published *Sentimental Tommy*. Buchan is gently mocking.

'Divus' Johnston

149 *The Golden Hynde* was a charming hardback periodical published by two young ladies from an address in Wigmore Street. It ran for only two numbers, in December 1913 and June 1914. The title was explained as being from the smallest ship of Drake's fleet, in the hope that the venture would bring back treasure 'that will bring joy and health to many little lives that would otherwise be sad and dull', for all proceeds were to go towards sending poor London children for holidays in the country. The first number, which resulted in £7 3s. 7d. being sent to the Children's Holiday Fund, opened with Buchan's story, and included a short piece on Indian railway travel by E. M. Forster. The second number included Belloc's *Homeward* ('Lift up your hearts in Gumber! Laugh the Weald!') and three splendid pages by Buchan, *The Hynde Let Loose*, being three lessons in how to be witty and get your sayings quoted in the *Observer* of a Sunday.

150 The epigraph is from Suetonius' *Lives of the Caesars*, Book 1, *Divus Julius*, Chapter 88, describing the deification of Julius Caesar. In its original magazine publication, the story has its epigraph in English: 'The Emperor assumed the title of *Divus* or Divine, not of his own desire, but because it was forced upon him by a credulous people.'

159 In the course of a lecture on 'Some Scottish characteristics' on 7 February 1921, Buchan gave the outline of this story. There is an additional final sentence: 'Besides, I would never hear the end of it from the hecklers.' But before he tells the tale, he recalls how in historical fact, a hundred years before, a German expedition had set out to visit the central Mohammedan holy cities, where no infidel was allowed to set foot. After the use of all kinds of special influence, the expedition got to the forbidden city of Medina, where they found that the governor was called Thomas Keith and was a Scot.

The Wife of Flanders
171 *Outward Bound*, 'The Live Magazine with a World Outlook' edited by
    Basil Mathews, was an illustrated magazine with vaguely missionary
    leanings, seeking 'a real understanding of other races and nations',
    hoping to 'help to discover a way through these great international and
    interracial problems'. Buchan's tale opened many numbers, and his
    fellow-contributors included Rabindranath Tagore, John Drinkwater
    and Alfred Noyes.